NO
LOOSE
ENDS

NO LOOSE ENDS

A NOVEL

ROBERT FRANCIS CORWIN, M.D.

Mill City Press, Inc.
2301 Lucien Way #415
Maitland, FL 32751
407.339.4217
www.millcitypublishing.com

Printed in the United States of America

ISBN-13: 978-1-63505-596-2

DEDICATION

This book is dedicated to the memory of Sergeant Cullen Peterson and every soldier of the 143rd Regiment of the 36th Division. They were members of the Texas National Guard and known as the "T-Patchers." These men fought, bled, and many died in Europe during World War II so that we can live free today. Sgt. Peterson was assigned to the Medical Detachment of the 143rd Regiment. He was awarded the Combat Infantry Badge at Salerno in 1943 and a Bronze Star in the Vosges Mountain Campaign in 1944. We first met at my office when he became a patient of mine. Subsequently we became great friends, and he honored me by making me the custodian of his personal memorabilia collected during his military service. The spread eagle holding the *swastika* pictured on the cover of this book adorned a captured photograph album that had belonged to a German officer. The album was part of Sgt. Peterson's collection.

ACKNOWLEDGEMENTS

I am grateful to my family for their continued love, support, and encouragement. A special thanks to my daughter, Courtney Lee, who did her best to insure that the German words and phrases I used were correct and conveyed the appropriate message. I still accept responsibility for any errors in that department.

To all of my friends who, once again, had to endure my frequent non sequiturs on the golf course, at lunch, and other inappropriate settings, I apologize—but thank you for listening.

I really don't have the words to express my gratitude to Joe Flowers who always rescued us from computer emergencies. Honestly, without his expertise and devotion to two old people who are still computer illiterate, this book would never have been completed. More than once he had to retrieve multiple chapters that were sent into cyberspace when the wrong key was accidentally struck!

Thanks also to my very good friend, Lt. Colonel Royce W. Setzer, USMC (Ret.), for his years of active military service to this country and his aeronautical expertise and technical assistance. Without his input and flight experience, the PBY would never have gotten off the water.

My golfing buddy, Dr. Simon M. Bunn, deserves special kudos for serving double duty. Not only did he have to listen to me prattle on endlessly about my progress on this book, he also volunteered for proofreading duty. Thanks, old friend.

I can assure everyone who reads this book that without my wife of 52 years, it would never have come to life on the printed page. Sandy showed incredible patience, persistence, and unfaltering diligence in translating this story from "Bob-Speak" to some semblance of English. I hope she is still my best friend.

Once again, thank you, Kim Giles, for designing the cover of my book and for guiding us through the minefields of the publishing world.

I sincerely hope you enjoy this story.

No Loose Ends

PROLOGUE

A ten-year-old boy, George Ames, witnesses the destruction of a Nazi submarine off the coast of Long Island, New York, in September 1944. As the lone witness, he convinces himself that the events that took place on the beach after the U-Boat appeared and subsequently exploded were only figments of his imagination.

Ten years later, a chance meeting provides George with the opportunity to cross paths with one of the men who had surfaced in the U-Boat ten years before. At that moment, George realizes that what he had seen had actually occurred. That chance encounter served as a catalyst for a 20-year investigation involving American agents, friends, and even some South Americans. Included in the group were George and Alice Ames, Colonel Garnett Hill and his son James, Richard Eherenfeld, Bert Vogler, JoAnn Scarlett, Aaron de Silva, Esteban Kreutzer, and Juan Diaz.

George and his friends uncovered the disturbing and insidious Nazi plans for an American version of *Lebensborn* to lay the groundwork for a *Fourth Reich*. While foiling the *Volsung Project*, the group becomes aware of a few Americans with strong Nazi sympathies, who remain totally committed to the Nazi cause. They are aware that these sympathizers have strong ties to four South American industrialists. Both of these groups have remained under surveillance by an international coalition of agents. Everyone is waiting for the other shoe to drop. As Colonel Hill always admonished them, "Leave no loose ends."

A year had passed since the *Volsung Project* had been successfully terminated. The embryo of a *Fourth Reich* had been stopped dead in its tracks—or so they believed.

Chapter 1
March–1978

Dr. Esteban Kreutzer sat reading and grading student papers at a small table that was located against the wall of the faculty dining room. A cup of steaming black coffee rested on the table, and a large sweet roll occupied a paper plate near a stack of papers. He appeared to be engrossed in his task. He was lost in thought.

A sudden and unexpected voice intruded into his thoughts. It was a new voice—soft and most definitely female. Had one been paying close attention, it could possibly have been described as a bit sultry.

"Dr. Kreutzer, may I join you?"

Kreutzer looked up and turned in the direction of the voice. At first glance, she appeared to be in her mid-twenties. She had deep blue eyes and long, straight, dark hair. She was about five feet five or six inches tall with an athletic build. In a word, she was drop dead gorgeous.

Dr. Kreutzer was on a one-year sabbatical from the University of Buenos Aires. He had been a guest lecturer at the University of Texas in Austin for less than three months. His instant gut reaction to this woman was that this could easily spell trouble. Fraternizing with students, undergraduate or graduate, might be interpreted as cause for dismissal, or worse, at the University of Buenos Aires, and it was probably the same at UT.

"Of course, you may," he responded as he made an unsuccessful attempt to stand.

"Thank you. Please don't get up."

"And how might I be of assistance?"

The woman was carrying a cup of coffee and seated herself across the small table.

He looked at her for a moment and said, "Haven't I seen you in my lecture hall on occasion? If my memory serves me correctly, you usually come in a little bit late, leave a bit early, and always sit on the back row."

"Yes, I didn't think you noticed. Allow me to introduce myself. I'm Dr. Nancy Alvarez. I teach in the Department of Archeology and Anthropology."

An immediate and visible wave of relief came over Kreutzer. Seductive students pose a continuous threat to the well-being and security of college professors, single or married.

Nancy commented, "You look relieved. I'm sorry if I shocked you. You must have taken me for a student. That happens more often than you think. And, by the way, I've enjoyed your lectures immensely. Last October I attended your seminar on 'The Influence of the Church and the *Conquistadores* on New World Culture.' I thought it was an excellent presentation. Much of my research relates to the American Southwest."

"Thanks," was all he could muster for the moment. He was, however, quick to notice that she wore no ring on her left hand. She was beautiful, obviously intelligent, and he was entranced. He thought, "I believe I'd like to get to know this lady a little better."

As that thought flashed across his consciousness, Nancy said, "I have two tickets to the Music Department's production of 'The Mikado' for Saturday night. Would you consider being my escort for the evening?"

Kreutzer momentarily hesitated and thought, "What red-blooded male could refuse an invitation like that?"

He responded, "I certainly would. It would be my pleasure, Dr. Alvarez."

"Nancy, please. Do you prefer Esteban or Steve?"

"Either one is fine with me."

"All right, Steve, here's my address." She handed him her card.

"Dinner at 5:30, if that's okay with you."

"I am looking forward to it," he responded as he watched her make her way to the door.

Chapter 2
First Date

Steve was at Nancy's front door promptly at 5:30 on Saturday with two bottles of wine in hand. Since he didn't know what she was preparing for dinner, one was red and the other was white.

After showing him into the kitchen, she handed him the white wine to open because the wonderfully aromatic casserole she had made was full of moist chicken. She carried the steaming dish to the table and returned to the kitchen for a bowl of crisp green beans and a delightful salad of romaine, goat cheese, and dried cranberries.

"Oh, I almost forgot the rolls!" she exclaimed as she rushed back into the kitchen. The dinner was delicious, and they chatted easily and amiably as they ate.

"Would you mind telling me a little about yourself? Kreutzer is not the kind of name an Alvarez would expect to hear from an Argentine."

Steve laughed and began to explain. "I was born in 1941 in Buenos Aires. I never knew my father as he was killed in North Africa early in the War. I would be remiss if I failed to add that he had been a military officer assigned as an attaché to the German Embassy in Buenos Aires prior to the War. When my mother realized she was pregnant, they were secretly married. My father was soon recalled to Germany and sent to North Africa with Rommel's *Afrika Korps.*

"My mother was the only daughter of a wealthy, aristocratic, Catholic, Argentine ranching family that did not in any way condone the marriage of my parents, despite the fact that my father was Catholic. Unfortunately, he was also German. My mother's family was traditionally hidebound, rigid, and unforgiving. They considered themselves a superior breed and perceived the Germans, Catholic or otherwise, as barbarians who wore animal skins and carried spears. They pictured them wearing Viking helmets with horns, sailing down the rivers and the coast lines all over Europe, raping and pillaging everyone and everything in their paths.

"When the death of my father was conveyed to my mother through the German Embassy, very slowly and somewhat reluctantly, with a magnum dose of Catholic guilt, her family allowed her back into the fold with her baby son. Very soon, my grandparents forgot my 'unfortunate' heritage and grew to love me, their only grandson. I was raised on the family *estancia* with all of its benefits. I learned to ride, hunt, and shoot. They also taught me the workings of the ranch.

"My grandparents made sure that I was educated by Jesuits who taught me from preschool in Argentina to graduate school at Georgetown. Over their objections I was also taught to read, write, and speak German since there was and is such a large contingency of German expatriates all over South America. I speak English like an American and without any trace of an accent because one of the Jesuit priests, Father Joe, was an American from Ohio. Early on he became my mentor. I learned the idioms, polite slang, and street jargon. When Padre Joe finished fine tuning me, I was, for all purposes, a product of the United States of America. And as they say in New York City, 'Sometimes you can't tell the players without a scorecard.' Well, that's about it."

Nancy looked at her watch and said, "That's fascinating. But we'll be late if we don't leave right now."

"Do we have time to do the dishes?"

"We can do those later."

"Now that sounds promising!"

Chapter 3
September–1979

Steve ambled slowly toward his apartment deep in thought. A lot had happened in this last year. A year and a half of guest lecturing at The University of Texas had led to the offer of a full-time, tenured position in Austin. His relationship with the beautiful Dr. Nancy Alvarez had blossomed. He had already introduced her to many of his friends who lived in Texas. George and Alice Ames had invited them all to their ranch for a great party. She liked them, and they loved her. Life was good. He was settled in his new job and loving it.

Except for a colloquium on Friday, classes for that week had ended for him. It was a beautiful fall Thursday afternoon, and a big football weekend was on the horizon for the students, alums, and rabid Longhorn fans. The fall semester had just started, and Steve was already mired up to his knees in students' papers and faculty duties.

As he fumbled for his keys to unlock his door, he heard the phone ringing in his kitchen. Before he could get there, the answering machine had picked up. He recognized the familiar voice of Richard Eherenfeld leaving a message asking him to call as soon as possible. He grabbed for the phone, but Richard had already hung up. He immediately dialed his friend's number in Houston.

Richard answered on the first ring and said, "Steve, we need to talk. Are you free tomorrow?"

There was urgency in his voice that Steve recognized, and he could see his plans for paperwork going out the window. There was no "hello" or "how are you." This was not at all like Richard, the laid back, cool, collected CEO of Global Import/Export.

"Yes, I'm always available for you, Richard."

"Good, I'll fly up to Austin on Friday. Would 10:30 a.m. be okay with you? Can you meet me at the airport?"

"Sure, I have a colloquium in the morning, but I'll be done by 10. The students are only thinking about football anyway. I can make it."

"By the way, how's your German these days? See you tomorrow."

Steve sat in the kitchen in stunned silence. Then he said out loud to an empty apartment, "What do you make of that?"

Chapter 4
The Meeting

The twin engine Citation II with the Global Import/Export logo on its tail touched down on the tarmac at the Austin Municipal Airport precisely at 10:30 a.m. and taxied toward a private hangar. The engines were just winding down as the door opened and the stairs unfolded. Richard appeared and waved at Steve to come aboard. He wasn't smiling. Nothing about this felt right to Steve. To make matters even more suspicious, as he ascended the stairs, he saw the ever-smiling face of James Hill. Whenever James Hill showed up, there was bound to be trouble close behind. Still strapped into his seat was Dr. Bert Vogler, a physician from Fredericksburg, Texas. He and Richard had been assigned to G2, the Intelligence Unit of the 10th Mountain Alpine Division, during World War II.

James Hill worked for the CIA and had the reputation for getting his friends involved in what one might call—"situations." He had been promoted rapidly and was a senior member of his department although still in his early 30s. His title, if he actually had one, was classified. He is the son of Colonel Garnett Hill who had played a major role in unraveling the mystery of the *Volsung Project*.

Under his breath Steve mumbled, "Oh no, here we go again."

Fast handshakes all around and a quick hello was all there was time for before Richard said, "Sit down and strap in for take off."

Steve knew better than to ask, but he did anyway. "What the hell is going on?"

"We're going to get off the ground where we can talk and think clearly, remain uninterrupted, and can't be overheard."

The plane began to roll down the runway and in no time was airborne, heading southeast. The pilot leveled off at 7500 feet and seatbelts were unclasped. The plane was incredibly quiet.

Without any preliminaries, Richard began, "Steve, as you probably already know, after the termination of the *Volsung Project* that you helped us with, the parties involved in South America have been kept under very close surveillance. James has been promoted to a desk at Langley and is no longer operating in the field. At least that's what he tells me."

One look on James's smiling face told it all.

"Although he now operates from a desk, any and all information related to the principals who were involved with that project still comes to him for review. *Volsung* is and has been a dead issue for over a year. But I'm afraid some of our old friends may be up to something else now."

Steve replied, "Richard, the look on your face tells me that you're not kidding."

"Exactly what it is and where it's directed has yet to be clearly defined. But there has suddenly been an increase in the number of intercontinental telephone and radio transmissions between South America and the Middle East. I'm sure you remember the four guys in Buenos Aires."

Steve replied, "Let me see. Wilhelm Heinz has the mining, smelting, and casting operation. Walter Erdman has chemicals and explosives. Paul Strasse runs the heavy machinery fabrication plant, and, last but not least, the fat and not so lovable Otto von Ritter is into the illicit international arms trade."

Richard said, "That's about it, except that von Ritter has taken his son, Siegfried, as a partner. If you can believe it, he's even a more arrogant ass than his nasty father. Their international arms business is thriving."

"I remember them well, but as you know, I was only a messenger in that operation—a minor functionary at best," Steve answered.

"That's precisely why you're here," James said.

Steve looked out the window and saw nothing but the Gulf of Mexico's blue water below. He had no parachute. There was nowhere for him to go and nowhere for him to hide so he gamely said, "Let's have it! You've got me!"

James began, "The CIA and *Mossad*, Israel's intelligence unit, have good reason to believe that there has been a continuous, steady, massive arms build up throughout the entire Middle East and North Africa for some time. These sensitive areas include Syria, Lebanon, Iraq, Yemen, Algeria, and Libya. Even the Iranians, despite their distinct cultural differences, seem to be involved. This by no means excludes Egypt, Saudi Arabia and a few additional North African countries.

"We've been getting some information from a number of our people who are employed in the industries of the men we just mentioned. How they were insinuated is a story for another day. Suffice it to say, they hear and see things and pass on useful tidbits of information to us. These pieces and fragments are beginning to fill in a new puzzle."

Steve was beginning to get interested. He asked, "What's this all leading to?"

James explained, "Needless to say, an organized and well-coordinated religious/political *jihad* in the Middle East, occurring in all of the aforementioned countries simultaneously, would be a catastrophic event on the world stage. If it spread to the areas of Southeast Asia and the island nations of the Pacific, it would be cataclysmic. First, the State of Israel would be virtually wiped out. Next, the United States would be in deep shit. Up to its lower lip, I'd say. Europe, too, I guess. We can't even begin to estimate the impact or reactions from China, Russia, Pakistan, and North Korea.

"Out of this chaos, it is remotely possible that a *Fourth Reich* might evolve. But if it does, I seriously doubt that once the *jihad* starts, the Nazis will be able to control it. They'll be next on the agenda."

"I'm beginning to get the picture," a subdued Steve responded.

Richard interjected, "That being said, we may be in need of your services in the near future."

"You guys are nuts. You really think that I, all by myself, can stop something like you are describing? Cataclysmic is the right word. And you expect me to thwart this by sticking my finger in the dyke like the little Dutch boy?"

"I'll ask you again, Steve. How's your German these days?"

Steve looked at Bert and replied, "*Angemessen danke-schön.* But I haven't written, read, or spoken German in years."

Bert said, "Your response was entirely correct. It translates into English as 'passable, thank you.'"

Richard finally smiled and said, "You may be needing it soon. I would suggest that you brush up on contemporary, conversational German, especially the latest idioms. I'm sure there are a number of native German-speaking graduate students at the your university. Consider employing them to bring you up to speed over the next few weeks. You're a clever fellow. You'll come up with a workable plan, I'm sure. While you're at it, maybe you could familiarize yourself with a few of the dialects as well."

"That's a tall order on short notice," Bert interjected.

Steve responded, "*Ja. Ich verstehe!* I understand!" To Steve's surprise, his German was beginning to come back.

"Oh, by the way, how are you at Middle Eastern language—say Arabic and Farsi?"

Steve's response came in German. "*Schrecklich.* Terrible."

Richard said, "I guess it was too much to hope for. I believe you're getting the picture. Gentlemen, how about lunch in New Orleans? Let's keep this meeting to ourselves for now. Steve, you may confide in Nancy if you wish."

"*Verstanden.* Understood."

The plane banked sharply to the right on Richard's signal to the pilot and began its descent into New Orleans International Airport.

Richard announced, "Lunch is on me! Next stop is *Antoine's.*"

Chapter 5
I Know Nothing

Armed with a new challenge, Steve returned to Austin and was back at his apartment by four. There was a message on his answering machine from Nancy.

"Steve, call me when you get in."

Before returning her call, Steve gave serious thought to the option of telling Nancy about his little excursion to New Orleans with Richard and his friends. He made his decision. After all, Austin was a small town and someone might have seen him at the airport. Anyway, he had a premonition that she was somehow going to become involved in whatever was about to happen. Her assistance might be invaluable to them all. He picked up the phone to call her.

Nancy answered, and before he could say a word, she asked, "Can you come over for hamburgers tonight?"

"Sure, what time?"

"Is 6:30 okay?"

"You bet. See you then."

While flipping burgers in her backyard, Steve regaled her with the day's adventures with Richard, Bert, and James. She seemed fascinated and interested.

"I figured out quite a while ago that you would become involved again in some caper with those friends of yours. I'll assist in anyway I can. And to quote Sgt. Schultz on TV, 'I know nothing. I see nothing.'"

Halfway through the meal, Steve blurted out, "*Ach Scheiße, Mein Gott!*"

"What's wrong?"

"It's nothing, just something I need to do. I'll deal with it on Monday."

"Where, in Germany?"

"No, on campus."

Chapter 6
Chance Encounter

Bright and early on Monday morning, Steve marched over to the Administration Building, seeking the Registrar's Office. He planned to try to sweet talk the Registrar into giving him a list of native-born Austrian and German graduate students, along with their contact information. He knew it was confidential information, but "please," "thank you," and a nice smile sometimes could go a long way. He really didn't have the time or the patience to try to go through channels. He certainly couldn't walk up to the Registrar and announce that he was a spy for the CIA and, even though WWII had been over for more than 30 years, that he was on the hunt for Nazi agents lurking in the woodwork. That alone would have landed him in the funny farm. He would have been pronounced a genuine nut case and confined to a rubber room.

He opened the door to the Registrar's office and entered. The only occupant in the office was a young woman seated at a typewriter with her back to him.

"I'm Dr. Kreutzer. I'd like to see the Registrar, please."

As the young woman stood up and turned around, she exclaimed, "Dr. Kreutzer, how nice to see you again. The Registrar isn't in now. Can I be of assistance?"

"Becky Ames, what on earth are you doing here?"

"I work here part time on a work/study program. I'm in graduate school working on my Ph.D. in German Studies. I hope to go into government service when I'm finished."

"Really? Well, good luck."

Suddenly, Steve had a flashback. He recalled Alice telling the story about the incident at Indiana University when Becky was an undergraduate student. She had inadvertently come across some information that proved vital to the termination of the *Volsung Project.*

"Becky, I need a big favor, but I don't want you to get in trouble or get caught. Feel free to say no, but I can't answer any questions!"

"Agreed. I'll do what I can and ask no questions."

After telling Becky exactly what he needed, she said, "Have a seat. This won't take long."

In less than 30 minutes, Steve left with all of the information he needed.

"Remember, I was never here!"

In his apartment that evening, Steve spread out a map of Central Europe. He reviewed the information Becky had supplied. There were many German-speaking graduate students enrolled. He circled their hometowns and chose those he believed were the best prospects. One was from Kiel, two from Berlin, one from Essen, one from Hamburg, two from Munich, one from Stuttgart, and two from Vienna. There were six women and four men. The young women would probably be more patient, but the men could give him the current masculine slang that the women would either not know or be too embarrassed or reluctant to share. He began to formulate a workable plan. What would be the most efficient use of his time as well as that of the students?

Steve called Nancy and asked her to come over. She was always a master of organization. He showed her the map and explained the dilemma of trying to work all of these students into his schedule. Nancy came up with a solution in less than a heartbeat.

"Why not invite each student to your office for lunch and tape record your conversations. In short order you'll have ten tapes to listen to at your leisure. By listening to them over and over, you should begin to regain your proficiency with accents, speech patterns, and inflections. I'm sure the students would be happy to do anything for a free lunch!'

"Brilliant! Nancy, you're a genius. I knew you would figure this out. This is going to be quite a project."

Steve's first contact was the student from Kiel who had been briefed over the phone about Steve's desire to refresh his German language skills. She agreed to the plan and met him at noon the next day. After his secretary brought in lunch, they enjoyed a lively conversation, mostly in German. The arrangement seemed to work well, and Steve contacted and offered the same package to each student.

Soon he was armed with ten taped conversations including varied accents, inflections, slang, and pronunciations from various areas of Germany and Austria. That was enough to get the ball rolling, and the students all offered to come again if he needed them. He began listening to the tapes in the evenings, often falling asleep as the tape recorder played. Nancy had been an asset already. He continued to work on improving his language skills while waiting for the next contact from James or Richard.

Chapter 7
October–1979

Steve listened to the tapes every night.. His lids would eventually get heavy, the words became slurred, and he would drift off toward what was usually a very promising good night's sleep. Very late one night the phone rang, and he nearly jumped out of his skin. It was Richard.

Half asleep, Steve blurted out, "Dammit, man! Do you know what time it is?"

"Steve, a situation has arisen that demands our attention as soon as possible. I also have some other news that might interest you. Are you free for dinner in Houston on Saturday? Maybe Nancy would like to fly down with you and do a little shopping while we have our meeting. Afterwards, we can all go out to dinner. How about *Arthur's*? I'll have my plane in Austin at 9 a.m. on Saturday morning. You're both welcome to stay over at my place if the evening runs late, and I'll fly you back on Sunday."

Steve agreed to come. He promised to ask Nancy and to let him know if she was coming. Not much arm-twisting was necessary to convince her to go along, shop, and enjoy a great steak dinner at *Arthur's*. Nancy had just read a great review of the restaurant in *Texas Monthly* and was excited at the prospect.

Richard's plane was waiting for them at the airport when they arrived Saturday morning. It took off as soon as they boarded and fastened their seatbelts. As the plane leveled off Richard offered them coffee and kolaches. They really enjoyed that Czech version of a sweet roll. Steve preferred the flaky pastries filled with sausage while Nancy loved the ones filled with fruit.

Richard said, "Take a look at this. It was delivered to my office two days ago."

He handed Steve a plain white business envelope with the name Richard Eherenfeld typed on the front. Under it was the single word: **PERSONAL**. The envelope had been slit at the top. When Steve removed the letter, he couldn't believe what he saw. His knee-jerk response was, "Those bastards never quit, do they?"

On the letterhead was an all-too-familiar spread eagle with a *swastika* in its claws. Below the Nazi insignia, in the center of the page, were the capital letters: **R.E.** Below those initials, typed in capital letters, was the single word: *ERWACHEN!* Steve knew that translated into English it meant, "Awake, awaken, wake up." At the bottom of the page were the letters **W.H.** There was no stamp, postmark, or date. Steve held the letter up to the light, and, at the correct angle, he saw the Nazi watermark.

"It's the genuine article all right. It's the real McCoy! No doubt about it."

Richard asked, "Steve, what do you make of this letter? And, by the way, I've sent a copy to Bert."

Nancy interjected, "Do you want me to go to the powder room for a few minutes?"

"Actually, no. I'd rather you listened in on this, Nancy. I value your opinion. This situation is about to get complicated, and I think Steve is going to be heavily involved! You've become a member of the family."

"Oh my god!" Steve suddenly exclaimed. "Richard, don't you remember that phony list of Nazi agents you and Bert conjured up during the *Volsung Project?* Well, it just may be that those chickens have come home to roost."

Steve turned to Nancy and explained, "Bert and Richard fabricated and circulated a phony list of deep cover Nazi agents in the Western Hemisphere. But the only two names that were verifiable were their own."

Richard asked, rhetorically, "Who the hell would have ever thought they would use that list? After the mission was over we never gave that list a second thought. We missed that 'loose end' for sure."

"*Erwachen!* is a wake up call, Richard. It's your wake up call. Whatever is going on, this is a call to duty. My guess is that 'they,' whoever 'they' are, have need of your services."

Richard said, "I agree. My first instinct is to do nothing—no response at all. **W.H.** is obviously Wilhelm Heinz. I'll let him contact me."

"Have you alerted James?"

"No, but this is as good a time as any. I'll call him when we get to the office."

Steve agreed with Richard's decision not to respond to the letter. "Let him seek you out. If you don't talk, he'll have to. You also might check to see if there is a duplicate letter at your office in Buenos Aires."

"Good idea."

Chapter 8
The U-Boats

The plane landed at Hobby Airport and taxied toward a private hangar. Richard's black Suburban was waiting there and spirited the three of them off to his office. Getting through Houston traffic was a bitch on the best of days—and this wasn't one of them. On the way, at Richard's request, Steve began to regale Nancy with the story of the *Volsung Project*.

"The short version goes like this. Late in 1944 after D-Day, two U-Boats departed Kiel on the Baltic coast of Germany, headed around the tip of Denmark and out to the open sea. The one designated 'N' was destined for North America, the coast of Long Island, New York, where she was purposefully scuttled. The other, designated 'S,' went to Montevideo, Uruguay. You will hear more about that soon. Both were carrying gold that the Nazis had stolen. This gold was earmarked for the creation of a *Fourth Reich* to be established in the United States. Those plans were in the works even as the *Third Reich* was crumbling. Before U-Boat 'N' was sunk off the coast of Long Island, she discharged an important passenger, a doctor who was entrusted with the task of initiating a new version of the *Lebensborn* concept. In short, *Lebensborn* was a plan to create a new super Aryan race in America. Richard, Bert, James, and his father, Colonel Garnett Hill, along with George and Alice Ames, thwarted the plan rather cleverly. JoAnn Scarlett played a major role in permanently eliminating the threat. And we mustn't forget the assistance we received from a group called *Mossad*. Does that name ring a bell?"

"It does, indeed. What an intriguing story. It should be made into a movie."

As soon as they got settled in his office, Richard left the room to make a call to Buenos Aires, while Nancy continued listening to Steve recount the past adventure. When Richard returned, he smiled and said, "There is a duplicate letter at my office in Buenos Aires, but Bert has not received an envelope yet."

Steve offered, "In my opinion, that could mean only one thing. You obviously have something they really need."

There was a knock on Richard's office door, and his secretary ushered in his old friend, Juan Diaz. Captain Diaz was now in his early fifties and beginning to show a little gray at the temples. Richard introduced the Captain to Nancy and Steve.

Steve asked, "Nancy are you ready to do some shopping?"

"Yes, I am looking forward to a little retail therapy. I'll leave you men to discuss business, and I'll be back about five, if that's okay?"

Richard listed the names of a number of high-end shops he thought might interest her. Since Nancy's clothing allowance wasn't tied to her salary at the University, no store of any prominence had escaped mention. As she left, Steve observed a look in her eyes—the kind that women get when they plan to do some serious shopping. Panthers also get that look while stalking their prey. Richard gave Nancy a magnetic entry card and directions to his private living quarters above his office.

"Just let yourself in when you get back."

Chapter 9
Juan Diaz

Captain Diaz sat in a comfortable leather chair and began, "I have a story to tell that you may find hard to believe."

Richard stopped him. "Before you start, let me give Steve a little background information about you. Juan was an orphan raised by the Jesuits in Montevideo, Uruguay, prior to WWII. He was very bright, but cleverly hid it from the priests, lest they try to groom him for the priesthood. That idea was not to his liking. He was working the docks when he caught the attention of one of my men who captained a small coastal freighter. Juan was about 16 years old at the time. How he became my eyes and ears in Montevideo is another story. I'll tell you about that later if you are interested. He was also a key player in the *Volsung Project*. By that time, he was Captain of one of my largest cargo ships. Now he's in charge of the entire maritime division of Global Import/Export. Okay, Juan, let's hear your news."

"*Bueno.* You will recall, a few years ago you asked me if I had seen a U-Boat sail up the *Rio de la Plata* when I was a 16-year-old working the docks as a stevedore in Montevideo in 1944. I told you that we unloaded very heavy crates from a German U-Boat and placed them onto a small coastal freighter. The U-Boat then sailed away toward the mouth of the river, which is about 20 miles wide, and out into the South Atlantic. That was the last anyone saw or heard of it. Well, we may have just found her. Actually, de Silva may have found her."

"Go on."

"The U-Boat, 'S,' went south, all right, but not to the suspected secret Nazi U-Boat base in the Antarctic. After D-Day, the *Wehrmacht*, the *Kriegsmarine*, and Admiral Dönitz's U-Boats were under extreme duress, to say the least. Although they weren't down for the count, they were on the ropes. By that time in the War, no one had any interest in watching the South Atlantic or patrolling the coast of Argentina. There was nothing of any military importance remaining there. The German surface raiders that had terrorized the shipping lanes had long ago been swept from the sea. The PBYs and the Martin Mariners that flew coastal patrol had been assigned to other theaters of operation, specifically the Gulf of Mexico and the Caribbean where the U-Boats were quite vulnerable.

"Fernando de Silva, the nephew of the coin dealer, Aaron de Silva, is now the 1st Officer of one of Global's coastal freighters headquartered in Buenos Aires. Remember, Fernando had been my 1st Mate on the *Evita Peron* when JoAnn destroyed John Wolfe and his boat, *The Lorelei*, off the coast of North Carolina. About a month ago, he saw an unusual light emanating from the *Golfo San Matias* on a night run south to the town of Camarones. He noted and entered the light's position in the ship's log. The *Golfo* is on the coast of Argentina, just south of the *Negro* River and the coastal town of Viedma. There are no known settlements or communities there. About two weeks later, on the same run, he saw the light again. I must admit that curiosity got the best of me, and I enticed de Silva to join me on a little foray to the *Golfo San Matias* by plane.

"I arranged a meeting with Zac Lewis, Global's chief pilot in South America, and the three of us sat down to talk about our plans. After explaining to Zac exactly what Fernando saw and what we wanted to do, he agreed to fly us down to the *Golfo* in Global's PBY Catalina.

"As you may already know, Steve, Global has two sea planes and a first class pilot. The smaller plane is a Supermarine Walrus Mk 1. It's a WWII surplus single engine amphibian that can muster 680hp and has a range of 600 miles at a cruising speed of 135 mph. The British used this model extensively for air/sea rescue and submarine patrol in the Caribbean.

"The other amphibian owned by Global is a Consolidated PBY-5A Catalina flying boat. It can cruise at 135 mph with a range of 2,520 miles. Obtaining these two planes after WWII was Richard's idea and a stroke of genius. With the large coastal and transoceanic fleet that Global runs, both planes have served as ancillary support for our ships and crew.

"Getting back to my story, Zac was instrumental in assisting us in gathering the necessary gear for our foray. We were kind of fumbling around until he intervened and told us he had been in the U.S. Army Air Corps and had served with a photo reconnaissance unit during World War II. When we asked him why he hadn't told us that before, he responded, 'You guys were having so much fun I didn't want to spoil it for you.'"

"At his suggestion, in addition to the usual food, water, shelter, and survival gear, we took a black rubber inflatable boat with a 5hp outboard engine, extra paddles, and a pair of 8 X 50 Zeiss binoculars. He also recommended we bring along a quality 35 mm camera and a variety of lenses, including a 1200 mm telephoto lens. We added plenty of black and white high-speed film.

"Richard, I don't know what got into us, but we loaded up the PBY and took off for the 600-mile flight to the *Golfo* to scope out the source of the mysterious light. I guess I'm not finished playing the spy game.

"It was twilight when we identified the coastal outlet of the *Golfo*. As we passed over the entrance to the bay, Zac pointed to starboard and over the intercom yelled, 'down there.' He told us to get our camera ready and to open the starboard waist blister as he circled and made another pass. Below us was a long, thin, cigar-shaped vessel heading for shore.

"I exclaimed, '*Madre de Dios, Yo no lo creo.* I don't believe it! The last time I saw a sight like that was 1944, in Montevideo harbor.'" Fernando shouted, "Is that what I think it is?" Zac answered, "Damn right it is! You may have just found the mysterious missing U-Boat."

"Zac told us to keep shooting film as he made one more low pass. He confirmed my observation and said, 'You're right, Juan, there she is!'"

"It was getting dark, and as we made that last low pass, we saw what appeared to be a giant camouflaged curtain rising at the shore line. A bright light emanated from within what appeared to be a cavernous space at the water's edge. We had found the source of the mysterious light. Better yet, we had found the missing Submarine 'S,' although I was pretty sure I had seen a gun mounted on the forward deck that had not been on the U-Boat I saw in 1944.

"Zac completed the last pass, cleared the southern peninsula, and headed for the Atlantic. Once past the southern shore of the *Golfo*, the PBY banked again, and Zac began his approach to land. The sea was calm, and the plane touched down and taxied toward the beach. Zac throttled back the engines and lowered his wheels. As we made contact with the sand, he advanced the throttle slightly, and the PBY came out of the water like a duck. We all helped secure the plane with wheel chocks, stakes, and ropes.

"I told Zac and Fernando that I'd like to get a better look at that place where we saw the light. Zac volunteered to stay with the plane while Fernando and I took the rubber boat into the bay. We knew it was unlikely that we'd get any pictures that night because we'd be shooting directly into the light. Zac told us we needed to set up our camera with the telephoto lens at night so at dawn, the sun would be at our backs. If they raised that camouflage curtain in the morning, we might get some decent pictures.

"Fernando and I inflated the rubber boat, loaded our gear, and motored into the bay. We spent a miserable night on a small spit of land inside the bay. We ate an assortment of candy, crackers, and K rations. We set up our camera and waited for dawn. Zac faired a lot better in the plane overnight. With the arrival of dawn, as Zac predicted, the giant curtain began to rise, and I started shooting pictures as fast as I could. I shot three 36-frame rolls of black and white film. Then we got the hell out of there as fast as we could. We fired up the outboard motor, hugged the shoreline, and motored out of the protected area of the *Golfo* into the Atlantic toward the plane.

"As soon as Zac spotted us, he started the engines and turned the plane around on the beach. We deflated the boat and packed it into the plane with the motor and all of our gear. He revved the engines as the plane entered the water and retracted the wheels as soon as they broke free of the sandy bottom. The ocean was like glass. He turned the nose into the wind, and, smooth as you please, the plane was up and heading south. Zac made a wide turn to starboard and headed home.

"Let me show you the pictures we took."

Chapter 10
A Picture's Worth a Thousand Words

Richard cleared a space on his desk, and Juan spread out the photos. "Thanks to Zac, these turned out rather well and will paint a very interesting picture of what we are dealing with now. As you can see, the first half dozen enlargements show the U-Boat underway in the *Golfo*. We took them from the open blister of the PBY. The next series of 8 x 10's were taken at dawn the next day. They show the shore installation from which the bright light had emanated the previous night. We are looking at the bow of the U-Boat and can clearly see the outer doors of her torpedo tubes. From that angle, the sub has the appearance of a pig's snout."

Steve interjected, "I've heard that U-Boats were sometimes referred to in slang as 'pig boats.' Now I know why!"

"It's hard to believe what we're seeing!" Richard exclaimed. "But there it is—proof positive."

He stood, turned, and went to his bookshelf to remove a reference book that included every variation and model of WWI and WWII submarines. He turned to the chapter on German U-Boats of WWII, which included all the vital statistics, pictures, and profiles of every make and model of the entire fleet.

They all gathered around the desk and Richard said, "My guess is that the boat in your photographs is a type VII/C. It matches the pre-1943 profiles in this book. Look at this footnote. 'After 1943 all type VII U-Boats assigned to the North Atlantic were no longer armed with an 88 mm deck gun.'"

Juan said excitedly, "I believe we found her. She has to be U-Boat 'S.'

Someone has added a deck gun. I wonder where they got it?"

"I've got a pretty good idea," Richard mumbled, "von Ritter."

Juan continued triumphantly, "Look closely at these pictures. The U-Boat appears to be completely out of the water, secured on some sort of lift device or drydock. Gentleman, we are looking at a duplicate of a WWII submarine pen constructed to accommodate the last and only seaworthy U-Boat of the *Third Reich*. As you probably all know, the Allies purposely scuttled what remained of the German U-Boat fleet after the War."

The room went silent. Richard began to pace, repeating over and over, "I wonder? I wonder?" He suddenly stopped and said, as much to himself as to the others in the room, "Coincidence? Hell no! I don't believe in coincidence." The wheels were turning. Then he exclaimed suddenly, *"Erwachen!"*

Juan Diaz said, "What?"

"The damn letter."

Richard showed the letter to Diaz. The men all looked at each other, and Richard said, in a *sotto* voice, "I'd like to get a closer look at that installation."

Steve countered, "I believe, if you are just a little patient, you'll be invited to view the entire facility before long. This letter suggests to me that whatever this 'wake up' represents, it will eventually involve the maritime division of Global Import/Export."

Diaz said, "I concur with that assessment. I'll bet a steak dinner that we'll find out very soon what they want from you. Meanwhile, I think we all need to lay low and exercise patience and restraint for now."

Steve glanced at the clock and said, "It's almost five. Nancy should be getting here soon. Let's have a drink while we wait for her."

The group agreed and entered the private elevator to Richard's apartment one floor above. They were on their second drink when Nancy appeared with an armload of packages.

"Sorry I'm late," she announced as she exited the elevator thirty minutes late. "Houston shopping is the best."

"Looks like you've had a very productive afternoon," Steve commented.

"Yes, indeed, and now I'm ready for a glass of wine and dinner."

The company's Suburban awaited them, and they were off to dinner at *Arthur's*. The men chose salad, steak, and twice-baked potatoes. All of that shopping had made Nancy hungry, and she added a lobster tail to her order. No one had room for dessert.

Steve and Nancy decided not to stay overnight. They both had mountains of paperwork waiting in Austin. Richard alerted his pilots, dropped Captain Diaz off at the apartment, and picked up Nancy's packages. Steve and Nancy told Juan how happy they were to have met him.

"Likewise," he responded, "and I have a feeling we will be seeing each other again soon."

On the way to the airport, Richard and Steve regaled Nancy with the story of Juan's trip to the *Golfo* and the serendipitous discovery of the U-Boat and its hiding place.

The plane, with its engines running, was waiting on the tarmac. Nancy and Steve started up the stairs to the plane. She turned to Richard and said, "Sound's like there's an adventure brewing."

"Absolutely," Richard replied. "Colonel Hill told us a few years ago that the opera isn't over 'til the fat lady sings.'"

Steve added, "I don't even think we know the name of this opera yet—let alone the characters."

The door closed. Nancy and Steve were filled with curiosity and anticipation, but they still snoozed all the way back to Austin, full of good food and wine, and worn out from a busy day,

Chapter 11
The Girl on the Swing

Classes were over for the day, and Nancy and Steve decided to take a walk around the campus before dinner. As they ambled along, she asked, "What's your take on the significance of the discovery of the submarine and the meaning of that cryptic letter Richard received? Surely it's just coincidence, don't you think?"

Steve responded, "I was just asking myself the same question. But I have no ready answer. It appears to me that the Nazis in South America haven't quite given up their dream of a *Fourth Reich*. However, let me suggest an off-the-cuff scenario—a 'what-if,' so to speak. First, let's accept the fact that, at this moment in time, most of the western world's opinion will no longer openly accede to those prejudicial concepts of anti-Semitism on a wholesale basis. No one will support the kind of prejudice that went unchecked in Europe and allowed the Holocaust to occur. Today everyone knows that almost all of the nations of the Middle East do not agree with the concept that the State of Israel has a right to exist. Many of their leaders openly continue to deny that the Holocaust ever happened. They resent the Jews, the State of Israel, and, for that matter, the United States of America. Many Muslim countries are continually calling openly for *jihad* and the eventual extinction of both countries."

"Okay, I agree. There are still some people concentrating their efforts on trying to eliminate Israel and possibly, sooner or later, planning to turn their full attention to us."

"Right! Due to the ineffectiveness of the U.N. Security Council and efforts behind the scenes by pro-Nazi and pro-Muslim factions, I can conceive of a scenario where the Nazis, keeping a low profile, could possibly get someone else, the Muslims, to do their dirty work for them. A *jihad* might be just the smokescreen needed to mask the emergence of a *Fourth Reich*."

"I'm not sure I'm totally following you."

Steve explained, "At present there is an undercurrent of unrest in the Middle East. We know that is the case from the communications Richard's group has been monitoring. I'm talking about the makings of a holy war, a *jihad*, a 20th century crusade against the infidel Christians and Jews. It has been smoldering for centuries. The State of Israel is now the prime target."

"So what you're telling me is that the Nazis might orchestrate a *jihad* in order to accomplish at least some of their goals and not put a single soldier on the field?"

"Think of it! The Nazis are no where to be seen, thus completely blameless."

"Oh my God! You don't have to paint any more of that picture!"

"By George, I think she's got it!"

"Okay, Professor 'Iggins, I've got it! But how does the U-Boat fit into this picture, assuming it fits at all?"

"That, my dear Miss Doolittle, is the $64,000 question. I just don't know. However, I think if we exhibit a modicum of patience, we'll find out soon enough."

Nancy laughed and said, "I'm getting hungry. Where would you like to go? My treat!"

"How about that place where they serve you a ten-pound block of Swiss cheese to fill you up before you get your meal?"

"Of course, *The Old San Francisco Steak House*. But are you sure you are interested in the Swiss cheese, or the young girl in the short skirt that swings overhead, ringing a bell with her toe when she gets high enough?"

"Funny girl! Let's go!"

On the way home, Steve thanked Nancy for dinner. "The steak was great."

"Right. I noticed you never took your eyes off the girl on the swing."

"I was just trying to imagine you up there."

"Sure."

"Well, I guess it's time to head home and plug in my nocturnal German lesson."

The next morning, Steve realized it was time to schedule another round of lunchtime interviews. He had practically memorized the original ten tapes. He asked his secretary to make the calls for him. She decided to start with the women. As it turned out, this round of lunches was reduced to six. Four of the students had conflicts, but promised to reschedule if needed.

The first student was Magda Bremmer from Kiel. For the first time the entire conversation was conducted completely in German. The hour passed quickly. Over the next couple of weeks the remaining sessions went just as well. The next student was Adelheid Kopp from Berlin, followed by Angela Berg from Vienna. Then came the men. Emil Richter was from Munich while Wilhelm von Hipper was from Stuttgart. The last conversation was with Fritz Schuster from Hamburg. Each student was impressed with Steve's progress in conversational German. He was very confident that his skills were returning and that the Jesuits would have been proud of him.

Steve called Nancy. "Hey, I've completed my last scheduled meeting with the German-speaking students. They all said I was doing well."

"Keep listening to those tapes. Who knows when you'll need to use your German skills."

Steve was a thorough and patient man. He didn't know exactly what he was preparing for, but he intended to be ready. He didn't have to wait long.

A few days later, the anticipated phone call came.

"Steve, it's Richard. Heinz called requesting a meeting with me in Houston at my office."

"When?"

"When are you free? I'll want you here."

"Is Saturday morning soon enough for you?"

"Yes, I'll call him back. My plane will pick you up Saturday at 9 a.m."

'That will be fine."

Steve called Nancy to tell her about the meeting.

"Sounds interesting." She asked no questions.

Chapter 12
The Contact

Steve landed at Hobby on Saturday morning and was driven directly to Richard's office by the pilot who explained that Richard had gone to meet Heinz at Houston International Airport and would join him after taking the South American to lunch.

Heinz greeted Richard somewhat formally giving him a nod and an almost imperceptible click of his heels. Then he offered a perfunctory handshake.

"Strange," Richard thought, "since we are old hunting buddies." Then he remembered that old habits die hard and that old Teutonic habits don't seem to die at all. On the way into town, the pair reminisced about their last dove hunt, and they made tentative plans for another one. Richard suggested an early lunch. Heinz enthusiastically agreed and immediately suggested *Leibman's*. The mention of that restaurant immediately put Richard on alert.

Richard thought, "First mistake, Heinz." Then he asked, "Wilhelm, have you been to Houston before?"

"No, no! It was recommended to me by a friend in Buenos Aires."

Heinz's recovery was quick—but not quiet quick enough.

Richard thought, "A kosher deli? How ironic. Either you've been here before, or you already have eyes and ears here watching and waiting. Regardless, it's time to stay alert. The ball is now in play."

Heinz continued, "I believe it will be a safe place for us to talk, since I understand the atmosphere there is mildly frenetic and loud enough to keep our conversation from being overheard."

Richard said, "I agree."

He thought to himself, "There's no way for us to bug the place on short notice. But since he chose the spot, his people must be in position already. That's what I'd do if the situation were reversed. I've forgotten how paranoid the rest of the world really is. Everyone is bugging everyone else. Half the world is spying on the other half. I'll make sure I keep the conversation light during lunch. That will drive them crazy."

The Suburban stopped in front of *Liebman's*. Richard and Heinz exited, and Richard gave the driver's window a short rap. When the window was lowered a few inches, he ordered him to take Heinz's luggage to the hotel and to pick them up in an hour or so. Then he dismissed the driver with a wave of his hand. It was an arrogant gesture—very Teutonic. Richard was playing his role to the hilt.

They each had huge pastrami on rye sandwiches with dark mustard and large dill pickles. Dark beer was the perfect beverage for the lunch they had chosen. Heinz seemed to want to start a conversation several times, but Richard, aware that they were probably being recorded, steered the topics toward the arts and fine restaurants available in Houston.

The Suburban was waiting by the curb when they exited the deli. They were driven directly to the *Westin Oaks Hotel*, which housed Richard's offices and his penthouse apartment. The doorman opened the door for them, and they went directly to the reservation desk. The clerk said, "Here's your key. You're already checked in, and your luggage is in your room, Mr. Heinz."

Then Richard said, "Why don't you freshen up? I'll call for you at 3 p.m."

Heinz agreed, and as they approached the elevators said, "I think we should conduct our business in Spanish from now on."

Steve met Richard in his office that was fitted out with well-hidden, sophisticated cameras and microphones attached to recording devices located in the apartment on the floor above.

"Steve, I'd like you to monitor my meeting with Heinz from my apartment. I sense he's very paranoid."

"With good reason," Steve laughed.

"Really. He even wants our conversations conducted in Spanish."

Richard knocked on Heinz's hotel room door promptly at 3 p.m. He inserted the magnetic key in the elevator, and it took them up to the corporate offices of Global Import/Export. Heinz, carrying a black brief case under his arm, nodded curtly to Richard's secretary as she opened the private office door for them.

Richard said, "Rose, we won't be needing you this afternoon. Why don't you take the rest of the day off?"

Now, Heinz and Richard were very much alone and secure, or so it appeared. Before Heinz sat down, he took a slow turn around the office. Ostensibly, he was admiring the artwork and decor, as well as the view of Houston's downtown. There was an original Albert Bierstadt painting on one wall and a number of original Frederic Remington and Charlie Russell bronzes displayed around the room. Behind Richard's massive desk was a special cabinet that held a complete state-of-the-art McIntosh stereo system with each component housed in its own oil-finished walnut case. The components were equipped with half a dozen dials and meters, each casting a turquoise light. As Strauss's *Alpine Symphony* was playing softly, one could see the needles on the meters move ever so slightly.

Finally satisfied that the room wasn't bugged, Heinz found a comfortable chair and sat down. "Very nice office, Richard. I like your choice of music."

"Thank you. Are you a fan of Richard Strauss?"

"Very much."

Heinz seemed to relax a bit, and as they had previously agreed, the conversation began in Spanish.

"Well, Heinz, what do you have on your mind?"

"I'll get right to the point. As you are now fully aware, I know what you are, and I have known it for a couple of years. You are one of the last of our deep-cover agents, a residual of the *Third Reich*."

"Really?"

"Yes, and don't toy with me. I'm here on serious business for *The Reich*."

"Which *Reich*, and what's the password?"

"Es gibt keinen verdammten Passwort."

Obviously frustrated, Heinz had spit out the last statement in perfect German.

"Mistake number two," Richard thought.

"Correct, there is no password," Richard countered in Spanish. "No sense of humor either," he thought, "that, too, will never change."

Steve caught every word of that short, sharp exchange.

"Now, Heinz, let us get on with your business."

Heinz began, "Recently there was a meeting in Montevideo of the few remaining members of the upper echelon of the *Third Reich*."

Richard's countenance revealed nothing. He just gave a slight nod knowing that if he said nothing, Heinz would eventually spill the beans and tell him everything.

Heinz continued, "You are aware by now that our agenda for the formation of a *Fourth Reich* as conceived in 1944 is no longer feasible."

"Yes, I see that clearly."

"We now have a better plan—a much better plan! We intend to finish what our glorious *Führer*, Adolph Hitler, and the men of the *Third Reich*, were unable to finish.

"An army of men, women, and children in many Muslim countries are being recruited to join a worldwide *jihad* against Israel and the United

States. Of course it will take time to organize the *jihad*. Our little enterprise will be the catalyst necessary to initiate and support the movement. We intend for you and your company to have a ship built—a very special ship."

"Really?"

"I have some sketches in my briefcase that will give you an idea of what we need. The ship must be fabricated by a legitimate firm and must be ordered by a corporation actively engaged in commerce all over the world. This enterprise must not raise even the slightest degree of curiosity.

"I've come to you for two reasons. First, you are one of us. Second, you and your company meet all of our criteria. Your reputation is spotless."

"Well then, let me see the sketches."

Richard studied them for a few minutes and said, "This looks like the drydock we have at our shipyard, but it seems to have engines. Is it a mobile, self-propelled drydock?"

"Exactly!" Heinz blurted out as his voice seemed to go up a full octave. And that's not all! It will also be rigged to function as a container ship that will be able to carry cargo to all parts of the world."

Richard commented, "I'm no maritime engineer, but I can see the practical possibilities for Global Import/Export in the commercial world."

"Wait, there's more!" Heinz was now excited, almost to the point of agitation.

"Really?" Richard thought, "He's about to wet his pants!"

"Yes! Our plan is quite simple. We have a U-Boat that can deliver men, raiding parties, *jihadists,* and munitions all over the world, quietly and undetected."

"Hold it right there, Heinz. You have a U-Boat—a WWII U-Boat?"

"Yes."

"And just where do you keep this U-Boat, if I might ask?"

"About 600 miles to the south of Buenos Aires there is a community of German ex-patriots living on the edge of the Golfo San Matias. They service and maintain the U-Boat in a pen that was specially built in 1944. They have been there ever since the War ended. But I'll tell you more about that later.

"The ship we want built will harbor and service the U-Boat as it sails the seven seas, wreaking havoc and supporting the *jihadists* who will foment unrest and indiscriminately attack government buildings, civilian gatherings, and military installations around the world. These *jihadists* are willing to die for their cause, I understand. For killing the infidel they believe they will receive their reward in heaven: 72 virgins."

Richard thought, "Yeah, 72 virgins of undetermined age and sex."

"Inside the container ship/drydock we will be able to launch and retrieve our U-Boat. We can send her anytime and anywhere in the world on whatever mission is required. We will have the capacity to deliver arms and men to disrupt governments all over the globe. This will create instability, panic, and financial disaster, especially for the Jews and the United States. Out of this chaos a *Fourth Reich* will emerge."

"And exactly what do you expect from me?"

"Along with my sketches, I have here the exact specifications of our type VII/C U-Boat. We need you to contract with a shipyard to draw up plans and build an ocean-going container ship that will also function as a drydock, service facility, and home base for our U-Boat." Heinz handed Richard a small notebook.

Richard opened it. On the first page were the dimensions of the type VII/C U-Boat hand-written in precise German script: length, 67 meters; beam, 6.2 meters; and draught, 4.8 meters. The final critical dimension was the distance from the keel to the top of the periscope housing, 11.2 meters. The following pages contained details of what else the ship must be fitted out with, specifically space for the crew and maintenance staff, room for supplies and torpedoes, and ample accommodations for the passengers/raiding parties. Details providing space for ample arms and munitions storage were also included.

Heinz asked in a authoritarian voice, "Now, what do you think?"

"Very interesting," Richard said quietly. But he thought, "Jesus H! Twisted, but ingenious—a U-Boat sailing the seven seas with a floating homeport. It will be a real *Flying Dutchman*. I've seen this act before when the German's sent out surface raiders disguised as merchant ships in 1939. It was effective, for a while."

He said aloud, "I'll have to do some research. I believe it normally takes about 18 months to build a container ship. If we intend to maintain secrecy, the final outfitting of the drydock facility may have to be completed in Buenos Aires at Global's shipyard."

"Good, good," said Heinz.

"Heinz, you—I mean we—will need to build a ship about 300 meters long. I'd estimate its cost roughly at $250 to $300 million. Where will we get the money?

"From the Arabs, of course."

"Will your Muslim bankers fund the project when they find out the cost?"

"Yes, they have an inexhaustible supply of gold."

"Really?"

"Not gold as in coins, ingots, or bars. I am talking about black gold: oil!"

Richard stood and said, "Can I offer you a drink?"

"Yes, please. A little *schnapps* will be fine, thank you."

Chapter 13
The Dream Lives

"Heinz, I have a few more questions," Richard said as he moved to the couch.

Heinz was really animated. "What do you want to know?"

"Where will you find a crew to operate and service the U-Boat?"

Heinz's eyes lit up as he said, "Toward the end of the War in Europe, von Ritter, Erdman, Strasse, and I were ordered by our superiors to identify and recruit capable U-Boat officers, sailors, and mechanics who were trained to operate and maintain the U-Boat that was already secreted in South America. All of them were loyal members of the Nazi Party. We brought them and their families to Argentina and settled them in the community we had constructed and camouflaged inland from the shore of the *Golfo San Matias*. As they have grown up, the children learned the skills of their fathers. They believe as we do. They are all loyal to the cause. The area was totally uninhabited before they arrived. They have been completely isolated there since the War and are supplied by air. Herr von Ritter has half a dozen WWII DC 3s, and he flies in supplies two or three times a week. There is also a well-camouflaged airfield and several warehouses that contain his cache of arms. So you see, we are presently developing a new solution to an old problem—*die verdammte Juden* and their promised land.

Richard responded in perfect German. "*Unglaublich*, that's unbelievable. Anything else, Heinz?"

"No," Heinz proudly announced.

"Well, that does it for me. I've heard enough for the time being. It's time to consider dinner. I thought you might enjoy a good German meal. We have a great restaurant here. Have you heard of *Rudi Leschner's*, Heinz?"

"I don't believe I have, but it sounds wonderful. I've worked up quite an appetite "

"I suppose you'd like to rest a bit after your long flight, so I'll call for you at six. There's someone I'd like you to meet. He'll be coming to dinner with us. Spanish is his native language so we can continue our conversation."

Richard escorted Heinz to the elevator door. When it opened and Heinz stepped inside and turned around, there was a very definite look of smug satisfaction on his face.

"See you at six," Richard said as the elevator door closed. He entered his office and was just hanging up the phone after making reservations for dinner when Steve emerged from the circular stairway that connected the office to Richard's apartment upstairs. It was hidden behind what looked like a closet door.

Steve could hardly contain himself. "Oh my God! That was an earful. What do you think?"

"The same as you, I'm sure. They are all demented, crazy as hell, and also very dangerous. Sounds like they intend to destroy Israel and the Jews if it's the last thing they do."

"He certainly made that plain enough."

"Well, part of it is true. This project will be the last thing they attempt to do. Since hearing those plans, I've been thinking. The residents of that colony of ex-patriot Nazis have been isolated for over 30 years. My guess is that they are all still hardcore and have raised their children to be the same. It appears that no one knows of their existence, and, even if they did, I seriously doubt that anyone in Argentina would give a damn. I'd bet everyone in the colony still speaks only German and lives in a toxic atmosphere of intense Nazism. They all probably live and breathe only to service, preserve, and operate the U-Boat for the Fatherland. They probably believe they are the last bastions of hope for the *Fourth Reich*."

"Otto von Ritter and the others were very clever to keep the colony well-supplied yet totally isolated. That being said, we are left with myriad problems to solve. If we do successfully destroy the U-Boat and its crew, we will still have to destroy the colony. It's mandatory that we dispose of the breeding ground and all of its inhabitants—men, women, and children. I'll bet all of the older children are fully indoctrinated and have already taken the Blood Oath of the *Hitler-Jugend*—the Hitler Youth. What do you suggest? Must they all be killed?"

"Steve, that's going to be a messy business. It's highly unlikely that any of the children over the age of three or four will be salvageable. Someone will have to make that decision when the time comes."

"Yes, I agree."

Richard continued, "And while we are at it, let me add to our list of hurdles. We must also deal with warehouses full of arms and ammunition, von Ritter's private air force, and the four industrialists."

"And let's not forget the Argentine government. Who knows how much of this story they're aware of?"

"None of these problems are insurmountable."

"Okay, but let me add one more speed bump. Have you considered what will happen to their companies when we eliminate Heinz and his buddies?"

"Oddly enough, that problem was solved years ago. Their boards have already been infiltrated by some of our people who will be in place to take control of them. But while we've been talking, I've been thinking. I have the beginnings of a plan to thwart the Nazis and to eliminate that nest of vipers—all of them. And the best part is—if all goes well—they will finance their own destruction. After Heinz leaves, we will gather our troops—James, JoAnn, and Nancy—to fine tune and work out the details.

"Get cleaned up. You're coming to dinner. You'll need no cover story. You are what you appear to be—a history professor at the University of Texas who was born in Argentina. Over dinner, and at my insistence, you will reluctantly tell Heinz your story. I want you to emphasize the fact that your father was German and that your grandparents never approved of him. Make up just one little white lie. Because of their disapproval of him they, never allowed you to be taught German by your Jesuit teachers. Then let the conversation go where it will."

"Right!"

"I want you there so that I can introduce you as my 'go to' guy, a loyal party member, and the man I trust at the Houston end of this operation."

"I understand."

"A word of caution, Steve. I'm intentionally not going to use your last name. Don't offer it to him until he asks."

Chapter 14
The Invitation

Steve and Richard arrived at Heinz's door at precisely 6 p.m. As they walked toward the elevator, Richard began the introductions. He gestured towards Heinz and said to Steve, "I'd like you to meet one of our leading industrialists in Buenos Aires. He is Wilhelm Heinz, the president of Argentina's largest mining, smelting, and casting operations."

They entered the elevator, and as it descended to the parking garage, Richard continued his flattering introductions.

"Wilhelm, may I introduce you to Esteban. He is a professor of history at the University of Texas in Austin. He is a fellow Argentinian and also my right hand man and a loyal party member."

After exiting the elevator, they walked to a brand new white BMW. Richard thought that using his German-made car would be a nice touch.

"Very nice," Heinz commented as he buckled in for the 15-minute drive to the restaurant.

Upon entering the darkened restaurant, they were warmly greeted by Rudi Leschner, himself. He directed the *maitre d'* to seat them in a small private dining room as Richard had requested when he phoned for the reservation. The three men settled around the table and perused the menu. Heinz seemed very pleased with the available selections. They all decided on pork schnitzel, spaetzle, and cucumber salad. Red cabbage and pan-fried potatoes would also accompany the meal. The waiter immediately brought them a basket of fragrant, warm bread with butter.

Richard asked Heinz to select the beverage, and he chose the *Paulaner Original Münchner Premium Lager*. It turned out to be an excellent choice, and the waiter kept their steins full.

While they were enjoying the bread, butter, and beer, Heinz turned to Steve and said, "Tell me a little about yourself, Esteban."

At first, Steve seemed a little reticent to speak, but Richard encouraged him to go ahead. As he began his tale, Richard locked his gaze on Heinz who appeared to listen intently. He seemed very interested.

"In 1939 my mother fell in love with an army officer who was assigned to the German Embassy in Buenos Aires. Unbeknownst to her parents, they met in church and somehow made arrangements to spend time together. When she realized she was pregnant, they married very quietly. Shortly thereafter, he was recalled to Germany, and that was the last time she saw him. This marriage and the pregnancy did not please her parents. They were embarrassed that she had not adhered to the strict rules their social class embraced. It is true that he was Catholic—but the wrong kind. He was a German Catholic. That was very unsatisfactory to them. My mother was turned out of the house and lived in a hotel until I was born. She had inherited some money, but, with a new baby, hotel living was not a good option. She needed help and turned to a married friend who took her in. Soon after that, she received word through the German Embassy that her husband—my father—had been killed in North Africa. When my grandparents heard that news, they swallowed their pride, relented, and allowed us to return to the family *estancia*. After all, I was their only grandchild."

As he came to the end of his story, Heinz inquired, "I'm sorry. What was your father's name again? I don't think I caught it."

"Kreutzer. His name was Kreutzer. He was a Captain, I think. That's all I know of him."

A momentary flicker of recognition seemed to cross Heinz's face.

"One more thing. The Jesuits educated me, but my grandparents, because of their prejudices, forbade the priests to teach me to read, write, or speak German. Although I loved them, I always resented their attitude toward my father and his people. I think that might be the reason I am drawn to the cause."

A slight smile crossed Heinz's face, and he turned the conversation to dove hunting. Suddenly, with a burst of enthusiasm, he exclaimed, "Richard, why don't we invite Esteban to hunt with us in Argentina? We need some new blood. I'm a little tired of George and von Ritter telling tales to each other."

They both looked at Steve, and Heinz asked, "You do hunt don't you?"

"Yes, indeed I do—every chance I get."

Heinz countered rather robustly, "Good! Good! Then it's settled. We shall include you in our little group. Don't you agree, Richard?"

Richard nodded his head while keeping a poker face. Inside he was grinning from ear to ear. They all enjoyed the dinner and topped it off with warm apple strudel and coffee. When they were finished, Heinz said, "It's been a long and productive day, *meine Freunde*, and I have a 6 a.m. flight in the morning."

"Yes, let's get going," Richard agreed as they all rose from the table and headed outside where the BMW awaited with the valet opening the doors as they approached.

As they were ascending in the elevator at the hotel, Heinz said in a rather conspiratorial voice, "As soon as I get home, I'll start making the necessary financial arrangements for you and the ship, Richard. I assume you'll be in touch when you've had time to formulate a plan."

Steve offered his hand to Heinz who shook it vigorously.

"See you in Argentina for the hunt, Professor Kreutzer," Heinz said as he closed the door to his room.

For Richard and Steve the evening wasn't quite over. Richard said, "I think we need to rehash today's events. Are you up for it?"

"I'm good."

Chapter 15
What's In a Name?

They settled into comfortable chairs in the living room of the apartment. Richard said, "Did you happen to notice the immediate change of expression on Heinz's face at the mention of your father's last name?"

"Yes, as a matter of fact I did. Then he couldn't wait to invite me to hunt with your party."

"My guess is he knows something. Dollars to doughnuts, he called Buenos Aires as soon as he closed his door. I can check on that in the morning. Do you still have contacts within *Mossad* in Argentina? I recall that you were involved in some way with them during the *Volsung Project*."

"As a matter of fact, I do. I keep in touch with them from time to time. Why do you ask?"

"I'm a little uneasy about this whole affair. Heinz and his Nazi friends are paranoid as hell. I'm certain they have me under surveillance. In spite of the fact that my name is on their list of deep-cover agents, I'm not sure they really trust me. But, they need me and my company must remain squeaky clean. Their paranoia runs deep. At dinner tonight, when Heinz suddenly perked up at the mention of your name and offered you an invitation to hunt with us, the hair on the back of my neck stood up."

"I agree. It was abrupt, impulsive, and curious. You seem to have something on your mind. What the hell is it?"

"I believe you need to contact your friends at *Mossad*. See if they can provide us with all the information they can find about your father and his family—all the way back to the first day of creation, if possible. I don't like surprises, and I think Heinz and company are planning one for us."

"Now who's paranoid?"

"Not paranoid, just cautious. Ask them to deliver the information in a diplomatic pouch to the Israeli Consulate here in Houston. Then the Consulate can deliver it to me by courier."

Steve nodded. "Richard, how much damage do you think these screwballs can do with no conventional army and a single obsolete U-Boat?"

"Let me put it this way, Steve. As you are fully aware, there are literally millions of restive, young Muslims out there with no jobs and no prospects. *Jihad* is the only thing on their minds. They are continually being indoctrinated to hate all Westerners, the United States, and Christians, as well as Jews, the world over. In particular, they're all intent on destroying the State of Israel. It's probably the only thing all the Muslim sects can agree on.

"They're combat-ready at a moment's notice, with very minimal logistical support required. In the field, their equipment consists of a prayer rug, a vest full of explosives, and an AK-47 with a full magazine or two. They can operate in small cells or independently.

"They're not looking for medals. Once they begin a mission, no one expects them home for dinner. As I said before, their reward will be 72 virgins—age and sex unspecified They require none of the trappings that plague every modern army. They need no medical corps, no commissary, no Red Cross, and certainly no Geneva Convention.

"Just imagine, for the sake of argument, that five *jihadists* walk into the emergency rooms at five major hospitals in Houston. Each detonates an explosive device. Not only would the devastation be enormous, but panic would ensue. The entire medical delivery system in the area would be paralyzed. Multiply that by the number of hospitals in every city and state. Preposterous, you say? Think about it. How many young, willing prospects are already living in this country? Worldwide, there must be thousands and thousands of men, women, and children willing to sacrifice themselves. It is expected of them. They believe in their cause. They can act independently or in small cells as terror units."

"Oh, crap! I've got the picture. They want to use the U-Boat to transport these *jihadists* all over the place. No one will know when or where to expect the next attack."

"Well, for sure this boat that Heinz and his cohorts want me to build to serve as a mobile submarine base and cargo ship may be what they want, but I intend to help them get more than they're expecting. As soon as we can figure a way to get them all in one place at the same time, we'll eliminate that whole damn nest of Nazi bastards once and for all. Steve, you realize that if the *jihad* begins in earnest, there will be no stopping it. The Jews will be first, the Christians next, and the Nazis will be right behind, even if they don't believe it. The *jihadists* will eliminate whomever they decide is unworthy."

"Yes, that picture is clear enough."

"I believe my next assignment is to find someone to draw up some plans and build us a very expensive boat with Middle Eastern oil money."

"I'll make that call to my *Mossad* contact in Buenos Aires first thing tomorrow."

"Great, time to hit the sack."

Chapter 16
The Plan Emerges

By the time Richard was up and dressed the next morning, Steve had already called the Israeli Embassy in Buenos Aires to set the wheels in motion to investigate his family history. Since Heinz had seemed so interested in the name, Kreutzer, they wanted to head him off at the pass.

As they sat down for a quick breakfast, Richard said, "By the way, I did check with the front desk to see if Heinz made any interesting calls last night."

"Did he?'

"Indeed he did. He called the German Embassy in Buenos Aires. The plot thickens."

After they ate, Richard drove Steve to the airport for his flight back to Austin. Upon returning to his office, Richard put his plan in motion. His first call was to James Hill. He filled him in on the meeting with Heinz and asked him who he should contact for advise about building the ship needed to carry out the Nazis' nefarious plan. Without hesitation, James gave him the name and private phone number of his friend at the U.S. Naval Academy. Captain Willard Pike had formerly been a member of ONI—Office of Naval Intelligence. As such, Captain Pike had helped James's father, Colonel Garnett Hill, get some vital information a few years before that was critical to putting a stop to the *Volsung Project*. Richard lost no time in making the call.

"Captain Pike speaking, how may I be of service?"

"Good morning, sir. My name is Richard Eherenfeld. How are you?"

"Quite well, thanks. What can I do for you on this fine day? Our mutual friend, James, has already alerted me to expect your call."

"That was quick."

Richard gave Pike the short version of the project, and Pike immediately suggested they meet in Annapolis.

"I think I know just the man who can help you solve your dilemma. Can you fly up to Lee Airport here in Annapolis on Wednesday? I'll meet you. Just call and give me an approximate arrival time."

Curiously, Richard slipped back into military jargon for a moment and replied, "Roger that."

When Richard's company plane landed at Lee Airport on Wednesday, Captain Pike and his driver were there to meet him.

"I made an appointment for us to see our professor of Marine Engineering and Design. He's young, but a real cracker jack. I told him what you needed, and I think he'll be able to solve your problem in short order."

Their Jeep passed through the front gate, salutes were exchanged, and they headed directly to the building that housed the Engineering and Drafting Department. Entering a large entryway, they climbed two flights of stairs. Lieutenant Commander John Ericsson greeted them and ushered them into his office. The first thing Richard noticed sitting on his desk in a glass case was a scale model of the Union's Civil War gunboat, *The Monitor.*

Richard outlined the situation, his requirements, and gave Ericsson the dimensions and displacement of the U-Boat. Ericsson listened intently. The engineer took out his calculator and began to work.

He thought for a few minutes and said, "You'll probably need a ship roughly 300 meters long with a beam of 51 meters. Equipped with the proper propulsion system, she could do between 10 and 25 knots on the open sea. At present, there are three shipyards on the top of my list that I believe could fill the bill. The first is Crandall Drydock Engineering. It's located in Boston. Next there is *Krupp Germaniawerft*, located in Kiel, Germany. Another good choice would be The Israel Shipyards, which are located in Kishon—a part of the Port of Haifa.

"Okay."

Commander Ericsson continued. "Trying to keep your project a secret will be like trying to hide an elephant in the living room. Your best bet, in my opinion, is to work with the Israelis. They have a staff of excellent marine engineers. They do good work, and they know how to keep things secret. But here are the phone numbers for all three.

"The usual time to completion for a ship like this is about 15 to 18 months. However, I sense a bit of urgency about this unusual project. If one had unlimited funds and enough men to work around the clock, a ship like this could be completed in about 180 days. Our shipyards turned out Liberty Ships for WWII in that time frame. I hope I've been of some help to you, Mr. Eherenfeld."

"Oh you most certainly have," Richard said as they all stood up. "I've heard of the Liberty Ships, but I didn't know they required three shifts a day. By the way, are you by any chance related to John Ericsson referred to in Civil War history books as the 'irascible genius' of marine engineering who designed *The Monitor?*"

"Yes, indeed. He was my great-great-grandfather."

"Very interesting. Thanks for your assistance, Commander."

"Before you leave, Mr. Eherenfeld, I've just had another thought. If the name on the contract to build your ship was that of a neutral company, your secret might keep a little longer."

"Thanks again, Commander, you've been more than helpful."

Captain Pike escorted Richard back to the Jeep, and they returned to Lee Airport. On the flight back to Houston, Richard began to mull over his options, weighing the pros and cons in his mind. Commander Ericsson had said that with adequate numbers of men and the proper incentive, it would be possible for a shipyard to construct the ship in about 180 days. He continued to review his options over and over. Suddenly, it all became crystal clear to him.

He blurted out, "By God, Ericsson is right! I'll have the Israelis build the damn ship right under the Arabs' noses. If Heinz and his people begin to get nosy, they'll be looking for a ship that will take 15 to 18 months to build and have Global's name on the contract. Worldwide, there are probably 30 or more shipyards building container ships. Kishon would be the last place on earth the Nazis would think to look, especially if some friendly entity would contract for the ship to be built. Transfer of the ownership of the vessel can change at the time of delivery. I can't wait to see how Steve and James react to this plan. If it works, and we get away with it, they'll call it a stroke of genius. If it doesn't work, they'll say I was 'mad as a hatter.'"

As soon as Richard returned to his Houston office, he asked Rose to set up a conference call with James and Steve as soon as possible. When he had them both on the line he said, "Time for a council of war, gentlemen. Steve, please bring Nancy. James, I think it's about time to call up the heavy artillery. Ask JoAnn to join us, as well. I'll fill everyone in on the details when we meet. Rose will arrange a date suitable for everyone."

Chapter 17
Road Trip

While Steve and Nancy were having dinner at her place on Thursday, he brought her up to date with regard to the weekend meeting with Heinz and Richard. He told her that Richard was calling a council of war and had respectfully requested her presence at the meeting.

Nancy said, "Count on me. I assume he'll be sending his plane for us?"

"Yes."

"Good."

"I don't know what your role will be, but I know you'll be a great asset to the project. Nancy, I've been thinking."

"Very good. My congratulations, professor. Thinking is worthy of a C+ in my class."

"Thanks for the vote of confidence. Things are about to get a bit dicey with this U-Boat project. Would you consider getting away this coming weekend? I've been dying to visit your ranch."

"Now, that's a great idea! You get an A+ for that one. I'll call Maria and alert her. She'll make all of the arrangements, get the house ready, and stock up the refrigerator. Remember, Steve, out there we observe the old world house rules. Maria's old-fashioned and very Catholic. Separate bedrooms will be the order of the day. If she even suspects we are sleeping together, she'll have a litter of kittens on the spot."

Steve responded, "Why, of course, anything for the sake of propriety. I'll pick you up after your class on Friday."

"Fine, I'm looking forward to it."

The weather forecast for the weekend was perfect for some outdoor activities, with the highs in the 70's and lows in the 50's. But this was West Texas, where the weather can change on a dime and give you a nickel change.

They headed west toward Nancy's ranch, which was fairly isolated with the nearest identifiable point on the map being the "thriving metropolis" of Cleo. Cleo consisted of a dilapidated roadside convenience store that sported a single, antiquated gas pump. Inside, however, the proprietor had stocked an eclectic assortment of items. Ammunition in obsolete calibers, beef jerky, *Twinkies*, and even snowshoes could be found on the shelves.

As they passed the store, Nancy said, "My parents haven't lived on the ranch in years. They prefer their home on the western edge of San Antonio. Most of their neighbors there consider themselves to be the last of the 'Old Spanish Aristocracy in Texas.'"

Thirty minutes later, they approached the ranch gate that had been left open for them. Nancy exclaimed, "Good old Joe. He thinks of everything."

"How long has he been foreman of the ranch?"

"Both of them have been here for as long as I can remember. My father designed and built their home to be a duplicate of the main ranch house on a slightly smaller scale."

As they parked the Suburban, Maria and Joe came out to meet them. There were hugs and kisses all around. The four of them spent nearly an hour talking and eating lunch. They devoured the ham and cheese sandwiches Maria had prepared and caught up on the news of other ranchers in the area. Afterwards, Steve and Nancy excused themselves and drove on to the main house about half a mile down the road. Tucked on the seat between them were a pot of chili and a basket of fresh tortillas that Maria had made and sent with them for dinner.

As they were bringing in their bags, Steve asked, "May I use the phone in the house?"

"Of course! Do you need to make an emergency call?"

"Well, it's not exactly an emergency, but I am very curious about some information I'm waiting for from Buenos Aires. I'll pay for the call."

"No you won't. Have at it."

Steve dialed the string of numbers he knew by heart. After a few rings, a voice on the other end said, "Israeli Embassy."

"Let me speak to Ari, please."

"One moment, please."

"Ari here. How can I be of service?"

Ari, this is Esteban Kreutzer. I called about a week ago concerning some genealogical research regarding my father and his family. Do you have anything yet?"

"Fortunately for you, the Germans keep meticulous records. The information is in a diplomatic pouch on its way to Richard Eherenfeld's Houston office as we speak, *Herr von Kreutzer.*"

"Many thanks. I owe you a big one. But what the hell is this *Herr von Kreutzer?*"

"You'll see soon enough my friend. *Adios.*"

Nancy asked, "What was that all about?"

"At dinner the other night, Heinz seemed to visibly react to the name, Kreutzer. Richard and I both noticed it. It seemed as if it had struck some kind of familiar chord with him. He knows something that we don't. Nancy, sadly I know nothing about my father. I don't even know his first name."

"That is sad. Can I assume you were speaking to a *Mossad* agent?"

"Bulls-eye!"

Showing Steve the ranch took most of the afternoon. Nancy drove the beat-up old ranch truck and found an abundance of wild life, including some really large bucks, a bumper crop of quail, a small herd of antelope, and a few jackrabbits. The sunset was spectacular. They ended the tour in the barn where Steve picked out the horse he wanted to ride the next day.

When they returned to the house, Nancy warmed up the chili while Steve opened a couple of beers. They enjoyed a real ranch dinner in the tranquil setting. When they were finished with the dishes, Nancy showed Steve to one of the many guestrooms down the hall from the large master bedroom that would be hers.

"Why so many guest rooms?"

"The weather changes so rapidly, and often severely, out here that most of the ranchers build a few extra rooms that can accommodate stranded visitors."

The room Nancy had chosen for Steve harbored a huge humpback trunk in one corner.

"Now that trunk looks interesting. Have you ever looked to see what's inside?"

"No way. That's Mother's. It's been in the family for over 150 years. There's no telling what's inside, but it's hands off without her permission."

Nancy said goodnight, and left Steve in the very comfortable room. He took a shower, unpacked his bag, and disturbed the bed linens sufficiently so as to suggest that he had slept there. Then he went on a little tour of the house on his own. Halfway down the hall, he met Nancy.

"Looking for something?" she asked.

"As a matter of fact, I am. To be specific, I'm looking for you."

Steve awoke to the smell of frying bacon and heard Nancy call, "Breakfast is ready!"

He entered the kitchen and said, "It's a beautiful day. Let's go for a ride after we eat."

"Sounds good to me."

After a nice long ride, they finally worked their way back to the barn. They unsaddled and unbridled the horses, gave them a rubdown, and fed and watered them.

Nancy suggested, "How about lunch, a beer, and a football game?"

"That works for me."

As Nancy headed for the kitchen, she asked, "Why don't we have our friends out here for a few days after Christmas? We could celebrate the New Year."

"That's sounds great to me. But hadn't you better consult with Maria first?"

Chapter 18
Play Lose Me

Richard had not slept well Sunday night. He was anticipating the delivery of the diplomatic pouch with Steve's genealogical information, but that wasn't what had kept him awake. He was convinced that Heinz's people had him under surveillance. Rose had set up a meeting for him with the Israel Shipyards in Haifa. The dilemma nagging at him now was how to get out of Houston without being spotted. In this case a little paranoia was a good thing. He certainly didn't want anyone seeing him board an *El Al* flight. He picked up the phone and called Steve.

"The diplomatic pouch hasn't arrived yet. When it does, I'll have my pilots fly it up to Austin. That's not why I called. I need your help." Richard explained his concerns about slipping out of Houston without being detected.

Steve responded immediately, "Call the Israeli Consulate in Houston. Ask for Kalish. I'm sure my contact will be able to help you."

"Thanks, Steve." Richard hung up the phone, dialed a number, and a pleasant female voice answered.

"Consulate. How may I help you?"

"This is Richard Eherenfeld from Global Import/Export. May I speak to Kalish?"

"Certainly, sir. One moment, please."

After a few moments, Richard was surprised to hear the voice on the other end of the line say, "Sarah Kalish, how may I be of service, Mr. Eherenfeld?"

At first he was surprised that "Kalish" was a woman. Then he remembered that all Israeli women serve in the Army and make damn good soldiers. He regained his composure and said, "I'm a friend of Esteban Kreutzer. He gave me your name and thought you might be able to help me."

"Tell me what you need. I hope I can."

Richard explained the situation as briefly as he could.

"Give me a couple of hours and your phone number. I'll get back to you."

Precisely two hours later, Kalish called him back. "I've come up with a plan. Everything you require will be delivered to the Global Import/Export hangar office at Hobby Airport by noon tomorrow. Let's go over the list together to be sure we have everything. I'll be sending you an *El Al* flight engineer's uniform and cap, a slightly worn brief case, and an Israeli passport. Just give me the correct sizes. You're scheduled to travel to Ben Gurion Airport in Tel Aviv on *El Al* Flight 1117 from Houston International Airport. You will be traveling under the name Marty Golden. You are a flight engineer and, as such, will be flying with the other officers in the cockpit. Your code name is 'olive.' From this moment on, the Nazis won't be the only ones having you under surveillance.

"Oh, and one other thing. Why don't you spend the night at your office at Hobby? I will arrange for a taxi driven by someone from the Consulate, a *Mossad* agent, to pick you up Wednesday morning at 4:15 a.m. to take you to Houston International. Anything else?"

"Sounds like you've thought of everything—a simple but very clever plan. Many thanks, Sarah!"

As promised, everything on the list was delivered as ordered to Richard's office by noon on Tuesday. He awoke at 4 a.m. and dressed in his *El Al* uniform. Everything he would need for the next few days was in his carry all. The taxi arrived on time and took him directly to Houston International.

Everything went off without a hitch. No one had followed the cab. As the driver opened the cab door he said, "Go directly to the *El Al* counter, show them your passport, and ask for security. They'll get you to the plane."

"Thanks."

As promised, security escorted him directly to the *El Al* flight personnel lounge where the crew was assembled. When they read his name tag, they nodded warmly. Obviously they were expecting him. The aroma of hot, fresh coffee filled the lounge. Richard took a cup and helped himself to several of the fresh pastries.

Richard fell into lock step with the other members of the crew for Flight 1117. When the call came for them to board the plane, they were escorted by a security detail.

"So far so good," he thought as the cockpit door closed behind him. Richard finally began to relax as soon as the plane was up and heading toward Tel Aviv. A flight attendant knocked on the door and gave Richard an envelope that he opened immediately.

The message read, "Take a cab to the Crowne Plaza Hotel in Tel Aviv when you arrive. It is about a 20-minute ride. There is a reservation in the name of Marty Golden at the hotel. Check in. You will be contacted there."

As he settled into a cab outside of Ben Gurion Airport, Richard thought to himself, "Steve was correct. Kalish has planned this out to the very smallest detail. I'd bet this driver is a *Mossad* agent, too." At the hotel, he checked in and was taken to a suite on the top floor. The bellman deposited his carryall inside the room and left immediately without waiting for the usual gratuity for such service. There was a man sitting on a couch. He rose and extended his hand to Richard as the door closed.

"*Shalom*, Richard. Just call me Jake. I understand we have some business to transact regarding some nautical equipment."

Richard responded, "*Shalom*, Jake." He immediately flopped into a chair and motioned for Jake to do the same.

Jake, who was an American-educated Israeli began, "So far, all we know is that you are interested in contracting with our company to build a ship for your company. We understand that it is to be an ocean-going, self-propelled drydock with dual purposes. Purpose one, a mobile drydock. Purpose two, a commercial container ship. Am I correct?"

"So far so good."

"Would you care to elaborate any further or give me some additional details?"

"No, not at this moment. By the way, could you show me some identification to prove you are who you say you are?"

"Do you read Hebrew?"

Richard didn't answer, but accepted the ID card offered to him. Everything on the card was in Hebrew, except the picture. Of course he couldn't read it. The picture was Jake, all right. He turned the card over, and taped to the reverse side was a piece of paper with one word on it. Olive. He handed the card back to Jake and said, "Okay, Jake, where would you like to discuss this project?"

"Suppose we take my car to Haifa? You can show us your plans or whatever it is that you have in that briefcase. I'll introduce you to our chief marine engineer and designer, Eric Benjamin. It's a 90 km trip. It'll take us about an hour.

Chapter 19
The Secret

The office building was a seven-story structure made of steel and glass. To be more precise, the windows were actually made of polycarbonate. This building could withstand a rocket attack, and the windows could absorb multiple hits from .50 caliber armor-piercing projectiles and RPGs. In other words, the building was bullet and bombproof. It was a fortress, and Richard suspected it might be housing more than a simple marine engineering facility for a shipyard.

Richard and Jake took the elevator to the third floor. When the steel doors opened, they entered a well-lit, cavernous room filled with drafting tables. In the far corner of the room facing Kishon, a part of the Port of Haifa complex, there was a spacious office equipped with a drafting table and a large steel desk. Standing behind the desk was Eric Benjamin. He was an American marine engineer working for Israel Shipyards Ltd. His office wall was papered with degrees and honors. Two diplomas immediately caught Richard's eye. One was from MIT while the other was from Cal Tech.

Richard held out his hand and said, "*Shalom.*"

Eric returned the greeting and wasted no time. "I have a very general idea of what you're asking us to do. May I see your sketches?" He took them, spread them out on his desk, and studied them for half an hour. Richard and Jake remained silent as they sat in comfortable chairs and helped themselves to coffee from the carafe on the side table.

Finally, Eric broke the silence. "I think I have a clearer idea of what you need. Now I have a few questions, and I need some more details."

Richard was about to answer when Eric held up a hand and said, "Before you begin, you need to know that I am also with *Mossad* and that I'm aware, at least to some degree, of the situation in Argentina." He started to pull out his credentials.

Richard said, "No need to do that. I believe you. How much do you know? I'll fill in as many of the blanks as I can as we go along. Are we secure here?"

Jake laughed, "Secure? We're as snug as a bug in a rug!"

Richard gave them a fairly complete assessment of the U-Boat and the colony of ex-patriot Nazis living near the *Golfo san Matias*.

Jake then took up the narrative. "Mossad has been aware of the colony for some time, but not the U-Boat. I think we can now understand the reason for perpetuating that isolated colony of Germans. They needed to keep the U-Boat operational. But we don't understand to what end. Where is this all going? We are also quite familiar with the four industrialists in Buenos Aires, as well. In the not too distant past, there had been a plan to initiate a *Fourth Reich*. That's no secret either. How they intend to do it has so far eluded us. Can you fill us in?"

"You may be too close to the problem," Richard said.

"Possibly," said Eric. "What do you think is going on?"

"One of the four Nazi industrialists, von Ritter, has been actively supplying arms to rogue elements and *jihadists* throughout North Africa and the Middle East."

Eric and Jake nodded.

Richard finally spelled out the plan. "Our belief is that when the time to strike seems propitious, there will be a call for a worldwide *jihad* against Jews and Christians. The Nazis will be next on the list, but I'm not sure they have figured that out. At this time, the *jihadists* have no leader powerful enough to unite them all. However, that could change. For now, the four Argentines want this ship constructed to be a mobile drydock and container transport owned and operated by my company, Global Import/Export. The principle reason for choosing us is that we are squeaky clean and above suspicion—not to mention the fact that they believe I am a deep-cover Nazi agent—a holdover from World War II."

Jake said, "We are already aware of the increase in coded chatter over the air waves. Much of it is directed either to or from the Middle East. It is a bit troubling. So, we ask again—why a self-propelled drydock hidden in a container ship?"

Richard said, "Have you fellows forgotten your history lessons and how devious your adversaries still are? Remember the *Atlantis* from 1939? She was a German surface raider disguised as a merchant ship that roamed the South Atlantic. Her mission was to fly a neutral flag as she approached unwary neutral and enemy merchant ships. As she drew closer, she would raise her German Battle Ensign, pounce on the unsuspecting merchantmen, and sink them. I think they're about to try a variation of that trick, but they are using a floating drydock/U-Boat pen hidden inside a working commercial container ship."

Eric jumped in, "My God! The damn U-Boat will never be seen. They'll be able to land spies, fully armed raiding parties, and *jihadists* anywhere and everywhere in the world and keep them supplied. They will create havoc worldwide. They will be able to strike at will. She'll become a 20th Century *Flying Dutchman*, a ghost ship sailing the seas that never puts into port."

"That's exactly what I thought when Heinz first made his proposition!" Richard said.

"It's down right diabolical," Jake agreed.

Richard continued, "It will create as much chaos in the shipping lanes as Captain Nemo did in Jules Vern's *20,000 Leagues Under the Sea.*"

"How interesting," Eric remarked.

Richard explained, "They hope precipitating *jihad* in the Middle East, North Africa, and possibly worldwide, will create a smoke screen for the rise of the *Fourth Reich*."

"They're completely demented," Eric shouted.

Richard said, "Demented or not, that seems to be the plan as I understand it so far."

Jake added, "Even though Israel just agreed to peace with Egypt in March, depredations and hostile incursions by PLO forces based in Lebanon continue to harass us."

"Now I get the picture," Eric said. "Let's get back to the plans. I see from Commander Ericsson's notes that he estimated a ship with the length of 300 meters and a beam of 50 meters or so. We also have the dimensions of the U-Boat as well as her displacement numbers. One crucial factor will be the requirement that the entire container ship be able to fill all of her ballast tanks simultaneously in order to gain an additional 10.7 meters or 35 feet of depth—evenly and uniformly—so the submarine can successfully dock. That will tax our engineers a bit. I'll assign our best men to begin some preliminary plans in the morning. The usual time frame for the plans to be completed is about three to four weeks. I sense a need for speed, stealth, and silence in this project. I think we can accommodate you with preliminary plans in about one week. Normally construction time to build a ship like this is 15 to 18 months if there are no hitches. However, with the proper incentives, that time could be abbreviated significantly. I understand that during WWII with people working around the clock, Americans produced Liberty Ships at a rate of one every 180 days. Today our technology is better."

Richard was impressed. "That sounds promising."

Eric said, "Jake, are you sure we should get involved in this?"

"Hell, yes!"

"Here's the irony of it all," Richard continued. "The Nazis want this to be hush-hush. They claim they don't want to know where the ship is being built or by what company. I don't believe or trust them. They'll get antsy and start snooping around as soon as the money has been deposited in a Swiss bank. Commander Ericsson had an idea. As added security, is it possible to have a friendly, neutral company contract to build the ship?"

"Great idea, Richard! I'll call our old friend Nicholas Alexander Poulos, the Greek shipping magnate," Jake responded. "He's always in the market for another big ship. He's been of service to *Mossad* many times before."

"How can we be sure he can be trusted?" Richard asked.

"After what he saw those people do to his family and his village during the Nazi occupation of Greece in 1941, let's just say he has an old score to settle," Jake responded.

Richard admonished both men, "You do understand that the Nazi industrialists and their bankers must not find out who is building their ship or where it is being built?"

Jake asked, "Where is the funding for this enterprise originating?"

"You'll never guess. It's your convivial neighbors who roam the deserts to the South, East, and North of you—the men in long white robes and *keffiyehs*. They're funding the ship with oil money—black gold. Neither they nor Heinz and his friends know that you're building it. Commander Ericsson said you do excellent work and can keep this project a secret longer than anyone else on the planet. So here we are."

Eric said, "All right, let's talk numbers. My rough estimate is that this ship will run in the neighborhood of $200 million to $250 million. Maybe more. Don't hold me to that exact figure."

Richard smiled, "Let's round it off to $300 million. What the hell! That's just pocket change to your neighbors."

Eric suddenly said, "Jake, have we lost our minds? Are we willing to build this ship and turn it loose to sail the seven seas with a U-Boat full of

Arabs and Nazis in its belly? Those people are as crazy as hell! You're liable to Start WWIII, or worse yet, Armageddon! Richard, are you really serious about allowing those people to roam the world unchecked? Out with it! What the hell do you know that we don't?"

"Simply this. You are going to build it. And my people are going to sink it in the middle of the South Atlantic!"

"Are you out of your damn mind? Sink it after we build it?"

"I'm happy to say, yes! And we will do it with all hands on board. That's all I can tell you now, but be patient. I promise I will reveal all in time. For now, just trust me and build the damn ship. Begin laying the keel as soon as the plans are on paper. I'll need my demolition expert to meet with you immediately so you can coordinate the placement of the explosives and their detonators during the building phase."

"So do I understand you want us to build a floating time bomb in our own shipyards?"

"It might seem that way, but I can assure you that the explosives are inert and that you will be in no danger. My demolition expert will brief you on the particulars."

Jake said, "If we build it and those Middle Eastern bankers or Argentine Nazis find out about this, your life won't be worth two Argentine *centavos, amigo.*"

Then it's settled. You build it, and let us take care of the rest. How soon can you have those plans available?"

Eric thought for a few minutes. "About six or seven days. My men will be working overtime.

"Eric, could you possibly fly to Houston to show my team the plans next week?"

"Yes, I think so."

"Then it's settled. Kalish's plan worked like a charm. How about sending me home the same way I got here?"

Jake agreed, "Right, but might I suggest that we book you on a flight that lands in Atlanta or at Dulles, just in case your Nazi friends are waiting for you in Houston?"

"Good idea! Atlanta would be great. I'll have my plane meet me there. I'll make the call when I'm in the air."

"Your uniform has been cleaned and pressed, Flight Engineer Golden. Now let's all go out for a late dinner and then get you back to your hotel in Tel Aviv."

Chapter 20
The Plans

The flight back was much less stressful. Everything that was needed to insure the anonymity of the enterprise had been put into place. After landing in Atlanta, Richard trooped into the lounge with the *El Al* crew, changed clothes, and returned the Flight Engineer's suit, hat, and briefcase. A security officer escorted him to the gate where his Citation II was parked. As the plane headed west to Houston, he called Rose to verify next week's meeting.

"Glad to hear you're back," Rose said. "I've scheduled the meeting for Thursday. Nancy will be able to attend, and JoAnn understands that it's a command performance for her.

"Good. Eric Benjamin will be flying over on Wednesday to go over the preliminary plans for the ship. He'll be staying with me."

As soon as Richard returned to his office, he called Steve. "I have a sealed diplomatic pouch on my desk addressed to you. Shall I have my pilot fly it up to you today?"

"That would be great. I'll meet him at the airport any time after 4 p.m."

The next call Richard made was to Heinz in Buenos Aires. Heinz answered his phone on the second ring, and Richard could hear the anticipation in his voice.

"Richard, you have something for us, yes?"

"Wilhelm, how are you? I believe it is time for us to meet with regard to our business enterprise. Could you arrange a short hunting trip down there? Make it over a weekend in about two weeks, if possible."

"Of course, how many will there be in your party?"

"There will be three of us—Kreutzer, me, and a special guest from Texas."

"Excellent! I will bring the rest of our party."

"By the way, before the hunt is over, I'll need to have a written confirmation that the entire amount—in American dollars—has been deposited to a numbered account in Switzerland. Of course, I'll also need the number."

"It will be arranged by the time you get here. Can you give me a figure now?"

"Yes, but understand that it is only an approximation. You must tell your bankers that due to the rather unusual requirements of this particular project, additional funds may be required."

"I understand. Give me the figure."

"I'll need $300 million deposited in a *Credit Suisse* account in Zürich. I must be able to confirm that before anything can start. In fact, I need to confirm it before the hunt is over."

Chapter 21
The Conference

Seated at his desk at Israel Shipyards, Eric Benjamin looked out the window at the ships in various stages of construction. He was thinking, however, of his newest project. He turned to Jake and said, "I'll be flying to Houston at 4 p.m. on Tuesday with some plans. I'll arrive Wednesday and have a meeting with Richard and his colleagues planned for Thursday. Do you intend to come with me?"

"No, I can't possibly be of any assistance to you regarding plans. Besides, it's unwise to tie up too many *Mossad* agents in one place unless it's absolutely necessary."

"I agree. You'll know everything that transpires when I return. I'm giving the crew the go-ahead to start laying the keel now. With an all-out effort, running three double crews, I'm hoping we can have this ship completed in six months."

"I'll leave that up to you. I'm only taking care of security for this project, and I think we've covered all the bases. Have a safe trip."

"Thanks. Going *El Al* should be safe enough."

Indeed, it was. Eric arrived in Houston without incident the day before the meeting and spent the night with Richard. They had a chance to go over the plans before everyone else arrived.

On Thursday, Steve and Nancy arrived at Richard's office at 11:30 a.m. A few minutes later James came in. He was escorting a well dressed, very attractive, and fit looking young woman. She had short dark brown hair and green eyes. Everyone turned to look as they entered the office. Richard said, "Everyone, I'd like you to meet JoAnn Scarlett. JoAnn, this is Eric Benjamin, Chief Marine Engineer at Israel Shipyards. Eric, JoAnn is our resident demolition expert. She has just been promoted to Major."

"Well, I'll be damned," Eric exclaimed. "I had no idea you were a woman."

"I hope you won't hold that against me. I understand your firm is building the ship I'm supposed to blow up. Is that correct?"

"Indeed, that appears to be the case."

"Hold on a minute, you two," Richard interjected. "I haven't introduced JoAnn to our other guests. Please meet Dr. Steve Kreutzer and Dr. Nancy Alvarez."

"Pleased to meet you, as well," JoAnn laughed.

James interrupted the pleasantries. "This is about the wildest caper I've ever heard of!"

"It wins first prize with me, as well," Eric replied as he opened the cylindrical container. "Here are the preliminary blueprints. We can study them right here if it's all right. Stand here close to the desk so you can see, JoAnn."

Richard cleared his desk, and Eric unrolled the blueprints, placing paperweights on all four corners to keep the plans flat. He began, "For now, I'll not go into too much detail about the type and horsepower of the engines. The ship will be slightly smaller than Commander Ericsson estimated. The length of the ship will be 260 meters, just over 850 feet. The beam will be 40 meters or 120 feet. Her deck will be equipped with overhead hoists and cranes. The entire deck will be able to accommodate standard commercial containers and cargo. The engines, located behind the bridge tower, will be 85 feet from the stern. The drydock bay that will house and secure their type VII/C U-Boat will be equipped with six overhead hoists, machine shops, and ample storage compartments for ammunition and torpedoes. There will be adequate room for crew's quarters below decks, forward of the bridge and superstructure.

"As you can see, there will be 24 paired compartments with baffles and a double set of two-way pumps in each compartment. Each pump will reside in its own housing. The safety margin of clearance required for a successful U-Boat docking is 10.7 meters or 35 feet. Questions?"

Steve asked, "What's the approximate time to completion?"

"Richard and I had that discussion in Haifa. The economics of the project will allow us to employ three double shifts. A little less than six months will be our target date. That should derail any snoops looking for the ship. They will be looking for a ship with a completion date of 15 to 18 months. I might add that the countdown has already begun. The keel is being laid as we speak."

JoAnn was studying the plans intently. Then she asked, "May I speak, Mr. Benjamin?"

"Of course, Major. But I'll tell you now, I'm going to build this pregnant whale to be totally seaworthy, and you are going to have to work like hell to send her to Davy Jones's locker with her baby."

"That's just it. I'm toying with an idea. Hear me out. Could you and your staff come up with a plan to alter and reduce the number of structural supports and still make her seaworthy? You would be creating a vessel that would carry a much lighter cargo load. Perhaps we wouldn't even have to completely fill all of the containers. We could probably fool the Nazis. That might also reduce the construction time even further. She would be sort of a *Trojan Horse*. She just needs to look like a container ship. Keep in mind: she only needs to be strong enough to make it across the Atlantic to Buenos Aires one time and then into the South Atlantic. Remember, we're only planning on a one-way trip. Her first rendezvous with the U-Boat will be her last. Reducing the number of supports would certainly make my job a lot easier—yours, too."

There was a murmur of understanding from the others in the group. Eric said, "I believe I see where you're going with this, Major. I'll work on it."

"I'd like to be on the spot as additional details in the plans develop and construction begins so I can observe the process from stem to stern," JoAnn continued. "This is a unique opportunity for me. As you are aware, I've demolished an existing ship, but I've never been in on the planning stage for the destruction of a vessel that's under construction. And this is by far a much larger ship. Would it be possible for me to be assigned to the Israel Shipyard in some capacity?"

James interjected, "She does have a degree in engineering. Does that count?"

Eric laughed, "Indeed it does. We can take you on as a consultant for the duration of the project. We'll just add your salary to the cost of the ship. We'll make arrangements for you to stay in a suite at the *Crowne Plaza Hotel* in Tel Aviv, and you will have three English-speaking body-guards/drivers living in the adjacent suite 24/7. You'll be able to come and go as you please and will also have an unlimited expense account."

"Don't you think that's a bit extravagant for a consultant?"

"Not at all," Richard said. "Your advice has probably already saved us some construction costs, and the people funding this project have deep pockets. They just pump it out of the ground on demand and convert it to cash as needed."

JoAnn retorted, "Really? If that's the case, I believe I'll need to make a trip to *Tiffany's* and then to *Lord and Taylor* to get outfitted for my debut in this demolition derby. By the way, what's the style in a shipyard in Israel these days?"

"Very funny, JoAnn," James piped up.

"I thought so."

Steve and Nancy hadn't said a word. They just listened and smiled.

Chapter 22
Family Tree

Eric rolled up the plans and replaced them in their carrying case. He and JoAnn continued to talk quietly. Richard waited until everyone settled down. "Now there's one more item on my agenda. Steve, would you mind sharing the information *Mossad* collected with regard to your family? I think it will be very useful to us all."

"I'd be glad to. In 1815, following the Napoleonic Wars, one of my ancestors was of great service to a Prussian prince. For services rendered, the family was rewarded with land and a *Schloss*, or castle, in Bavaria, and we became instant nobility. The title, '*von*,' was added to our name to indicate that distinction. Apparently, at some point, my father dropped the '*von*.' My father's first name was Walter. He was born in Neuss, a city in northern Germany on the Rhine River. He was the younger of two brothers. Johann was older by ten years. Apparently, he was also an ardent Nazi and retained the '*von*.' He has a degree in Chemical Engineering. Before and during World War II, he was one of the top research scientists at I.G. Farben. He now lives in Wiesbaden with his wife, Helga. How Heinz came to know the name, Kreutzer, or von Kreutzer, is unclear. That's all we know so far. Hopefully more of a connection will be made as we move forward."

Richard agreed. "I think the fact that Heinz and his buddies assume you have real connections to the Nazi faction of this project will come in handy."

James asked, "How about me? Will I come in handy?"

Richard laughed, "You already have—by bringing JoAnn on board.

Just give it a little time. I'm not quite sure at this point, but I know something will come to mind. Steve, you keep working on your German. I've reserved rooms for each of you on the fifth floor here in the hotel. I've also taken the liberty of making reservations at *Alfred's* for dinner at 7 p.m. How does a delicious beef tenderloin dinner sound to you, Eric?"

"Great! I've been missing that kind of fare!"

"All right then, everyone go freshen up a bit. I hope you'll find your accommodations satisfactory. Let's meet back here at 6:30."

There was a chorus of thanks. Most everyone in this group was a seasoned veteran and always traveled with a wardrobe change, an overnight bag, and a passport. Steve had filled Nancy in on the SOP—Standard Operating Procedure. It was also no surprise to either James or JoAnn when they found themselves in adjoining rooms. Steve and Nancy had similar arrangements.

Chapter 23
It's Biblical

"This one's no cake walk," JoAnn said out loud as she headed for the bathroom. James was just lying on the bed thinking.

Standing in the hot shower, JoAnn wondered if she should incorporate the demolition charges into the skeletal structure of the vessel during construction or add and disguise them later. If she incorporated the explosives into the skeletal structure, the radio frequency receivers would have to be installed at the same time. JoAnn finished her shower and flopped on the bed in nothing but a large towel.

She thought out loud, "Obviously, it's not just the mother ship we want resting three miles down at the bottom of the South Atlantic. We also want that U-Boat down there—hopefully in bits and pieces. The demolition of the U-Boat will require an entirely different plan."

Richard and Eric had gone upstairs to Richard's apartment to shower and change for dinner. Like JoAnn, Richard also did some of his best thinking in the shower. As the spray of hot water pounded his head and shoulders, he thought that it might be a good time to check in with Heinz about the hunt and the financing. Still in the shower, he suddenly shouted out loud, *"Jonah!* By damn, I'll call this project *Operation Jonah!"*

As soon as he put on his bathrobe, Richard picked up the phone and called Heinz on his private number in Buenos Aires. Heinz, with Teutonic promptness, answered the phone on the second ring.

"Richard, good to hear from you. All is well, yes?"

"I've just contracted for a large order, and I think we need to work out the details. Were you successful in arranging the hunt?"

"Yes, of course. There will be me, three of you, von Ritter and his son, and I'll fill the remaining slots. Seven or eight should make a nice party, *nicht wahr?* The hunt is on for the weekend after next. We can hunt for one or two days, as we please."

"Good, I'll be in touch when we arrive in Buenos Aires."

Next Richard called Steve's room. When Nancy answered the phone, he asked if she and Steve could make room on their calendars to hunt birds in Argentina the weekend after next with Heinz and his 'band of merry men'? "It's a one or two day hunt. We'll have to take a flight out of Houston on Thursday, hunt Saturday and maybe Sunday, and return on Monday. I have a plan that I'll share with you later."

"Let me check. Hold on."

Steve was just stepping out of the shower when Nancy asked, "Is there any reason you can't leave next Thursday to hunt in Argentina with Richard and the 'Boys from Buenos Aires'? We'll fly back to Austin on Monday."

"No, I'll make arrangements for my graduate assistant to teach the class until I get back."

"Richard, we're clear to go Thursday at noon."

"Fine, I'll have my plane pick you up. May I speak to Steve a moment?"

"Sure. Here he is."

"How's your German, Steve?"

"Ziemlich gut."

"Good. See, you in half an hour for dinner."

Their dinner at *Arthur's* was served in a private dining room on the second floor. The round table was set with sparkling white linens under a crystal chandelier. Richard explained to the group, especially Eric, that *Arthur's* had become a favorite with German Consulate personnel and the Argentine community in Houston. "They are very fond of the Argentinian beef served here."

No one discussed business at dinner. They were too busy enjoying the food that was excellently prepared and served. There were crab cake appetizers, Caesar salad, beef tenderloin, lobster, and potatoes Anna. Even after such a big dinner, they all enjoyed baked Alaska and coffee for dessert. Afterwards, they all returned to Richard's office to cap off the evening with snifters of brandy. The conversation continued in earnest.

Richard began. "James, I'll contact you as soon as I have something specific for you to do. JoAnn, I'll be working on our overall plan of attack. Meanwhile, you and Eric will need to be working closely from now on. By the way, I've named our enterprise *Operation Jonah*."

Eric said, "That's positively Biblical! I approve."

Richard continued, "If I know my adversaries, Steve, they will test you by trying to trick you with incorrect information. It might be something as simple as an incorrect name or date. Don't fall for any of it. Remember, you know nothing about your family! I may be barking up the wrong tree and over-reading the situation, but it's possible that Heinz and his friends may be planning a little family reunion down there to test you.

"Nancy, you, Steve, and I have a date with some very nasty characters in Argentina. You are both new faces to them. I'm counting on you. Nancy, your task is to charm the von Ritters, father and son. I've a feeling you will be the belle of the ball there. Look, listen, and remember as much as you can. You may get some valuable information."

"In that case, I have some serious shopping to do, as well. Steve and I are both leaving early tomorrow, so we'll say goodnight. Thanks for a wonderful dinner, Richard. It was nice to meet all of you. Eric, have a safe trip back to Israel."

Eric responded, "Nice to meet you as well. You are all doing Israel and the rest of the world a great service. I am proud to be a part of *Operation Jonah*. There's much work to do. I'm also leaving early in the morning, and I'll be anxious to hear from you, JoAnn."

JoAnn smiled and said, "Have a safe flight home, Eric. I'll stay in close touch. I've already started thinking and making detailed plans for a successful demolition on the high seas."

They all said goodnight. Walking down the hall to their rooms, JoAnn said, "James, I'll need a diplomatic passport and attaché case, pronto. I'll be doing a lot of traveling, and I'll need the absolute security that a diplomatic bag affords me."

"I'm your genie. Your wish is my command. I guess I'm already handy."

After everyone left, Richard felt unsettled. He placed a recording of Dvorák's 9th Symphony on the turntable in his office and hit the switch. As the arm silently rose, drifted over the record, and landed, ever so gently, the music began to play. He settled into his favorite leather chair, put his feet up, closed his eyes, and replayed the 'von Kreutzer' scenario. He was bothered that he couldn't make any connection between Heinz and his interest in Kreutzer. "It appears that there are several pieces missing from my chess board. I can't seem to find them."

Chapter 24
The Trip

Richard had flown down to Buenos Aires a few days before the hunt to take care of some business for Global Import/Export. As planned, his Citation touched down in Austin just past noon on Thursday. Nancy and Steve were ready and waiting. As soon as they boarded, the pilot said, "There are sandwiches and drinks in the cooler. Help yourselves."

After receiving clearance, he taxied out onto the runway and positioned the plane for takeoff. It was a short flight to Houston International where they settled into very comfortable first class seats on their American Airlines flight to Buenos Aires. They were served a lovely dinner, and, after several glasses of wine, they slept during the remainder of the ten and a half hour flight.

Richard greeted them upon their arrival at customs at *Aeroparque Jorge Newbery*. After they collected their luggage, he escorted them to a black Suburban with a Global Import/Export logo on the door. Nancy thought, "Richard must have stock in General Motors. He seems to have Suburbans all over the place."

"Let's go back to my office for a short pre-hunt briefing. We'll pick up a quick lunch and then hop on the company plane for our flight to the hunting lodge. We should be there in two hours—just in time for cocktails."

Richard's Buenos Aires office was located on the top floor of a very modern 15-story glass and steel structure in the dock area. Unlike the Houston office, the furnishings were spartan. They took seats around the table in the center of the room.

Richard began, "Heinz has put together the rest of our hunting party. It will consist of Heinz, Otto von Ritter and his son, Siegfried, and two additional men whom Heinz has conveniently failed to name. These are the mystery guests I spoke of earlier. I'm willing to bet there will be a little surprise or two waiting for us. Be on your toes. I have a premonition, and I don't like premonitions or surprises. Put on your game faces. Remember, Steve, you have no romantic interest in Nancy, and I'm only interested in securing oil leases from her.

Nancy jumped in, "Well, I may have a little surprise for all concerned as well. Don't be shocked or over react."

Steve responded, "Oh really? Just what the hell are you planning, Nancy? Are you going to hunt in a bikini or in the nude?"

Richard interjected, "Now there's a pretty picture!"

"No, no, nothing that dramatic. Just relax. You're both dirty old men."

"Let's get serious, Nancy. Your cover story, just like Steve's, is simple because it's true. You're Dr. Nancy Alvarez, a professor of Cultural Anthropology at the University of Texas in Austin. Steve is just a colleague and a friend. Remember you have no romantic interest in each other. You will probably be under observation the entire weekend. Don't slip up. You own thousands of acres of land in West Texas and control all the mineral rights. Much of the land came to your father's family as a land grant from the King of Spain in the 1500s. The rest came from your mother's family, also as a Spanish land grant. Fortunately for all, both sides of your family retained all of the mineral rights. They were probably hoping to find gold there early on. Now they are delighted with the prospects of oil. As far as our hunting partners know, my interest in you is strictly a business arrangement. I want to exploit your mineral rights—the oil to be specific. As a West Texas girl, you love to bird hunt and had expressed your desire to hunt dove in Argentina. You've heard the shooting is fabulous down here. Questions?"

Nancy answered, "No, the picture is clear enough."

"Good! With a little luck, and if Siegfried von Ritter's taste runs towards beautiful women, you might be able to charm some valuable information out of him about his arms dealing.

"Steve, count to five before you speak. I don't trust those men. Be on your guard. Here's a final admonition. Remember that you don't speak, read, or write German. Those Nazi bastards are paranoid. One of their favorite tricks is to switch from Spanish into German in the middle of a sentence. I expect that Heinz or one of the others might try to engage you in a conversation about your family. Remember, you know nothing. Using incorrect names of family members and incorrect dates is another one of their favorite ploys. Now, how about some lunch before we head for the plane?"

Richard took them to one of his favorite cafés where they enjoyed a taste of local cuisine. They shared a platter of assorted ham, chicken, and cheese *empanadas*. A creamy caramel flan was perfect for dessert. The black Suburban picked them up and took them to the company plane. After a two-hour flight, they landed on a well-maintained tarmac runway that was owned and operated by a very exclusive sportsman's club called *Little Bavaria*. Steve thought, "Why not? If the shoe fits..."

A five-minute drive in the club's van put them at the lodge about 45 minutes before the cocktail hour. Porters attended to their luggage. Richard said, "Let's get cleaned up and meet in the bar about 6:30."

They were escorted to their respective rooms. Each of them had a private room, decorated in a very comfortable but rustic decor, and all three of them wondered just where the listening devices were hidden.

Chapter 25
The Gathering

Richard was the first to arrive downstairs. As the advance guard, he positioned himself at the bar so he could keep a weather eye out for Heinz and the rest of his party. Steve joined him a couple of minutes later. They soon spotted Heinz and von Ritter, the elder, with a rather portly young man following at his heels like a puppy.

Richard thought, "That has to be Siegfried."

Across the spacious room, and from a different direction, two new faces appeared. Richard whispered to Steve, "Do you know those two?"

As they approached, they appeared to be walking in lock step. Their posture was erect, and they carried themselves like military officers. They each had a distinctive military bearing.

Steve whispered back to Richard, "Not offhand, but they are definitely military or ex-military."

The older of the pair seemed to be in his late 70s with short gray hair. His suit fit him like a military uniform. The younger man was in his late 40s. As they crossed the floor, side-by-side, there was something about them that made both Richard and Steve uneasy. They seemed to be heading towards Heinz. Richard still couldn't put his finger on their names. Then it came to him.

He said, under his breath to Steve, "They're the Beckers!"

Heinz approached and said, "Richard, you remember Otto?"

They shook hands. "Of course, *Herr* von Ritter."

The introductions continued, "This is his son, Siegfried." Then he introduced the other two men. "This is Colonel William Becker and Mr. Gunter Ehrlich."

"So, they're using different names," thought Richard. "How nice."

Before Richard could utter a word, Heinz said to the group, "And this is the man I told all of you about, Kreutzer. Professor Esteban Kreutzer. He is originally from Argentina." They all greeted each other with smiles, handshakes, and slight nods of their heads. There was a noticeable absence of any heel clicking.

Fortunately, Steve had been briefed about Richard's prior involvement with the group that had been involved with the *Volsung Project*. He recognized their names. Suddenly, the room went quiet, and all heads turned toward the person who had just entered the room and was approaching the group.

"*Mein Gott,*" Siegfried and Otto said softly in unison.

"Good evening, gentlemen. May I join you?"

Nancy had arrived, and she was stunning. She wore an expensive peasant blouse, a colorful long, flowing, Mexican skirt, and a pair of hand-tooled custom boots made of some exotic leather. Around her neck, she wore an exquisite squash blossom necklace of turquois and gold that drew everyone's attention to her low cut neckline. She had just stopped the show. She was drop dead gorgeous! Somehow, Richard and Steve were able to mask any obvious expression of delight. After all, they had been given ample warning.

Richard immediately spoke, "Gentlemen, allow me to introduce Dr. Nancy Alvarez." The men in the Heinz party each introduced themselves in turn.

"Pleased to meet you all," she said in her best West Texas drawl. I really hope I'm not intruding in this all male outing."

There was a chorus of, "No! No! Not at all."

Heinz continued, "Of course, not. We're all glad to welcome an attractive addition to our party. What will you have to drink? I'll get it for you."

"Macallan on the rocks, please."

Heinz was his usual charming self. Becker and Siegfried couldn't take their eyes off Nancy, and they homed in on her. Otto's gaze also kept shifting towards her as he spoke to the group with his usual bluster. Everyone had a drink and was engaged in conversation. They appeared to be a very convivial group. No one would ever have guessed the real reasons for this gathering.

Richard sidled over to Steve and said, "I think we both need another drink. Walk slowly, I want to give you some details about Becker and Ehrlich.

"Gunter Erhlich is actually the father of Colonel William Becker, Jr. In fact, his real name is William Becker, Sr. He uses 'Gunter Erhlich' to hide his true identity. He's a chemical engineer and a devout Nazi. In 1944 he was a full colonel in the U.S. Army Chemical Corps, assigned to the Picatinny Arsenal/Lake Denmark Naval Air Station complex in New Jersey. He facilitated John Wolfe's entry into the United States by submarine. Wolfe brought the semen specimens that were to be used in the *Volsung Project*. Those specimens were supposed to produce the nucleus for a new Aryan race and the beginning of the *Fourth Reich*. He was also the man who had access to, and could insure, a continuous supply of the liquid nitrogen required for the preservation and storage of the semen specimens. Wolfe took half of the semen specimens to North Carolina with him when he left the Army. The remaining half was left in New Jersey. When JoAnn destroyed half of the specimens, his namesake, the very same Colonel William Becker with us today, was on active duty in the Army and was the only person who could access the second batch of specimens that was still preserved in liquid nitrogen in New Jersey. Becker, the younger, gave the specimens to another undercover Nazi agent who transported the semen to Wisconsin. Luckily, we tracked them down, and JoAnn and James eliminated the remainder of the 'Aryan' specimens as well." As they approached the bar, their conversation stopped.

"Scotch on the rocks," Steve said to the bartender.

"Make that two," Richard added. With fresh drinks in hand, they ambled slowly back towards the group. Richard continued his tutorial on the Beckers. "After the War, Becker, Sr. worked for Hercules/DuPont. That's when he began to travel to Mexico and South America. He would fly to Mexico City as William Becker. Using a different passport, he traveled to Montevideo and Buenos Aires under the name of Gunter Ehrlich. He came home in the reverse order. We all concluded that he was the man in charge of the *Volsung Project*. With the timely destruction of the last specimens, the *Volsung Project* was permanently terminated, but it appears that none of this group has given up on the idea of a *Fourth Reich*."

Steve whispered, "So this is the surprise—the itch you couldn't scratch. I think you were right on target after all. You suspected that they might try to lay an elaborate trap for us. I think this proves it."

Their conversation concluded with the sound of the dinner bell. The first ring announced to all that it was time to finish their drinks and begin drifting toward the dining room. As one might expect, the lodge called *Little Bavaria* looked like its name suggested. High, dark, thick beams crisscrossed the room with braces added to support the roof. Animal heads, horns, game birds, and weapons of all kinds were mounted on the walls. Over the entrance to the capacious dining room, there was a display of hunting paraphernalia from the Bavarian *Schwarzwald* that certainly added to the ambiance. Mounted above the mantel that capped a massive stone fireplace were short hunting swords, cross bows, spears, and sabers. The hall was a cross between an armory in a Bavarian *Schloss* and the den of a *Jägermeister*.

The second bell rang signaling everyone to take a seat at the table. The menu for the evening included fresh shrimp, tossed green salad with bleu cheese dressing, and an entrée platter of venison, pheasant, and dove. Red cabbage, fried potatoes, and thick slices of fresh rye bread accompanied the meal that was served family style. That type of service was very conducive to conversation, and there was plenty of that. The group designated Heinz as the spokesman to choose the wines for the group. He did an admirable job. Warm apple strudel, topped with mounds of luscious whipped cream, capped off the meal.

Chapter 26
Twisting the Tiger's Tail

After dinner, the group gathered near the massive fireplace to get better acquainted. The conversation remained on the light side. Becker and Siegfried von Ritter, totally smitten, once again zeroed in on Nancy. Heinz, Otto, and Ehrlich spoke jovially with Richard. Steve remained more of an observer than a participant. He made no attempt to join the conversations and didn't try to compete with the two wolves on the hunt. He just watched and listened.

Steve overheard Nancy ask Siegfried about his line of work. That seemed to evoke a cascade of information. He began to babble about supplying arms to the entire world and every revolutionary group therein. He continued to elaborate on the types of weapons he had in his arsenal. Nancy shifted gears and said something to the effect that it was nice that a father and son could work together.

Then she turned, looking directly into Becker's eyes and said, "How did you choose the military as a career? Was your father in the army?"

"Actually, my father was in the army for a time during WWII," Becker answered as cool as a cucumber.

Then Nancy pressed the button, "Did you ever have an opportunity to work with your father? I mean, you're in the army, too. Could you do that in the army?"

That question caused Colonel Becker to blanch momentarily. Both Nancy and Steve saw his reaction. Nancy continued her stream of thought without missing a beat by adding, "Oh! How stupid of me. You would have joined the army much later, wouldn't you?"

"Yes of course," he responded, "We were in the army at different times."

Steve thought, "Damn, that was gutsy. She certainly knows how to twist the tiger's tail."

As it was getting late and everyone had finished their drinks, Heinz announced that breakfast would be served at eight in the dining room. The group began to disburse and head for their rooms.

Richard and Heinz paired off. They had a little business to discuss. Heinz opened the door to his room and motioned for Richard to enter and sit down.

Richard said, "Heinz, in order to initiate our enterprise, as we discussed, I will require $300 milion American in a numbered account at *Credit Suisse*, and you will give me a written confirmation and the number of the account before we leave the lodge. I will have sole control of the account. No construction will begin until I have possession of the entire amount. Remind your bankers that, due to the rather special requirements of this project, the initial amount may not cover the entire cost. Additional funds may be required. My company will make arrangements for the construction of the ship. After launching and delivery, I will arrange to complete the registration and ownership paperwork. We can discuss further arrangements and the final disposition of the ship later."

Heinz spoke up, "May I inquire which company you are planning to employ for the construction of the ship?"

"No, you may not! Once the $300 million has been deposited in Switzerland, this enterprise is no longer of any concern to you or your financial backers until the ship is delivered to me. If we are to keep this operation secret, the fewer people who know what I'm doing, the better. If you and your bankers are uncomfortable with this arrangement, or if it's a matter of trust, remember that you called me, Heinz! I can assure you that you will be receiving exactly what you want—a container ship housing a drydock for our precious U-Boat."

In a way, Heinz was taken aback by Richard's forcefulness. On the other hand, he was thinking, "Now I can see why this man was on our deep-cover list." Aloud, he said, "Very well. I'll make the call immediately, and you will have written confirmation and the number before you leave *Little Bavaria* on Sunday."

"By the way, Heinz, I need to take a closer look at the U-Boat facility in the very near future, and I'm planning to bring Steve with me. Will that be a problem?"

"No, not at all. But why Kreutzer?"

"I repeat, the less information out there, the better to keep our secret. Let's just say I need someone I can trust at my end."

Heinz rose, extended his hand, and, with a slight click of his heels, said, "Then I bid you *guten Abend.*"

Richard opened the door and left the room. After the door closed, he smiled and said under his breath, "Nice touch, Heinz."

Chapter 27
The Hunt

Nancy looked out the window of her room at *Little Bavaria*. The dawn had brought a spectacular display of color. Pink, gray, and baby blue mixed with orange, yellow, and red all reflected off the scattered clouds. The colors were continually changing, coming and going, heralding the actual sunrise. She, however, was the only one in the group who was awake to witness it. She had set her alarm early so she would have time to wash her hair and get ready for the day's activities. She really enjoyed bird-hunting and was looking forward to that, as well as the interaction with the other people in the hunting party. She had thoroughly enjoyed her interchanges with Becker and Siegfried the previous night and was anticipating what was to come today.

The breakfast buffet was served at the very civilized hour of 8 a.m. There were pancakes, waffles, sausage, ham, bacon, sweet rolls, toast, butter, and assorted jams and jellies. The chef prepared eggs to suit the individual taste of each patron. There was steaming hot coffee in a multitude of flavors and varieties. The fare was appealing to the large contingent of *Norte Americanos* who frequented the lodge. The lodge staff members were all instructed never to use the word—*gringo*.

The men in the party were already seated when Nancy made her grand entrance at 8:15. She wore a pair of tan, custom-made, lace-up hunting boots. Tucked and bloused into her boots, like a paratrooper, she had on a pair of khaki slacks, topped by a tailored khaki shirt, tapered at the waist. It was snug in all the right places—not too tight but just right. Needless to say, she had the desired effect on all of the men in the room. Once again, every head turned her way.

Richard thought, "Her little surprises just keep on coming. She really will foul up Otto von Ritter's concentration. He'll be crossed-eyed by noon. The poor bastard won't be able to make half of his shots today."

By 10:00 a.m. they all had chosen their guns. They piled into the hunting vehicles—skeletonized Volkswagens—and rode out to the fields. Otto had requested that Nancy be stationed on the line to his left. He wanted to keep one eye on her. It was, of course, the only reason for the request. There were plenty of birds, but Otto was not on his usual game. He finally shot his limit late in the afternoon. Nancy had hardly missed a bird. The men, especially Otto, were very impressed with her shooting prowess.

At dinner that evening, Nancy wore a baby blue cocktail dress, and, once again, all eyes were on her. During the cocktail hour, von Ritter was full of excuses. He claimed he had a foreign body floating in his shooting eye most of the day. No one laughed, lest it precipitate an apoplectic fit. Rumor had it that, when angered, he literally turned purple with rage. No one dared challenge him. As usual, he considered himself the champion of the hunt. Everyone knew that the foreign body he spoke of was Nancy.

Steve was sipping a scotch and water before dinner when he spied Gunter Ehrlich approaching. Steve thought, "Oh, shit, here it comes." The hackles went up on the back of his neck. He steeled himself for whatever was about to occur. He tried to recall everything that Richard had told him the night before.

"This is the guy everyone thought was the key man behind the *Volsung Project*. It's obvious that he and Heinz are as thick as thieves. Otherwise, why would he and his son be here at all?"

Ehrlich broke the ice. "Esteban, or would you prefer Steve?"

"Steve is fine." "I understand your father was the military attaché to the German Embassy in Buenos Aires about 1939 or 1940. Is that correct?"

"I didn't expect Ehrlich to be my inquisitor," Steve thought. "I would have guessed it would be Heinz. They are tricky bastards. That was definitely not a question. It was a statement of fact, and he damn well knew the answer. I am very confident that Ehrlich has no inkling that I know his true identity and that he is a native-born American, a retired U.S. Army Colonel, a hard-core Nazi, and a traitor to his country of birth."

Not waiting for an answer, Ehrlich continued, "I understand he was killed while fighting with Rommel's *Afrika Korps*."

"That's the story I was told as a child. Sadly, I never knew him."

"Yes, of course. Tragic, and you never knew any members of his family?"

"No. I know nothing at all about his family. It was forbidden to speak of him in my grandparents' home. When I was a child, my mother's family forbade anyone to speak of my father, and I was forbidden to learn to read, write, or speak German. My mother never spoke of him, and I don't even know my father's first name."

"Walter, your father's name was Walter."

"Thank you for telling me."

"Ah yes. Well, I knew his older brother—your uncle Klaus. Allow me to fill in some of the blanks for you."

Steve nodded, smiled, and said, "Please, I'd appreciate that." But, he thought, "If this is your first attempt to trip me up with deceptions, you get an 'F' because my uncle's name was Johann."

"Your name, Kreutzer, can be traced back to the Crusades. Your family came from northwest Germany near the city of Neuss, located on the Rhine. They were Catholics, I believe, but continued to live in a predominantly Lutheran part of Germany. Sometime in the mid-15th century the '*von*' was added to the name. The '*von*' indicates that the family had acquired land or a *Schloss* or both."

"Really–in the mid-15th century? Bullshit," Steve thought, "that's your second mistake!" But he responded, "How interesting. Exactly what is a *Schloss?*"

"Oh, forgive me," Erhlich replied. "I forgot. You don't speak German. A *Schloss* is a castle or manor house. Klaus von Kreutzer was a top research chemist for I.G. Farben. During the War, he was instrumental in the development of synthetic fuels and lubricants for the *Third Reich*. By the way, I'm also a chemist, and I am familiar with his work."

"That's impressive. Synthetic fuels and lubricants were important to the *Reich*. If I understand history correctly, reliable sources of petroleum were always in short supply for Germany."

"That is correct. I also worked at I.G. Farbin. Although we were in different departments, we collaborated on projects from time to time. We seemed to have a great deal in common."

Steve thought, "I'll just bet you did."

"Didn't I.G. Farben make that poison gas. What was it called? Oh yes—Zyklon-B, wasn't it?"

"Yes, yes, and unfortunately a few misguided souls went off on a tangent and committed unpardonable atrocities with it. But, that's all in the past. I.G. Farben was, and still is, a huge company. During the War they were finally able to mass produce synthetic lubricants and fuels, but it came too late. After the War, the company contributed a great deal of money to the rebuilding of Germany."

"I'm sure it did."

"After the War, he came to America with a group of high-level German rocket scientists in 1946. He was part of a U.S. government top-secret project called *Operation Paper Clip*. He eventually returned to the Fatherland. Steve, if you're at all curious about your family, you might want to investigate this lead. I seem to recall your uncle mentioning that he had a wife. Helga, I believe, is her name. They have an estate somewhere in Bavaria. I believe your uncle and his wife are presently living in Wiesbaden."

"How interesting! Thank you for that information. I will certainly check it out."

Out of the corner of his eye, Steve noticed Becker sidling up to join them. Steve went into attack mode.

"Colonel, are you still on active duty?"

"No. I put in my twenty and retired. The Army was changing rapidly, and I wasn't happy with the direction it was taking. Now, I'm a stockbroker on Wall Street. I buy and sell securities for a very select group of clients."

Steve thought, "Yeah, and I'll bet every last one of them is a Nazi."

"It's interesting work, but one must stay alert to follow a rapidly changing market."

Steve replied, "I'm sure. I prefer the life of an academic. I'm presently working on a book about Coronado and his exploration of the New World."

The dinner bell rang for the second time, interrupting the conversation and summoning all the guests to dinner. Not to be outdone by the feast the night before, the chef presented an all-German menu including pork schnitzel, sauerbraten, bratwurst, warm German potato salad, spaetzle, red cabbage, and sauerkraut. Each table had a large basket filled with an assortment of freshly baked breads and rolls. There was a variety of light and dark beers on tap. The waiters kept the steins filled. For those who had any room left, there was a dessert buffet. The stars of the buffet were fruit tarts and Black Forest cake. First in line for the sweets was Siegfried, and hot on his trail was his *Vati*, Otto. Like father like son.

Chapter 28
The After Dinner Chat

After dinner, Heinz and his little party assembled near the fireplace. Everyone had a drink of some sort in hand. Once again, Siegfried cornered Nancy and began to regale her with a cascade of information. He told her where he obtained the weapons and from whom. He revealed the names of those who he had to bribe at various military installations and posts. He rattled off names of the dealers who supplied arms to dissident political factions. He appeared to be using actual names of contacts and countries. The information continued to pour forth. He was willing to say anything to keep her attention.

Nancy was trying to assimilate and remember everything. She hoped that when she returned to her room later, she would be able to record what he had revealed. Her training as an academic was coming in handy. She had listened to many lectures and had become adept at remembering small details and facts.

Siegfried continued to babble on. "We have half a dozen DC-3s. My father bought them from the Americans as surplus after WWII."

Nancy asked, "Where do you keep this air force of yours?"

"We have camouflaged warehouses and an airfield about 900 kilometers south of Buenos Aires. There is a community of ex-patriot Germans living there, also. No one knows about them. They are completely isolated. We fly supplies in to them two or three times a week. That's where we store the 'products' we have for sale. It's much too dangerous to keep all that stuff in Buenos Aires." He leaned closer to her and whispered in a conspiratorial fashion, "We also have American RPGs, surface to air missiles, and a small supply of poison gas."

Nancy couldn't believe he was spewing forth all of those details. "Really! Poison gas? What kind of poison gas?"

"The very best: Zyklon-B. Have you ever heard of it?"

Nancy responded hesitantly, "I'm not sure. I think so." With the untimely arrival of William Becker, drink in hand, the conversation abruptly ended.

Heinz, Otto von Ritter, Ehrlich, and Richard were engaged in a conversation about hunting, guns, and shooting. Ehrlich seemed to be there more as an observer than a participant. As conversations evolved within the group, Steve watched Ehrlich as he continued his own surveillance. It appeared to Steve that if Ehrlich had been looking for the fly in the ointment, he had failed to find one. Nancy played her role. Steve kept his mouth shut.

Then Ehrlich approached Nancy and asked, "Did you enjoy the hunt today?"

"Indeed I did, and I want to thank you and your friends for allowing me to join your party. It was a privilege. It's not every day a girl gets to do what I did today. It was an experience I'll never forget. I hope I wasn't too much of a distraction."

Ehrlich replied, "Not at all. Not at all."

"I'd love to have a group picture for my scrapbook. Do you think that could be arranged?"

"Of course, by all means."

Ehrlich went over to Heinz and said a few words. Heinz immediately went to the front desk and spoke to the concierge. In a few minutes, a photographer arrived and jockeyed them all into the proper position for a group photograph. After a few shots, the photographer smiled at Nancy and said, "I'll choose the best one and have a print ready for you in the morning before you check out."

"Thank you so much," Nancy responded.

Heinz approached Richard and said, "I hope you will be successful in your business enterprise. I refer to Nancy's oil leases."

"She's had a wonderful time on the hunt and has enjoyed everyone's company. I feel sure that the outcome will be favorable. I trust that our outcome will be just as favorable, Heinz."

"Don't worry, I'll have the number and written confirmation as you requested before you depart in the morning."

The entire party gathered together to say their farewells, as they would all be leaving *Little Bavaria* at different times in the morning. Ehrlich once again suggested that Steve take the time to look up his uncle in Wiesbaden when he got home. Siegfried looked like a lost puppy as Nancy left for her room. Becker remained polite while saying his goodbyes. Richard shook hands with each participant and thanked each of the men for a fabulous hunt.

The next morning Richard, Nancy, and Steve met for breakfast. As they were checking out, the desk clerk handed Richard a sealed envelope from Heinz that contained the confirmation and account number that he had promised to deliver.

Nancy was also handed an envelope. The clerk said, "The photographer left this for you. It's the picture of your group that he took last night."

They didn't see any of the other members of the party as they left the lodge. The van took them to the airfield where the Global plane, engines turning, was on the tarmac waiting for them. On the flight to Buenos Aires, Nancy feverishly scribbled in a small notebook. She was trying to fill in the outline she had started the night before, hoping she could recall every name, place, and type of weapon Siegfried had mentioned. Two hours later they were back in Buenos Aires.

With a four-hour wait until their commercial flight left for Houston, they stopped by Richard's office so he could catch up on some paperwork. Then they decided to pay an impromptu call on Aaron de Silva. Richard wanted Nancy to meet the coin dealer who also had been instrumental in the demise of the *Volsung Project*. For Steve, it was a reunion with his old friend who also had *Mossad* connections.

"I'm glad you stopped by. I was about to call you, Richard, to let you know that Heinz has had guests in long white robes recently. My people have had him under surveillance."

"They must be the bankers. Good to know."

They spent an hour listening as de Silva recounted the tale of his part in the *Volsung Project*. Nancy was fascinated. Then they returned to the airport for their flight back to Houston.

Once settled into their first class seats, she resumed recording every detail she could remember. They did not discuss any of it on the flight home. The post mortem of the weekend would be conducted at Richard's office in Houston. They catnapped off and on. Steve caught Nancy awake and asked, "I'm curious. Where did you get that fabulous turquois and gold necklace? It's quite a work of art."

"There's a shop in Tucson, Arizona, owned by an old Navaho artist who occasionally works in gold. He's a long time family friend. As you know, most of the Navaho craftsmen work in silver."

"Well, it's a beautiful piece."

"Thanks. It's one of my favorites."

The following morning, back in Richard's Houston office, they began debriefing each other and reviewed the notes Nancy had made. There were names, military bases—foreign and domestic—and all types of equipment, most of which meant little to Nancy, but was of value to Richard. She mentioned the DC-3s and the camouflaged warehouses and the secret airfield, as well as the Zyklon-B.

"That's where the U-Boat is based," Richard said.

"Oh, one more thing. Are you aware that there is a colony of ex-patriot Germans living there? Siegfried also volunteered the information that supplies are ferried into the colony two or three times a week by the DC-3s."

"Yes. Eric and Jake told me about that colony when I flew over to Israel to meet them. Apparently, their *raison d'etre* is to preserve and man the U-Boat we are calling *Jonah*. Nancy, that's a nice piece of work. Thanks. The picture is becoming much clearer. By the way, our ploy about us making a deal regarding your thousands of acres of oil land appears to have been convincing. Heinz bought it hook, line, and sinker."

Nancy handed Richard the group photograph from the hunt. "I think you should keep it. It might come in handy."

Steve asked, "Did you really have to tweak Becker's nose about the virtues of father and son working together? Praising the von Ritters in warm friendly terms and then turning it on Becker and the military connection with his father was a bit bold and brazen. I actually saw him pale for an instant, but you continued your stream of conversation uninterrupted, and he remained clueless."

Richard said, "You do like to play close to the edge of the cliff, don't you?"

Nancy just smiled.

Richard said, "The last order of business for us, Steve, is our visit to the U-Boat base. I've requested permission from Heinz to visit there, and I included you. I told him that I needed a man I could trust at my end. It seems you passed the test, since I encountered no resistance from him. I'll call Heinz in the morning to set it up."

"I'll look forward to that. But, I really would like to get back to Austin today. Could you set that up?"

"Yes, of course. I'll call Hobby right now. The pilot will be ready when you get there. Thanks to both of you for a job well done."

After they left for Hobby, Richard, armed with the phone number of

Credit Suisse in Zurich and the account number containing the $300 million American dollars, was ready to begin moving the money.

Chapter 29
The Check's in the Mail

Richard made a call to *Credit Suisse* to confirm the $300 million was indeed in the bank. His next call was to a secure number in Haifa.

"*Shalom*. Eric speaking."

"*Shalom*, Eric, it's Richard. The money is in the bank. How much will you need right now and where should I send it? I'll make the transfer immediately."

Richard listened as he wrote the name of the bank and the account number on a pad. "Consider it done."

Richard called *Credit Suisse* again and transferred the entire $300 million to a private numbered bank account in the Cayman Islands. Then he transferred $150 million to the numbered account in the bank Eric had designated. The last item on his agenda was to open an account in a Houston bank for JoAnn. He deposited $50,000 for the expenses she would incur. "It's a small price to pay."

The link between Richard, Heinz, and the Arab bankers was severed completely. Now, the money was untraceable. Richard's Cayman account was obviously in a name other than Global Import/Export. With the funding of *Operation Jonah* complete, the wheels could begin turning faster.

A call to James was next on the agenda. "James, we need to meet in my office. How soon can you and JoAnn be here?'

"Is early tomorrow afternoon fast enough?"

"Yes! Excellent."

It was time to think, plan, and plot. James and JoAnn arrived just past noon the next day. "How about lunch? I'll send out for sandwiches and drinks from the deli," Richard greeted them as they entered his office.

"Great," responded James. "Now what's on your mind? Things must be really popping."

Richard delivered a condensed and succinct version of the hunt, including a description of Nancy's outfits, her antics, and a brief synopsis of the conversations that had transpired the nights both before and after the hunt. JoAnn and James began to laugh.

"You may think it's funny now, but you weren't there to witness her acts. Having said that, she did glean some vital information from Siegfried about his sources and suppliers. He also spilled the beans about the kinds of weapons he's selling around the world. Otto, his father, is a very dangerous man, but Siegfried is one scary bastard! He's not only a little crazy, he's totally stupid. Imagine him giving up all of this valuable information just to curry favor with a pretty woman. He has warehouses full of all sorts of small arms, ammunition, cases of RPGs, and stinger missiles. To top off his laundry list, he has a store of Zyklon-B. And let me add a small surprise bonus for you both. In attendance at this little drama were none other than Colonel William Becker, Sr., in the guise of Gunter Ehrlich, and his son, Colonel William Becker, Jr. Nancy had the presence of mind to request a group photo. Let me show it to you."

No one spoke for a long moment. Then James let out a long, low whistle and whispered, "No shit!"

JoAnn asked, "Richard, do you have a plan or is this just a brainstorming session?"

"I'm afraid the latter for now."

Suddenly JoAnn's face lit up like Times Square on New Year's Eve, followed by a grin that wouldn't quit.

James just shook his head and said, "Whatever plan just popped into your head, I trust bodes ill for our adversaries. Would you care to share it with us?"

"Actually, I wouldn't—not until I've thought it out thoroughly."

"Okay, just hold that thought," Richard grinned.

"Richard, what's my role in this little enterprise?" James asked.

"I'm not quite sure yet. If you'll give me just a little more time, I promise I'll put you to good use."

"Nuts!"

"Hold on there! Wait a minute! I don't know what I was thinking! I've got it! You can start right now with the list of names and bases that Nancy acquired from Siegfried. Put together a small select team and quietly begin an investigation. Then make preliminary preparations to shut down some of von Ritter's suppliers here in the good old U.S.A."

"I'll get on it right away. After we take out the suppliers here at home, we'll start overseas. This is what I've been waiting for! Just my cup of tea!"

JoAnn spoke up, "Richard, I've just received my diplomatic passport so I can start traveling to Israel. More specifically, I need to meet with Eric Benjamin to discuss the ship's construction and how I plan to sink her. By the way, the paperwork just came through confirming my promotion to Major. It's official now."

"Congratulations!"

"I'll fly to New York tonight. Maybe I can get in a little shopping tomorrow before continuing on to Tel Aviv. I'll need expense money."

Richard reached into his desk drawer and removed a checkbook that he handed to JoAnn. You have a $50,000 account for travel and expenses. Try not to spend it all in one day. If you need more, just ask."

James smiled and said with a grin, "I don't suppose I get a checkbook, too, do I?"

"We'll see about that later."

"Just kidding, Richard."

"I know. I wasn't."

Chapter 30
Haifa

JoAnn was exhausted from her day of shopping as she boarded the *El Al* plane for Tel Aviv. She hated long flights. It would take ten and a half hours, but she would be comfortable in first class. "Those Middle Eastern financiers can afford the very best. All the better for me."

Jake had never met JoAnn. He was waiting for her as she stepped off the plane. As the passengers headed for the baggage area, he identified her immediately. She had a diplomatic briefcase chained to her left wrist. He approached and said, "*Shalom*, my name is Jake. Welcome to Israel."

She returned the greeting and immediately asked, "May I see your identification?"

He handed it to her and asked, "Do you read Hebrew?"

JoAnn just shook her head, took the card, and turned it over. Taped on the reverse side was a small piece of paper with the word 'olive' on it. She immediately returned the card, grabbed her suitcase off the carousel and said, "Let's go!" They left the terminal and went directly to a waiting black sedan with dark tinted windows and diplomatic plates. Once inside, they were off to Haifa. JoAnn immediately unlocked the briefcase from her wrist and said, "That's a relief." Upon arrival at Israel Shipyards, Jake escorted JoAnn directly to Eric Benjamin's office.

"Good to see you again, Mr. Benjamin."

He motioned for them to sit around a table and offered them cups of fresh, steaming coffee and some pastries. Jake spoke first, "Major Scarlett, as a matter of protocol, may I see your passport and Military ID, please?"

JoAnn obliged and passed both documents across the table. Her diplomatic passport was in order. Then both men examined her Military ID card that was laminated in blue plastic. All it took was a cursory look at the ID before both men recognized that it was not the standard US Military ID.

Jake said, "Major, this is, to say the least, a rather unusual Military ID card. Would you care to translate this for us? It's pure gibberish to my untrained eye. Let me add, I've never seen a card like this before."

"Of course. The card says, 'Scarlett, J.A.; 4791; F; SO; 04; MOS, Classified; SS, D, A, QX-SW.' It translates this way: 'name; serial number; sex; unit; rank; military occupational specialty; special skills.'"

"Hmm. Could you be a little more specific, Major?"

"Jake, you're mighty inquisitive."

"It's my business to be inquisitive. That's how we Israelis have continued to remain alive."

"Sorry. Yes, I'll break it down for you. I'm a Major in a Special Operations unit. That accounts for my low serial number. F means female, of course. My MOS is and will remain classified. SS means special skills. My special skills are demolition and assassination. QX-SW means I am qualified as an expert in small arms and hand-held weapons, domestic and foreign, with no exceptions."

"Well, Major, it seems you're to be our demolition expert on *Operation Jonah*. Welcome," Eric said.

"Yes I am and thank you, Mr. Benjamin. I'm your girl. Let's keep it informal. I'm JoAnn, and you're Eric."

"In that case, let's get to work, JoAnn."

Jake said, "We have some small apartments on the top floor of this building. We took the liberty of providing one for you so you can shower and refresh yourself during the day. It can get hot and sticky here. If you prefer, you may use the apartment whenever you desire rather than having to waste valuable time going back and forth to your hotel in Tel Aviv. Allow me to take you upstairs so you can clean up and rest after your long flight. Suppose we meet back here in two hours. We have a lot of ground to cover."

JoAnn's apartment window and balcony overlooked the harbor and shipyard. Her luggage was already in the room. The apartment was equipped with a refrigerator, a pantry, a small kitchen, and a stove. There was a living area with a TV and a bedroom with a few potted plants on the balcony. All in all, it was quite comfortable. She doubted that she would be spending much time in the hotel in Tel Aviv. She felt much safer at the harbor. After a hot shower and a nap, JoAnn was refreshed and ready for work. Jake was punctual, and they both went down to Eric's office.

Eric began the session, "You and I will be working closely together on this project, so I've assembled a special crew of draftsmen and blueprint engineers to work exclusively with us. As you are well aware, the sooner we complete the ship, the less chance there will be of a leak to the wrong people and the better for all of us. The ship, as requested, will look externally like any other container ship as she is being fabricated. Let's go into the model room."

The model room was adjacent to Eric's office. There were a dozen or more scale model ships of all kinds in individual glass cases. At one table, JoAnn saw two young men working on a scale model that resembled a WWII U-Boat.

Pointing to the model submarine the men were building, she asked, "Jonah?" Eric nodded.

"Then that must be the whale," she said, pointing to a scale model of a ship about four feet in length, displayed in the center of a large table. Around the table were six comfortable leather chairs. They all sat down.

JoAnn said, "It does look like a container ship to me. Is that really our baby?"

Eric began, "What you see before you is a scale model of a fairly standard, medium-sized container ship. The real ship will measure a fraction less than 260 meters long (850 feet) and will be quite capable of ocean travel worldwide. Now, let me disassemble the model and show you some of the finer points of her construction."

"Damn!" JoAnn exclaimed. "This is just like a James Bond movie. 'M' takes James Bond to the lab to see 'Q.' You know, that guy who shows 007 how to work all the gimmicks and gadgets."

At that moment, Eric barked, "This is not a James Bond movie! This is serious business, Major!"

"Whoops!" JoAnn thought, "Just like 'Q.' No sense of humor, either."

JoAnn addressed both men in a more serious and subdued tone and said, "During your briefing about me, do you recall being informed that I also have an engineering degree from Purdue University?"

A moment of pregnant silence followed. Eric said, "I apologize. We completely forgot." At that moment, both men realized that JoAnn was no run-of-the-mill military officer. Suddenly they got her little joke. All three of them smiled and began to laugh. The tension was broken.

"Okay, gentlemen, I'll get serious. Eric, please go on."

Chapter 31
The Devil's in the Details

Eric began to disassemble the ship model. "Let's address the hull design and construction first. From the outside she appears to be like any other standard medium-sized container ship. However, on the inside, the hull splits at the forward tip of the docking bay. In other words, the docking bay for the submarine is flanked by a split hull design. The inside of the ship's hull is comprised of a series of paired watertight chambers or compartments. See here on the model? They function independently of one another. This ship will have 24 compartments, or chambers, on each side. Each chamber has a series of perforated baffles welded inside to minimize the force of the water shifting inside of it. Each chamber will have two pumps. In case of a failure of one pump, the second is a backup. Should a pump or compartment fail to fill or empty, the weight can be offset by flooding or emptying its opposite number. Thus, the ship is stabilized. A stationary drydock operates in a similar fashion. By flooding or emptying the compartments, simultaneously and uniformly, the ship will rise or sink to the required depth necessary for the U-Boat to enter the drydock. When the U-Boat is safely in her cradle, a catwalk can be extended on each side for easy access to the sub.

"In order for the U-Boat to gain access to the mothership, a hinged stern plate can be lowered using two massive hydraulic pistons while the ship's compartments are filling. From the dimensions, our engineers have calculated, 35 feet will give *Jonah* ample clearance to enter the docking bay. When the model of the submarine is ready, I'll demonstrate the process for you. Once *Jonah* is docked on her cradle supports, the compartments will be emptied simultaneously, and the ship will rise 35 feet. The U-Boat will be totally out of the water. What do you think?"

"Interesting. On the surface it appears to be quite workable. I do have a couple of questions for you, Eric. What if a third of the compartments fail to empty at the bow and a third fail to empty at the stern, but the middle third empties completely?"

"Interesting question. The ship might buckle in the middle from the excess weight, fore and aft."

"Will the mothership have a fully reinforced bottom and reinforced keel?"

"Yes, see here on the model?"

"Ingenious!"

Eric continued, "Moving on to the propulsion system, there will be two diesel turbo-electric engines capable of moving the mothership along at a cruising speed of 18 to 20 knots. The engines will be located on either side of the U-Boat bay. The machine shops as well as ammunition and torpedo storage will also be below decks, forward of the U-Boat and the engines. Four Gantry cranes will be positioned above the open scaffolding to reposition the submarine for painting and repair as needed, and to load torpedoes."

"Well, that's impressive, but keep in mind as you design and build her, that I'm thinking of ways to destroy both vessels. My plan is to completely obliterate both ships," JoAnn said.

Jake, who had remained silent up to this point entered the conversation. "Allow me to offer my most profound and sincere apology to you, Major. You are not what I expected at all. I had no idea what a devious mind you possess. I'm almost afraid to hear what you have in store for our enemies when you encounter them. I'm glad you're on our side."

Eric said, "I'm fully aware that is your mission, JoAnn, and we'll keep it in mind. As a matter of fact, I've been considering your ideas, and I have my engineers working on ways to reduce the number of supports required and to eliminate any unnecessary steps in construction. Although that will certainly speed things up a little, we need to keep in mind that those compromises are predicated on not overloading the ship and not encountering any violent storms or typhoons."

"I hope that during our planning sessions you don't mind if I continue to ask what may appear to be foolish questions. I will be continually looking for weak points in construction. I've decided it will be much easier for me to incorporate the explosives now rather than adding them later. The people behind this project aren't fools. We have no intention of allowing any of them to inspect the ship, but things happen and plans can change. I'm sure they already have people snooping around shipyards the world over. If they do, they'll be looking for a ship that will take 15 to 18 months to construct."

"Understood."

"I had an idea back in the States that continues to stick with me. I'd prefer not to go into it at this time, but I do have a couple of construction requests right now."

Eric said with a serious look on his face, "I'm listening." He took out a note pad.

JoAnn started, "Am I correct in assuming that the location of the Captain's bridge will be the uppermost level on the ship's tower and that it can be reached by an external elevator on the tower or by a series of gangways?"

Eric nodded, "Every level in the tower will be accessible by an elevator and gangways."

"Good," JoAnn continued, "I'd prefer the radio room be a separate compartment, but immediately adjacent to the Captain's bridge with a connecting door. I would like the observation lounge to be located one level below the Captain's bridge and to occupy the entire second level. I want it to run the width of the tower. I intend to furnish the lounge like the lobby of an upscale Paris hotel, equipped with a full bar and refreshment area. I want the lounge to be so comfortable and well appointed that none of the guests would have any reason to want to leave it. I'd like at least two large video monitors mounted there so our guests can observe the docking of the U-Boat in comfort. I'll need two pneumatic doors—one placed on each end of the observation lounge. Both doors must be airtight, equipped with heavy duty, self-sealing rubber gaskets, and fitted with a triple set of electronic locks. The windows must be made of bulletproof polycarbonate, heavy enough to withstand the impact from a fusillade of .50 caliber AP rounds. We also need to start thinking about mounting internal and external cameras and audio systems for the plan I'm still developing."

"I'll pass those requests along. Since we're talking about the tower, here's what else is in the works so far. The starboard half of the tower's third level will contain the officers' wardroom and sleeping quarters. The port half will be earmarked for the rest of the crew. The fourth level, called the boat deck, will house the German docking crew. Any other requests?"

"Yes, I'll need a set of three identical electronic control panels to detonate the charges. Can your engineers rig them up for me?"

"I'm sure they can," replied Eric.

JoAnn continued, "I've observed one weak point. It seems to me that a large quantity of air might get trapped in the compartments. The explosives will be detonated just below the waterline. The detonations in each chamber should leave a 20-foot hole in each compartment of the ship's hull. When the ship's chambers fill with water, I assume the ship will sink. Or will it?"

Both men just stared at her in amazement. Jake was thinking, "We've sorely underestimated her. She's no amateur. She knows what she knows and asks questions when she doesn't. She seems to have sized up the situation pretty well—even before we've finished showing her all the plans."

Eric replied, "To answer your question, JoAnn, yes, the ship will definitely sink. Eventually. Unless. . ."

"Unless what?"

"Unless, as you said, enough air remains trapped in the compartments to keep her afloat just below the surface. There is a remote possibility that the ship might float, partially submerged, indefinitely."

"Even with all 48 compartments ripped open with holes at least 20 feet long at or below the waterline?" JoAnn specified again.

"Yes. She may even capsize and still remain afloat."

"Ah, I was afraid of that. But I believe I can remedy that situation with a series of explosive charges placed at the top of each compartment. Water will enter the big holes in the sides of each one, and the air and water will be forced, like geysers, out of the holes above."

Surprised at her understanding of the situation, Eric replied, "That should certainly insure her sinking. Anything else you can think of?"

"Well, yes. There are two more things. First, I'd like to assist the engineers with the design of the cradle and supports for *Jonah*, if at all possible. That way, I can place and conceal the explosives and detonators inside. That should solve the U-Boat problem for us."

"I'm sure the engineers would be glad for your input. I'll arrange that."

"Secondly, I have questions about the crew. How many able-bodied seamen will it take to operate this vessel effectively as a container ship, excluding the Captain and the First Mate, who will also serve as the radio operator? I'm not counting the Germans who will board in Buenos Aires to ready the docking bay for *Jonah* and assist with the operation of securing her in the belly of the whale."

"No more than 15 men will do nicely. But we haven't decided if they will be Richard's men or ours."

"I have an idea," JoAnn said. "Do you want to hear it now or after dinner?"

"Now, while it's fresh."

"We'll need a foolproof way of getting all of the 'friendlies' off the ship and safely away before the action begins. At that point, all the Nazis will either be on *Jonah*, in the docking bay, or confined in the observation lounge. What if we equip the ship with two of those new 20-man, fully provisioned, motorized ocean-going lifeboats? They are completely covered and virtually unsinkable. They could safely carry our crew a long distance. Having two lifeboats—one on each side of the ship—leaves all options open."

Jake practically jumped out of his chair. "I'm absolutely blown away by your style. No pun intended. I don't ever want you for an enemy."

Eric stood and stretched. "That's enough for now. Let's get you to your hotel, and we'll all go out for dinner."

"You know, we could save a lot of time if we forget the hotel in Tel Aviv," JoAnn, said. "The apartment upstairs is fine. Any place to eat around here?"

"Yes, plenty of good places," Eric said smiling. "We'll pick you up at seven."

Chapter 32
The Investigation Begins

James decided to start his investigation using the list of domestic military bases Nancy had provided. He believed that the sources of supply for the illicit arms trade could only be explored under the guise of a routine general inspection, conducted randomly by the office of the Inspector General. He wanted to get started immediately. However, he realized that nothing could be revealed and no action could be taken until *Operation Jonah* had been concluded.

James stayed up late into the night organizing his plan of attack. By pulling a few strings, he had acquired from the Pentagon a comprehensive Quarter Master's manifest of weapons reported lost, stolen, or missing, as well as weapons retired or considered unserviceable. The list went back six months and was broken down by branch of military service.

Unfortunately, there were always a few men and women in the U. S. Armed Forces who were able and in a position to conveniently adjust inventories to add purloined items to the list of "lost, damaged, stolen, or unserviceable equipment.'" This was all done with appropriate "tokens of consideration" changing hands. Creative record keeping by the supply Sergeant was the key to a successful operation. The list included RPGs, Stinger missiles, .50 caliber machine guns, cases of small arms ammunition, AR 16s, Beretta pistols, and even the "obsolete" .45 caliber 1911-A1 automatic pistols. James had a map of the United States on his office wall. He decided to place red pins on each of the offending bases from the Pentagon's list. Then he placed blue pins on the bases Nancy had listed. Not surprisingly, when he finished that part of his project, many bases contained both colors.

The second list contained the names of as many military personnel as Nancy could recall. In spite of an influx of foreign immigrants in the U.S. Armed Forces after WWII, most of the names on her list were distinctly American. James studied the map. Right in the middle of Texas, a duo of pins caught his eye. "Why not start there?" For the time being, this was a solo endeavor. Actually, it was a rogue operation without any official sanction from the Department of the Army or any other government agency. At this point, he realized and understood that, if his operation were exposed, he could kiss his ass and his career goodbye. Fort Hood, an Army base in central Texas, would be a logical starting point. It was an enormous base and a full-blown IG inspection, supposedly originating in Washington D.C., would take time. Time was just what he needed.

He decided to begin his inspection on a very low key, so as not to arouse any suspicion in the minds of the black marketers. He certainly didn't want Otto and Siegfried von Ritter or their suppliers alerted. Fort Hood was indeed a good place to start since James knew the area well. He arrived on post dressed in civilian clothes and reported directly to the post commander, Major General William Boothe. The fact that Boothe knew and respected James's father, Colonel Garnett Hill, had been an additional reason for his choice.

Boothe was informed that this investigation was to be kept totally under wraps and not to be discussed with anyone. The nature of the investigation was not revealed to the CO, but he was assured that he was not in the line of fire, nor would he be held responsible for the outcome. This seemed to satisfy Boothe, and James was provided with an office in HQ. James explained that he didn't want or need an adjutant. "Please don't put my name on the door, but for the record, General, I hold the rank of full Colonel."

Within a week, James had already tagged one suspect. A Master Sergeant assigned to the armory was conveniently losing, returning, or destroying unserviceable weapons and parts. The attrition rates of some types of weapons and parts were significantly above the norm. There was also the occasional case or two of grenades, RPGs or Stingers that came up short in the shipments from the arsenals. The shortage usually showed up during transfer from the freight cars to the trucks or from the trucks to the warehouse and was easily accounted for. The Sergeant or dock master always blamed the discrepancies on a miscount somewhere along the line.

The data was accumulated slowly and quietly. As it turned out, Fort Hood had been the perfect place to begin. James was developing quite a dossier on the responsible parties. The problem there was much larger than he suspected. He was sure Fort Hood was just the tip of the iceberg and that additional "inspections" would be launched at the other bases he identified with the help of Nancy's list!

Chapter 33
U-Boat 'S'/*Jonah*

Richard called Steve. "We have a date with a U-Boat in three days. Can you make it?"

"Hold on. I'll check my calendar." After a short pause, he said, "Yes, I'll be free after 1 p.m. on Monday."

"Good! Tweak your German skills. I'll have my plane there at 1:30. We have a 5 p.m. boarding time on American Airlines to Buenos Aires. Then we'll take the PBY to *Golfo san Matias*."

"Okay, see you on Monday."

Richard made his next call. "Heinz, it's Richard. We can be in Buenos Aires on Tuesday. Does that suit you?"

"Yes. By all means."

"Then we can take the Global PBY if we can refuel down there at your airfield."

"Yes, we have an ample supply of aviation fuel available."

"Great! See you soon, Wilhelm."

Richard knew that the PBY had a range of over 2,000 miles and didn't need refueling for a round trip of 1,200 miles. What he really wanted was to see as much of the facility as possible. He wanted to get a good look at the airfield and the warehouses.

His next call was to Zac. "You're on alert. Get the ground crew started servicing the PBY. We're going back to the *Golfo san Matias*, and we will have guests going with us. We are about to make a house call on an aging U-Boat. We'll refuel down there even if we don't need it. I want you to take a good look at this place. Keep your eyes open."

"Roger that."

As Richard and Steve flew first class to Buenos Aires, they conversed in hushed voices. Richard said, "Steve, when we arrive at the U-Boat pen try to lag a little bit behind the party. Exhibit curiosity and remember— you don't speak German. Just try to mix with the crew and listen. The same rules apply there as they did on the hunt. Don't let them sneak up on you or surprise you. Count to five before responding to anything directed your way. Spanish and English only! Don't respond to any German at all."

"I've got it."

A company car, the ubiquitous black Suburban, met them and took them to Richard's office. Following a quick shower and a change of clothes, they went to inspect the PBY. Steve was anxious to meet Zac for the first time.

Richard phoned Heinz and said, "The plane is being serviced, and we will be ready to fly by noon. Let's meet at my office at 11:30. We'll have lunch before we leave. The plane can carry eight passengers comfortably, so there's room to accommodate additional guests if you care to bring a friend."

"I'll check and let you know. Yes?"

"No need to bother. Just bring whomever you wish. *Adios.*"

Richard had a sixth sense—a penchant for great anticipation. "Steve, you can bet your boots that Heinz isn't about to travel alone. He's too paranoid. Who he brings will be interesting. Care to guess?"

"I have no idea."

Promptly at 11:30, Heinz arrived, and as Richard had predicted, he brought a guest with him. It was none other than Gunter Ehrlich, aka Colonel Charles Becker, Sr.

The hair on Steve's neck stood up. "Oh crap! Here we go again. Now I really do have to be on guard."

After lunch they all walked to the plane. The Consolidated PBY Catalina was a venerable relic from WWII and had been the salvation for many pilots and airmen downed at sea. She sat on the concrete taxi ramp looking like a duck out of water. Introductions were made. Heinz handed Zac a map with the destination clearly marked in red ink. Obviously Heinz was unaware that this would be Zac's second visit to the U-Boat pen.

Everyone climbed aboard through the waist blister and strapped in. Zac started the twin Pratt & Whitney engines. When they were humming smoothly, he revved them and released the brakes. The plane started to roll, entered the water, and, as the wheels came up, they could feel the resistance and drag on the plane abate. The plane began to move smoothly across the water and picked up speed. The passengers were all given and put on headsets that had no communication capacity but acted solely as noise suppressors. Richard didn't want to give Ehrlich another shot at tripping up Steve. Conversation in the plane was impossible over the roar of the engines.

Zac hugged the coastline as the plane flew south. The view from the waist blisters was spectacular. Before they realized it, Zac was making his approach to the *Golfo san Matias*. He executed a smooth landing on the water and taxied toward the raised door of the U-Boat pen.

Zac said, "Richard, the port engine is running a little rough. If it's all the same to you, I'd like to run her up on that sandy beach we saw just outside the mouth of the bay to work on it. Oh, and please check on the refueling procedure for me, will you?"

A motor launch came out to meet them, and the four men exited through the open starboard waist blister and climbed aboard for the short trip to a well-camouflaged dock. As the group approached the sub pen, Richard gave Steve an almost imperceptible nod, and Steve immediately began to casually inspect the segmented overhead door.

A sturdy looking man of about 55, who stood just shy of six feet tall, met them. He was dressed in a Captain's uniform. "He's a bit tall for a U-

Boat commander," Steve thought. His hair was short and graying at the temples. He had the weathered face of a sailor, and introduced himself in Spanish as Captain Kuntzelmann.

"Please allow me to show you our U-Boat and our facility." Then he began addressing them in English with almost no trace of any accent. Almost was the operational word. There it was once again—a change in language.

Richard looked at Steve, who in turn gave him a brief nod. It was a warning to Steve to be on guard: "These men were purposely switching languages back and forth, and they might suddenly introduce German into the mix. Watch out!"

Steve thought, "It appears that these Nazis are not finished playing games. Gunter Ehrlich has coached them well."

"Gentlemen, follow me," Kuntzelmann ordered.

Inside, Richard and Steve followed Heinz and Ehrlich on the narrow catwalk that ran the length of the submarine at deck level on both sides. It ended at a suite of offices and the radio room. The submarine was out of the water, resting on hydraulic lifts. Steve fell a few steps behind as planned.

Richard noticed the 88mm gun mounted on the deck just forward of the conning tower. He thought, "They've added that. It wasn't on the U-Boat when it was seen in 1944." They climbed the ladder in order to enter the conning tower. Richard noted that on its second level, there were mounts for a pair of 20mm anti-aircraft guns. These had been added after arriving at *Golfo san Matias*, as well.

Steve remained last in line, pretending to look at this widget and that gadget. No one seemed to notice or care that he was lagging behind the party. He walked softly and listened carefully. What he heard was not what he had expected at all. Instead of hearing many dissimilar dialects and pronunciations, representing the various regions in Germany, among the crew and maintenance personnel, everyone seemed to be speaking the same dialect. The dialect was a bit strange to his ear. He had never heard it on any of the tapes of the native German-speaking students that he had conversed with back at the University of Texas.

At first it made no sense. Then Steve realized that this strange little colony of Germans had come from all parts of their native land, but they had been cloistered and inbred here for three decades. They had raised families and had been prepared and trained for a single purpose. They were dedicated to maintain and man the U-Boat whenever the call came. Their close proximity and lack of outside contacts had led them to develop a German dialect unique to their colony.

Steve thought, "A common language and a common ideology. Wonderful! Who would have ever suspected? This looks like another incubator for the *Fourth Reich*."

He hurried along the deck, climbed the outer ladder on the conning tower, and half slid down the one inside. The conning tower contained the housings for two periscopes, a telescoping radio antenna, and a snorkel.

Steve caught up with his party, but only for a few moments. Then he began to lag behind once again—looking at this and that and listening. The crewmen were excited to have visitors aboard and were anxious to show them everything. Their boat was, as the British say, "all spit and polish." Every piece of machinery, gauge, dial, and fitting was immaculate and looked brand new. The master machinists and crew had seen to that. Steve entered the forward torpedo room. He was still a compartment or so behind the others and heard one of the crew distinctly say, a little too loudly in German, '*Dieses Mal werden wir diesen verdammten Juden und Amerikaner immer beseitigen.*'

Steve was caught by surprise, but didn't react. He thought, "I had no trouble translating that little outburst, you Nazi bastards. 'This time, we'll eliminate those damned Jews and Americans forever!' Really? Not if I have anything to say about it. All those language sessions with the students have indeed paid off. Richard was right again. These people have been indoctrinated since birth by those goose-stepping, old-guard, hard-core Nazis. All of those de-Nazification programs that the United States started after the War were bullshit. De-Nazification can only be accomplished at the business end of a Colt .45 Automatic, with two shots to the heart and one to the head. I've heard how the Nazis treated many British and American POWs. This nest of vipers is living totally in the past. There is a concentrated substrate of venom and hatred here."

The Germans, however, were quite polite to Steve and showed him around the U-Boat. They continued to tell him, in German, how well the boat had been kept up, repaired, polished, and battle-ready. After all, they had been told that their guests were very sympathetic to the Nazi cause. Steve continued to nod and smile, pretending that he had no idea what they were saying. He managed to keep his cool and show no emotion.

Steve finally caught up with the main party. They were inspecting the 14 torpedoes secured aboard. The boat also carried a full complement of weapons. In the arms lockers were racks of 88mm shells for the gun mounted on the deck. There was an assortment of small arms including 9mm Lugers and Schmeisser MP-40 machine pistols. In addition, there were four MG-42 machine guns, and ammunition belts were hanging everywhere.

Steve already had a bellyful of this crap, but, in addition to the tour of the U-Boat, they had also been invited to dine with the officers. This was considered an honor that could not be refused.

The four guests followed the Captain out of the sub pen and across a stone-paved courtyard to a building in the center of the compound. There they entered a large medieval-appearing hall. Steve had a feeling of *deja vu*. Inlaid on the floor was a huge *swastika*. Encircling it was an enormous round table that looked like a giant stone ring. There was a fire burning in an open pit in the center of the *swastika*.

"Oh my god," he said to himself. "This looks familiar. I've seen this before in a captured Nazi documentary film. The film portrayed Heinrich Himmler, head of the SS, hosting an Arthurian gathering in a medieval fortress called *Wewelsburg*. Himmler and his SS officers were enthralled with the legend of King Arthur and the Knights of the Roundtable. They called the fortress the 'Grail Castle' and often held pageants there. It was the perfect place for the SS chief and his minions to play out their fantasies. They were thoroughly obsessed with the occult, Arthurian lore, the Holy Grail, and the Lance of Longinus. These crazy bastards have constructed a replica of the banquet hall at *Wewelsburg*."

Kuntzelmann led Richard, Steve, Heinz, and Ehrlich to their places at the table. There were 24 places set, and at each place was a glass filled with red wine. There were 19 officers present, each standing behind his chair. Captain Kuntzelmann lifted his glass, and everyone followed. Some of the younger men could barely grow hair on their faces. The senior cadet officer, with his glass of wine extended at arms length, offered the toast: *"Blut und Ehre!"* A chorus of *"Blut und Ehre!"* repeated the toast. Richard and Steve almost choked as they swallowed their wine. They knew that toast was the motto of *dies Hitler-Jugend*—The Hitler Youth.

Dinner was served, but after the fervor they had just witnessed, Richard and Steve had little appetite. During the meal, Heinz began to regale Richard and Steve, who were seated on either side of him, with the history, plans, and preparations for this colony. "It began in the fall of 1944..." Heinz rambled on and on and on.

As the meal finally ended, Steve thought, "Enjoy it while you can. You won't be here for long, I hope! These people are Nazis to the core. They will have to be dealt with!"

Chapter 34
Back In Haifa

"I think it's still too early for me to make any definitive decisions about where to put the explosives," JoAnn said.

Eric agreed. "I think that when you see the detailed blueprint overlays we are working on, you will be able to finally decide the best to places to put them."

"I concur. By the way, Jake, does *Mossad* happen to have any HMX or ONC-C8 lying around?"

"How the hell do you know about that stuff? I thought it was top secret!"

"Hey, remember me—the one-woman demolition derby? And, I might ask you the same question."

"Oh shit! I humbly beg your pardon, my lady."

She smiled and said, "Well, don't let it happen again. So, does *Mossad* have any of either or both available?"

"In a word, no—neither one. Hercules keeps that stuff under lock and key. They are top security items."

"All right, then here's what I plan to do. I'll fly home tomorrow. I'll arrange to meet with the people at Hercules and acquire the explosives we will need. I'll have it delivered to the Israeli Consulate in Houston. Jake, I'll need some help getting the stuff aboard an *El Al* flight back here. Fifteen hundred pounds each of HMX and ONC-C8 will have to be crated, labeled 'medical supplies,' and, I hope, flown back here with me. Can you arrange clearance to have it all loaded on my flight—or on an *El Al* freight run? Believe me, it's totally inert. Without a detonator, it's as harmless as modeling clay.

Both men exhaled. Eric said, "I'll have the overlays ready for you when you return."

"Great! I'll book a flight right now. Who's going to take me to Tel Aviv?"

"I'll take you," Jake responded.

JoAnn boarded the *El Al* flight to Houston, settled herself into the comfortable first class seat, and attempted to get some sleep, which she did, albeit fitfully. Somewhere over the Atlantic Ocean she became restless and suddenly awoke. The embryo of an idea—a plan—was developing and beginning to mature. She smiled. It was dastardly, devious, diabolical and deadly. She couldn't wait to share it with Richard, Steve, and James.

Chapter 35
Houston

As soon as she landed, JoAnn called Richard. He and Steve had just returned from Buenos Aires. They were on their way to dinner where they planned to rehash the details of the inspection of the U-boat base and their visit to the "colony," as Heinz referred to it.

"Why don't you take a cab and meet us at *DaMarco's* on Westheimer?"

"Fine! I'll see you there soon."

Forty minutes later, her taxi arrived at the Italian restaurant. The *maître d'hôtel* ushered her into a private dining room, where she found Richard and Steve sipping red wine. As soon as the door closed, Richard rose, held out her chair, and poured a glass of wine for her from the open bottle on the table.

JoAnn sat down, took a sip of wine, and said, "Well, what's new?"

Richard said, "What's new? Are you kidding me?"

They all laughed. Then she said, "Before you tell me, let me tell you what I need. Steve, I need you to contact the Israeli Consulate here in Houston. Ask them to contact Jake in Haifa. I need clearance at both ends to transport the explosives when I fly back to Israel. Also, Richard, I have a list of items, electronics, and supplies I'll need. James should be able to cobble them together while I make a quick trip to Hercules Powder Company in New Jersey to arrange for the explosives. It's all to be marked 'Red Cross Medical Supplies,' and, if possible, it's to go on the same plane that I'll be on when I return to Tel Aviv. The stuff is completely inert without a detonator. I have no death wish. The compounds are top secret. I need to be able to board the plane without alerting anyone or creating an incident."

Steve buzzed for a waiter and requested a phone. As soon as the phone arrived, he made a call to the Israeli Consulate and asked for Sarah Kalish. A short conversation followed, and then he hung up. "Consider it done. Just give me your date of departure and flight number when you know them. The Consulate will relabel the crates *'Magen David Adom.'* That's the equivalent of The Red Cross in Israel. The mother lode will be in the belly of your aircraft when you leave."

"Thanks! Now, how about dinner? I'm famished!"

While they ate, Richard began to recount the visit to the U-Boat facility in great detail, only interrupting the narrative when the waiter appeared. When he ran out of breath, he said, "Steve, you fill in the rest of the details. I can't seem to eat and talk at the same time."

JoAnn sat quietly and listened as Steve recounted each and every detail he could remember, including the little outburst in German that had occurred in the torpedo room. She absorbed every detail. It was clear to her that this colony of Nazis was every bit as hard-core, anti-Semitic, and anti-American as their forebears. Every boy in the colony became a member of the *Hitler-Jugend* at the age of ten and had taken that organization's oath, *"Blut und Ehre."* She asked, "How many residents of this colony of ex-patriots are living there now?"

"I don't know the exact number," Steve answered.

"How have they been kept living in isolation so long? The War ended almost 35 years ago."

Richard spoke up, "Let me tell you what Heinz told me. There was a high level Nazi Party meeting in August 1944. The very next month, a group of men who were loyal to the cause were ordered to have a U-Boat pen constructed in *Golfo san Matias.* Until then, U-Boat 'S' was to remain hidden in a small inlet near the *Negro* River. The critical element in construction of the pen was the hydraulic lift system. It served to keep the boat out of the seawater when it was not in use, thus retarding deterioration of the hull. In addition they were ordered to construct warehouses and a well-camouflaged airfield.

"Heinz told me that as soon as the War ended, he and a few other men were ordered to select the people for the colony. First they needed at least 65 officers and enlisted crew from Admiral Dönitz's U-Boat command. They also needed top maintenance personnel, mechanics, and master machinists. They were all ordered to relocate to South America along with their families. Of course, most of them were willing, since Germany was a shambles. So it became necessary to find ancillary personnel including teachers, doctors, and nurses to support the colony. They all had to be loyal members of the Nazi party. From the very beginning, supplies have been flown in by von Ritter. Under no circumstances has anyone been allowed to leave the compound, except in cases of life-threatening medical emergencies. The result of this project has produced a covey of Nazis who have dedicated themselves to serving in every way necessary to establish a *Fourth Reich*. Their entire focus has been on maintaining and preserving that submarine so that somehow, someday, it might be used to further their cause. They are true fanatics."

JoAnn said, "Looks like we've got our work cut out for us. I've conjured up a plan I'd like for you to hear and assess. I'll wait until James is here tomorrow to tell you about it. For now, I have one question. Do we have access to any Zyklon-B?"

That was a conversation stopper.

"Christ, what the hell are you planning to do?" Richard asked.

"Later—just answer the question!"

Steve responded, "Yes, I know for a fact that the Israelis have some they captured from the Syrians."

"Can Jake get it?"

"I'm sure he can—for you!"

The conversation stopped for a few moments. Each of them seemed to be absorbed in thought. No one spoke. The mood lightened after dinner with the arrival of dessert, multihued blocks of *spumoni*.

Richard spoke first. "JoAnn, you're not planning to start WWIII are you?"

"No, those Nazis down south and their Middle Eastern friends seem to be the ones planning to start it. It seems to me that they're hell bent on establishing a *Fourth Reich*. It's been brewing since before the end of the *Third Reich*. I plan to put an end to all of this once and for all. I will terminate it."

Chapter 36
Arranging the Chess Pieces

The following day, James arrived from Fort Hood, and they all met in Richard's office. JoAnn took charge of the meeting. "James, I've compiled a list of electronic equipment I will need, including RF transmitters, receivers, and some additional items." She handed James several typewritten pages of requests. "I need them as soon as possible—say three days? I also need you to call Hercules to alert them that I am coming."

James glanced at the list and said, "I can have it ready for you in two. I'll get right on Hercules as well."

JoAnn then addressed all of the men. "On the flight back I had an epiphany. Many of the fine points need some work, but, basically, here's what I'm thinking. My plan is to get all of our adversaries in the same place at the same time. What I'd like to achieve is a smooth and seamless series of coordinated movements, resulting in the converging of the container/drydock ship, the U-Boat, the PBY, and the leaders of our adversaries—both Middle Eastern and Nazi. I still need to work out how to arrange the pieces on this chessboard and to determine how to best get them there. For those answers I'll need time and probably some input from all of you. Getting the right people to the right places at the right time will be tricky."

James said, "It's going to be like herding cats, JoAnn."

"I know," she responded. "But this will be the last gathering they will ever attend!

"Diabolical!" Steve shouted.

James asked, "By the way, Richard, what's going to become of that entire nest of vipers living in the little 'Naziland' on the *Golfo san Matias?*"

Richard responded hesitantly, "Uh—I haven't completely decided that question yet. That's going to take lots of thought."

"Oh, I almost forgot something, Richard," JoAnn added. "Eric asked me to inform you that he needs a transfusion of greenbacks for the project. Another $75 million will do for now. He's working three double crews around the clock."

"Okay, I'll make the call as soon as we adjourn."

Chapter 37
Ready

Steve returned to Austin, and James set about gathering the laundry list of items that JoAnn had requested. Included on the list were electronics, antennae wire, state-of-the art long-range radio frequency transmitters and receivers, waterproof containers, and many other items. To accomplish this task, James had to call in a few favors from his friends at Quantico.

In less than 48 hours, he had collected all the items that JoAnn needed. They were crated, marked "Red Cross Medical Supplies," and delivered to the Israeli Consulate in Houston.

Through another CIA contact, James had obtained priority authorization for JoAnn to have *carte blanche* at the Hercules Powder Company in Kenvil, New Jersey. JoAnn made a quick flight up there in a Global plane. The military liaison officer was very accommodating. She requested and was allocated 1,500 pounds of HDX and 1,500 pounds of ONC-C8. When she gave the officer the date to deliver the explosives to the Israeli Consulate in Houston, he gave her a very quizzical look.

"That's easier said than done!" he almost shouted.

They finally agreed that the entire shipment would leave Hercules by helicopter in six crates marked "Red Cross Medical Supplies" and would be flown to Fort Dix/McGuire Air Force Base. There they would be flown to the Texas Air National Guard Hanger at Hobby Airport in Houston and then transported by truck to the Consulate.

Jake had done his job in Tel Aviv, and Sarah Kalish had done hers in Houston. The six crates of explosives and the two of electronic supplies were relabeled '*Magen David Adom*'. All eight crates were held under tight security awaiting further instructions from JoAnn. When she returned to Houston, and knew her flight number, the crates were loaded onto a Penske rental truck and, under armed escort, delivered to the freight entrance at Houston International Airport. When JoAnn's flight was ready for loading, the crates were carefully transferred into the baggage compartment under the plane for the trip to Israel.

JoAnn boarded the plane with the rest of the passengers. She was exhausted from her whirlwind trip. She sat back in her first class seat, closed her eyes and thought. "Well, JoAnn Scarlett, here we go! *Operation Jonah* is about to commence. You're on your way to destroy an 850-foot steel container ship and a WWII German U-Boat. James and Sarah Kalish have done their jobs, and now I am sitting above a cargo bay containing 3,000 pounds of explosives and a couple of crates of assorted electronic gear and gadgets, each one of them marked with a big red Star of David. My parents would never believe this!"

During the flight, JoAnn continued going over her plans for a workable timetable of events. She had initially considered her adversaries nothing more than pieces on a chessboard. Now she was coming to realize that they were all different personalities who may not react the same way to a given situation. What she required was a foolproof plan for getting all the pieces on her chessboard into their proper positions.

Jake and two additional *Mossad* agents met her when she arrived in Tel Aviv. They escorted her through customs and into a black limo. They waited 30 minutes. Finally, the military truck with the eight *Magen David Adom* crates loaded inside pulled up behind the limo. The truck driver flashed his lights, and both vehicles pulled away from the curb. They moved out into the stream of traffic leaving the airport and headed toward Haifa and the shipyards at Kishon. The truck entered the service area to unload the crates, while the limo stopped in front of the office building of

Israel Shipyards Ltd.

Eric met her at the entrance to the building, and they went directly to his office. As she gazed out of the window she commented, "I see our little project is progressing quite well. Have the crates been off-loaded?"

"Yes, they are all down in the basement and quite secure," Jake responded.

"Well, congratulations, Jake. Getting those crates on the plane and over here without any fuss must have taken a little fancy footwork on your part."

"Thanks."

JoAnn breathed a sigh of relief, and they all sat down. "I have a very short list of modifications for us to consider before it's too late." She began to give them a brief outline of how her plan was taking shape. They listened with interest.

"I'd like to test each of the explosives on solid steel plates, welded seams, and riveted plates. I'd also like to test the seacock and bilge pump housings as well. The tests need to be conducted above and under water. Is there a secure place away from prying eyes that fits my needs?"

Jake enthusiastically answered, "That's a 'can-do,' Major. I know just the place. We have a base on the coast where we train the equivalent of your Navy Seals. To the east of the base there is nothing but desert. Let me assure you that the one thing we have in ample supply here in Israel is desert. If you would care to take some back with you, we'll be happy to package some up."

"So, you guys do have a sense of humor, after all?"

"Yes, on occasion."

"Oh, I almost forgot," JoAnn, asked innocently. "Do you happen to have any Zyklon-B available to you?"

Eric and Jake said in unison, "What?"

"You heard me correctly. A simple yes or no will be sufficient. From your reactions, however, I take it the answer is yes."

Both men nodded, and Jake said, "Yes."

Eric said, "We have the overlays of the plans ready for your perusal, if you're not too tired."

"I am truly bushed and could really use a good night's sleep before I tackle those. Could we start tomorrow?"

"That's perfect," Jake responded. "That will give me a chance to alert our demolition people to ready the test sites for you. See you tomorrow!"

Chapter 38
Set

Hunched over the plans the next morning, JoAnn started a meticulous examination of each and every detail. With a red pencil she carefully marked on the overlay every place she planned to place or incorporate an explosive charge.

As she studied the plans she began to talk softly. "The eight cradle arms or support braces for the U-Boat are mounted on two pairs of tracks running at right angles to each other. Together, with the overhead Gantries, they can adjust the position of the U-Boat's hull to suit docking requirements."

Both men just listened quietly and watched her work.

"I'll place explosives inside each one of the support braces. When the U-Boat is on board and resting on all eight arms, I'll be ready to detonate the charges. That will destroy the last U-Boat of the *Third Reich*, its crew, its support personnel, and maybe even a few other men important to them."

"One problem solved," Jake whispered softly.

"Now," JoAnn said, "let's have a look at the quarters for the support personnel and docking crew. Where are the torpedoes going to be stored?"

On the overlay, Eric pointed out the answers to each question.

JoAnn was completely zoned out. She remained silent as she worked. Occasionally she gave a slight nod or emitted a soft sigh. She worked through lunch. Her examination was thorough and took up most of the afternoon. She used her red pencil liberally on the plans. Finally she looked up, rubbed her neck, and said, "I'd like to get on with the testing of the explosives tomorrow. Is that possible? I can use the rest of the day to do some more calculations."

Jake said, "I have a demolition team on alert status. I'll call them now. You can either work here or at your apartment."

"The apartment will be fine. You've stocked it well. When I'm finished working, I'll eat and turn in early."

"Great. I'll have them pick you up at 0700. Test samples of everything you need will be available for you in the desert and at the coastal base. How much explosive will you need?"

JoAnn, still somewhat zoned out, said as much to herself as to the men, "Let's unpack the truck now. I'll take 100 pounds of each explosion. Since I'll be using transmitters and receivers set to three different frequencies to stage my detonations, give me a dozen of each frequency. That's probably all I'll require to determine the size of the charges needed at each point to complete the job. Send everything on ahead so that I can get started as soon as we arrive."

"Major, we'll have it packed, loaded, and on its way in a few hours." Indeed, an Israeli Army truck with an armed escort soon left Kishon loaded with 200 pounds of explosives, steel plates (solid and welded), support struts, pump housings, and the electronic equipment for test detonations. The driver was unaware of his load. He thought he was delivering medical supplies for *Magen David Adom*.

A military Jeep was waiting for her promptly at 0700 the next morning in front of the building. There were two strapping young men inside. Both were wearing a full complement of Sergeant stripes on their sleeves. JoAnn didn't recognize them but felt confident that they had not been randomly chosen. In fact, they were a team—a very experienced team. One of the men was very large. JoAnn observed that he was at least six feet tall and weighed about 250 pounds.

He offered his hand to JoAnn and shook hers vigorously. "Just call me 'Little David.'"

The passenger jumped out of his seat and offered it to JoAnn. He was much shorter and probably weighed in at 160 pounds. "My name is actually Joshua. But once I was partnered up with 'Little David' here, I quickly acquired the sobriquet of 'Goliath.'"

"Great to meet you both! Let's get going."

The Jeep headed northeast out of the city for half an hour and arrived at a small military post. There was a helicopter waiting for them. The pilot already had the rotors turning. In a few minutes, they were airborne, heading toward the desert to the south.

Chapter 39
Stuff That Goes Bang

The truck with the test samples and supplies was waiting for them when the helicopter arrived in the desert. JoAnn waited until the truck driver and his armed escort boarded the helicopter for the trip back to Haifa before she began to unpack the equipment. What was about to happen in that Israeli desert needed to happen in strict secrecy. As the chopper faded from sight, JoAnn and the demolition team started unloading the truck. She carefully separated the two different types of explosives and began cutting them into small pieces that she weighed and labeled.

Then the business at hand began. They tested the plates, welds, and riveted joints using different amounts of explosives and three different frequencies. By noon, JoAnn was finally satisfied that she had identified the correct weight of explosives needed to effect her mission. She asked her companions, "Are you both in agreement?"

"Yes," they responded.

"So am I. Let's move on to the underwater tests."

Little David said, "As John Wayne used to say, 'Saddle up.' It's a short ride to the coast."

They packed up all the equipment and loaded it into the truck. In less than an hour, they arrived at the gate, and with a salute were waved in by the guard. Obviously, Jake had called ahead and requested clearance for them to enter the base. A test area had already been prepared for them. These underwater tests would prove to be critical.

The two demolition sergeants and JoAnn, with the help of some of the

Israeli "Seals," rigged an underwater, A-frame testing device allowing her to detonate both types of explosives in varying amounts without having to reposition the apparatus after every explosion. As the underwater testing progressed, JoAnn was quite impressed with the results. It didn't take very long to convince her that under water, the HMX out performed the ONC-C8. She had made her choice. The jagged holes in the various metal plates left after detonation were impressive.

JoAnn said, "We'll use only HMX below the waterline and in the pump housings. The ONC-C8 will be quite satisfactory for the U-Boat cradle arms and everyplace on the ship above the waterline." Little David and Goliath nodded in agreement.

Goliath said, "I'm curious, what's the maximum range of those new RF transmitters and receivers, or is that a military secret?"

"The maximum range is top secret. However, we'll not be using the equipment at maximum range. All we'll require is a distance of two miles at the most."

The two Sergeants just stood there shaking their heads. Then they both said something in Hebrew. Since she didn't speak their language, JoAnn didn't catch any of it, but the essence of the response wasn't lost on her.

JoAnn returned to Haifa by helicopter, while Little David and Goliath drove the truck back with the remaining equipment. After breakfast the following morning, JoAnn, Eric, and Jake met again in Eric's office. "Jake, thanks for making all the arrangements for the testing yesterday. Everything went really smoothly. I'm ready to take another look at the blueprints now. I was beginning to second-guess myself. Blowing up a steel container ship is more formidable than eliminating an 80-foot, mahogany PT Boat like *The Lorelei*. Now I'm positive that I'm on the right track.

After going over the plans once more, JoAnn said aloud, "Eric, there are two pump housings in each compartment. I had planned to pack each pump housing with explosives. But on second thought, is it possible or practical to incorporate both pumps into a single larger housing unit? Is it too late to do that?"

"No, it's not too late. I believe we can accommodate your request. We're a little ahead of schedule as it is."

"Good, a larger housing would allow me to pack in even more explosives. I will triple or quadruple the charge of HMX. That will give us more bang for our buck. After the U-Boat docks and is resting on her cradle supports there will be a toast to the *Fourth Reich*. Then, I'll simultaneously detonate all of the charges in the cradle arms and in the keel of the ship. That will take care of the U-Boat and all of the personnel in the U-Boat bay. I have a surprise for the people in the observation lounge before I detonate the charges in the pump housings in tandem and sequentially. The explosions should tear gashes large enough to let in half the ocean in each ballast compartment below the true waterline. Simultaneously, I'll detonate the charges of the ONC-C8 that I've placed on the external surface of each ballast compartment's roof. Once the integrity of each of the hull's compartments has been completely breached, water will pour in below the waterline as water and trapped air are forced, like geysers, out of the holes in the roof of each compartment. Then—down she goes!"

Jake exclaimed, "That sounds like a plan to me!"

Eric asked, "Are you still considering doctoring the torpedoes after the ship gets to Richard's dockyards in Buenos Aires?"

"No, I've reconsidered. With these new explosives, it won't be necessary. Frankly, I'd prefer that everything be completed here at Kishon."

"I agree." He added, "By the way, I've already ordered the unsinkable lifeboats we spoke of earlier. We should also have the three electronic control panels ready to test when you get back."

"Well, I think our meeting is over. It's a pleasure doing business with you gentlemen. I'll be flying home late tomorrow, if you don't need me for anything else. I won't be gone long. I'll be back right after our New Year.

I'll be in touch when my travel plans are made. *Shalom!*"

After JoAnn left the room, Jake and Eric just sat there. They were speechless.

Finally, Eric turned to Jake and said, "That's one impressive lady!"

Chapter 40
The Fog Clears

JoAnn boarded the Boeing 747 heading for Houston and settled comfortably in first class. She thought, "Time to relax. There's nothing more I need to do until next year." She laughed quietly at her little joke. She was anticipating ringing in the New Year and relaxing at Nancy's ranch with James and the rest of the gang from the *Volsung Project*.

After the plane left the runway, she tried to relax, but her attempt failed. She had a lot on her mind and began to review the sequence of events that would be required to make her plan work. Although the final make-up of the crew had not yet been determined, JoAnn was favoring the Israelis over Richard's people, since they would already be in place and familiar with the ship. Everyone had agreed that Captain Diaz would sail the ship to Buenos Aires and de Silva would be his First Mate. Exactly where the ship was to change hands and become the property of Global Import/Export had not yet been discussed or decided.

She thought about the issue of getting all of the docking support personnel, machinists, and ancillary crewmen from the colony to the container ship in Buenos Aires. They would have to consult Kuntzelmann about the number. How would they be transported to Buenos Aires and then board the ship without being seen? Maybe von Ritter's DC-3s would be useful. That would require more thought and fancy footwork.

JoAnn turned her attention to the plan that would be required to get one group of Nazis into the ship's observation lounge and another group of them onto the U-Boat, almost simultaneously and seamlessly. It struck her that precision timing was essential. Also, everything must appear routine while getting the Nazis aboard the container ship and during *Jonah's* docking within the ship. "The trickiest part is that I have to think of a way to get the ship's crew off and into the lifeboats. Last of all, I have to get Captain Diaz, de Silva, and Richard off the ship. The makeup of each traveling group will take careful consideration."

She continued to shift the chess pieces around on her mental chessboard. Her first gambit was to put Heinz, the von Ritters, Becker, and Ehrlich together on the U-Boat. She immediately dismissed that idea. Richard must travel with Heinz, Becker, and Ehrlich. If there were any trouble, it would probably come from the men in that group. She thought, "That's good, but what do I do with the two Arab oil moguls? They'll certainly want to be there for the show, and we need them there. Of course—the PBY! I'll put them on the PBY. Richard can fly with them as well. I'm sure the Middle Eastern bankers would not take kindly to getting their robes soiled with grease and oil while packed into tight quarters aboard the U-Boat. That leaves Strasse, the two von Ritters, and what's-his-name, Erdmann, the other industrialist. They can sail on *Jonah* with Captain Kuntzelman."

For a moment she closed her eyes and continued to mentally wrestle with the logistics of the operation. She was totally absorbed in thought. Suddenly she blurted out loud, "I've got it!" She noticed that everyone in the first class cabin was staring at her. "Sorry! I've just had an idea."

A male voice in the back responded, "That's wonderful! Is it a first for you?"

"Jerk," she thought, "it may not have been my first, but, by damn, I believe it's one of my best. We'll use von Ritter's squadron of DC-3s to move all the ancillary U-Boat personnel and docking crew to Buenos Aires. They'll arrive at night and be bussed to the ship in Richard's dockyards under cover of darkness. Erdmann, Strasse, and the two von Ritters can fly back to the colony to board the U-Boat on a DC-3. Richard, Heinz,

Ehrlich, Becker and the two Arabs will take von Ritter's DC-3 to the colony. I'll need to talk to Zac about the PBY's range and fuel capacity. I believe that if we were to refuel on the high seas and transmit the pictures to the screen in the lounge, it will keep the guests there occupied until the U-Boat docking procedures begin. That, and a sumptuous spread of food and drinks, will help distract them."

JoAnn took out her notebook and pen and began to write furiously. She had a plan, and now she needed to consult with James and Richard. When she finished her outline and was finally satisfied, she leaned back, closed her eyes, and began to snooze. She had been asleep for about an hour when she suddenly awoke with a start. She was covered in sweat and panicky.

"What have I forgotten?" Then it hit her like a ton of bricks. "Oh my god, I've made no provisions for myself. How the hell am I going to get there?" Then the epiphany struck. It was logical, and it was brilliant! "If Zac gives me a few flying lessons before the operation begins, I could fly as his co-pilot. After all, I've had a few basic lessons in an Army Beechcraft T34 Mentor. Granted, it's not a twin engine PBY, but we have three or four months to bring me up to speed before the ship is ready to sail. At least he can teach me to keep the damn thing in the air. That would be infinitely better than hiding me stuffed in the plane's cargo compartment for hours. Problem solved!"

Again, JoAnn curled up in her seat. Just before closing her eyes, she thought, "We need to give this ship a name. What about *Stella Maris?* I'm pretty sure that in Latin it means 'Star of the Sea,' and before this project is over, she will become a supernova." Finally, JoAnn fell asleep for the rest of the flight.

Chapter 41
Houston

JoAnn woke up with a bit of jet lag as the plane began its final descent into Houston International. She cleared customs quickly and was met by James and Richard who were clearly glad to see her.

"How was your trip?" James asked.

"Very productive, but I'm starving. Could we go to your office, Richard? I'd like to brief you both on my plan and then give you time to think about and critique it. By the way, I've taken the liberty of naming the ship for you. How does *Stella Maris* sound to you? It translates as 'Star of the Sea.'"

James said, "I like it." Richard nodded his approval as well.

"Well, lets get going," Richard said. "Let me order lunch and have it delivered. You look as if you're about to explode if you don't get it off your chest."

"You've got that right."

Richard took their orders, called the deli from the phone in the company Suburban, and asked them to deliver the food to his office. Once seated, with a sandwich in one hand and her little notebook in the other, JoAnn began to outline her plan.

"I've laid out a fairly complete plan for you. But there are some points of information missing. Until I get them, I can't finalize anything. First, of course, I can't even estimate the date until we know when *Stella Maris* will be completed. Then we'll have to establish her actual cruising speed. Zac can give me the cruising speed of the PBY, and Kuntzelmann can give me the cruising speed of the U-Boat on the surface and underwater. Most importantly, until Diaz gives me the exact latitude and longitude of our planned rendezvous, I can't pin anything down, and the success of this operation depends on all elements making the rendezvous precisely on time.

"It's been quite a struggle for me to construct a plan to get everyone on *Stella Maris* and *Jonah*. Here's what I've come up with so far. I think it would be wise for Heinz, Becker, Ehrlich and the two Middle Eastern bankers to travel to the ship with you and Steve on the PBY."

"Don't count on Steve for this part of the operation. I'm working on a special project for him."

"That's fine. I'll make a note of that. We need to get the two von Ritters, Strasse and Erdman on the U-Boat. They can fly from Buenos Aires to the colony on one of von Ritter's DC-3s that will have just brought all the docking support personnel, machinists, and ancillary crewmen to board *Stella Maris*.

"Oh, a thought just struck me. Why not ask Kuntzelmann to invite the senior Hitler Youth officers from the colony to accompany the other guests on the U-Boat? I'm sure they would relish the opportunity to witness the historic moment firsthand—the birth of their glorious *Fourth Reich*."

Richard said, "I see where this is going, and I like it. Dammit, JoAnn, you do have a diabolical streak. Indeed, even though some of them are still teenagers, they have all taken the Blood Oath of the Hitler Youth and been taught to kill without remorse. I've given this issue some serious thought, and I doubt that any of them are salvageable. I've seen their performance on German WWII combat film captured after the War. At the end of the War, these 'kids' were actively engaged in the fanatical defense of Berlin against the Russians. They were quite effective, adept, and ruthless. Why not invite the DC-3 pilots to take a submarine ride as well? That will tie up another loose end."

JoAnn continued, "I hope to get some flying lessons from Zac before the ship is completed so I'll be able to fly as his copilot and keep the plane in the air if need be. Traveling to the rendezvous as his copilot, I can go first class and not have to hide crammed in the cargo compartment. What do you think?"

"Great ideas," James responded. "You have done a phenomenal job of thinking this out. I can't see a weak spot at all."

"I'm sure Zac will be more than happy to give you the necessary instruction," Richard added.

"I need to check with Zac about something else, as well," JoAnn said. "I need him to fill me in on the fuel consumption and the operational range of the PBY. We may have to refuel the PBY when we rendezvous with the ship in order to get back to Buenos Aires. However, even if the PBY can carry sufficient fuel to make it both ways, I've decided that watching the refueling exercise at sea on the video screens will create an additional diversion for our guests in the observation lounge. If we keep them occupied, they'll give us less trouble. I'd better make a note to call Eric and have him install two 600-gallon tanks with refueling hoses on the ship and fill them with aviation gasoline."

James said, "So far so good. It keeps getting better and better."

"There's more. After the PBY lands, the Captain's launch will be lowered by de Silva. He will be towing the line that's attached to the refueling hose. He will secure the line to a cleat on the plane's fuselage, pick up the guests, ferry them to *Stella Maris*, and escort them all to the observation lounge. This includes you, Richard. I'll remain in the copilot's seat while Zac attaches the hose to the gas intake and starts to refuel the plane. There will be external video cameras installed on the ship's bridge, port and starboard. All of this action will be caught on camera and played in real time on the video screens in the lounge. There will be three RF master control boxes. Two of the control boxes will be in the plane—one attached to the bulkhead behind the copilot's seat, and the other tucked under the copilot's seat in a waterproof case for quick and easy access. The third will be on the ship in the Captain's safe.

"Once the guests arrive in the observation lounge, they will be informed that Captain Diaz has ordered a routine lifeboat drill, for his crew only. It will be explained that the Captain is required by Maritime Law to check the integrity of his lifeboats on a monthly basis, and that this is the designated date for testing. That takes care of getting our crewmen off the ship. Our guests will be impressed by the luxurious lounge and the sumptuous buffet and bar.

"Just over the horizon, one of Richard's smaller ships will be shadowing *Stella Maris*. While the lifeboat drill is in progress with all of the crew on the lifeboats, de Silva will send a radio message to the U-Boat. *Kapitan* Kunzelmann will be ordered to prepare to surface. By now, everyone in the lounge should be glued to the video screens. The guests will be able to watch the PBY being refueled and the lifeboats being loaded and launched. When the U-Boat is given the final message to surface and begin the docking procedure, the external cameras will be turned off, and the internal cameras in the docking bay will be activated so the guests can watch the preparations taking place as the German docking crew prepares to lower the ramp, flood the ballast tanks, and ready the ship and the bay to receive the U-Boat.

"While this is going on, de Silva will contact Richard by phone from the radio room and inform him that he has an important call from Buenos Aires. As Richard leaves the observation lounge headed for the radio room, the lounge door will close behind him, and he will trigger the electronic device in his pocket that will lock and seal both pneumatic lounge doors. With the doors airtight and triple locked, no one else will be able to enter or leave the lounge.

"Richard, de Silva, and Captain Diaz will meet on the boat deck and take the Captain's launch to the PBY. By that time, Zac will have finished the refueling process, and the plane's tanks will be full. The refueling hose will be capped and set adrift. After Diaz opens the seacocks and the launch begins to take on water, he, de Silva and Richard will board the plane through the waist blister. With our three men aboard the PBY, gentlemen, *Stella Maris* will be totally devoid of 'good guys.' As I mentioned before, the video screens in the lounge will be filled with images of the docking bay. The U-Boat will have surfaced by this time and *Stella Maris* should be down the required 35 feet on an even keel. Everyone in the lounge will be watching as their beloved U-Boat 'S' is given the signal to proceed slowly into the docking bay. Kuntzelmann, Strasse, Erdman, and both von Ritters should all be standing on the conning tower by now. The rest of the U-Boat's passengers and crew will be standing on her deck. Hopefully, if all goes as planned, soon each of them will be holding a glass of champagne.

"When the U-Boat has completed the docking process and has been secured, Heinz, watching on the video screen in the lounge, will call for a toast to the birth of the *Fourth Reich* and to *jihad* which will be heard over the loudspeaker system in the docking bay.

"That's pretty much how we get all the bad guys on the ship and the good guys off the ship. Questions or suggestions?"

Richard and James turned their chairs toward JoAnn, looked her in the eye, and said in unison, "And then?"

"Exactly what do you mean by 'and then?' Are you kidding me? Do you think this is a serial cliffhanger at a Saturday matinee? Don't worry, you won't have to wait a week to find out what happens next. What the hell do you think? I'm going to blow the whole damn mess to kingdom come, that's what!"

"That's clear enough," said James. "I don't know why we even bothered to ask."

Chapter 42
R and R at the Ranch

Nancy and Steve were very busy at the University in December. There were term papers to grade, finals to give, deadlines to meet, and getting all of that information to the Registrar's Office. Christmas came upon them very suddenly, it seemed. After some frantic last-minute shopping, they made a quick trip to San Antonio on Christmas Day to visit her family.

After their fall visit to Nancy's ranch, Steve had suggested having a New Year's house party there for their friends. She had happily agreed, and Maria and Joe had thought it a wonderful idea, too. They had invited the principals who had participated in the *Volsung Project*, and they had all enthusiastically accepted. Nancy had planned for everyone to arrive at the ranch December 29 and remain through January 1.

Nancy and Steve were packed and ready to go at daybreak on the 29th. They wanted to be there before the other guests arrived. Maria had made all of the preparations. She had stocked the ranch with everything the guests might want or need and had planned all of the meals. She had been cooking and baking for days. Joe checked the tack room to make sure everything was in order for horseback riding. Then he cleaned the shotguns in case anyone wanted to hunt quail.

The ranch gate was open when they arrived. Their first stop was at Joe and Maria's. Nancy removed an armful of packages from the back of the Suburban and carried them into the house. She had brought Maria a beautiful soft, long wool skirt, a pretty blouse with billowing long sleeves, and a silver beaded jacket.

There was not much shopping around the ranch. She was anxious to have Maria try them on to see if they fit.

Steve asked Joe to come out to the Suburban with him. "This is for you, Joe," Steve said. Joe opened the long, skinny package. His eyes widened when he saw a fleece-lined leather gun case containing a Winchester Model 92. It was a 44/40-saddle ring carbine. Another package contained 100 rounds of ammunition. "Wow," Joe exclaimed, "let's try this baby out!" Steve and Joe took a walk behind the house while Maria tried on her new outfit and modeled it for Nancy.

Joe set up some tin cans on the back fence and then loaded the carbine. He took aim and, "Bam, bam, bam!" Three rounds fired; three cans hit.

"Good shooting, Joe."

"Here, you give it a try, Steve."

Again, there were three quick shots, and three cans fell.

"Very nice gun, Steve. Good for varmints, large and small."

"Nancy thought you might like it."

"She was right. It's the perfect gift."

Just then, they heard Nancy calling from the driveway. "We'd best head up to the ranch house. Our guests will be arriving very soon."

The ranch house was decorated perfectly when they arrived. Maria and Joe had set up a beautiful Christmas tree with rustic ornaments in the living room. The theme was carried out throughout the house, including the guest rooms. Also sprinkled among the baubles were religious representations that reflected the melding of the Spanish and Texan cultures over the years.

Maria had set up a beautiful lunch buffet. There was a large pot of chili on the stove that Nancy turned on so it would be hot when everyone arrived. The rest of the buffet consisted of blue corn chips, flour and corn tortillas, cheese, salsa, *pico de gallo*, and guacamole to accompany the thick and hearty chili. Just in case there was someone in the crowd that didn't fancy south-of-the border cuisine, there were all the fixings in the refrigerator for ham and cheese sandwiches.

Steve immediately went to his room and unpacked. The customary sleeping arrangements for Steve and Nancy prevailed. They continued the pretense of occupying separate bedrooms.

Nancy looked out the living room window and said, "There's a cloud of dust on the horizon, and I'll bet you a buck it's George and Alice."

"You're on."

A few minutes later, George and Alice pulled in. Nancy and Alice visited while the guys carried the luggage into the house. Nancy said, "Alice, what's new in your world?"

"Becky is working on her Ph.D. in German studies at Texas, but I believe you already knew that. She's meeting friends in New Orleans for New Year's. George is George. He's always on the trail of a new antique gun. Right now it's an engraved Colt pistol with ivory grips. That's all he could talk about on the drive out here. He's still a little boy. Sometimes it's hard for me to believe that he's a surgeon and can take people apart and successfully put them back together again."

"Most men are just little boys at heart."

Next to arrive were James and JoAnn, followed by Richard and Bert. There was hugging, handshakes, and the usual chitchat. Bert manned the bar and took drink orders. Then they gathered around the sideboard in the kitchen and began to assault the chili bar. With plates and bowls piled high they settled around the table and enjoyed the feast Maria had prepared. As everyone finished lunch, they began to migrate to the living room and lounged around the inviting fire that Steve had started in the huge fireplace.

"So Steve, "George asked, "how's your book on Coronado going?"

"Well, it's a long story. For the moment my book is in limbo. We're involved in a bit of mischief."

Richard had overheard that little interchange and took the floor. "My friends, I think it's time to bring you all up-to-date on our present endeavor. It began with a wake-up call that arrived at my office in the form of a single word on a piece of stationary with a WWII Nazi watermark. It was addressed to me, and, when I opened the letter, there was a single German word on it: *ERWACHEN*. There were two letters above that word: *R.E.* Below it were two more letters: *W.H.* For a moment, I was stunned. Then I realized that I was being contacted by our old acquaintance, Wilhelm Heinz."

Bert nodded. Alice and George said in unison, "You've got to be kidding!"

"Alice, do you and George recall that phony list of deep-cover Nazi agents we conjured up and distributed rather overtly, specifically to the Nazis involved in the *Volsung Project*? If you all remember correctly, the only verifiable names on the list were Bert's and mine. Apparently, we did such a good job that it's come back to bite us on the ass. Heinz and his playmates have concocted a plan involving me, Global Import/Export, and the missing U-Boat 'S.' I guess they didn't contact Bert because they didn't think a doctor landlocked in the Texas Hill Country could be of much use to them." Everyone chuckled at that.

They also had a few laughs when he related Nancy's antics at the hunt in Argentina. George, especially, got a kick out of that. "I guess you've replaced me as comic relief at the hunt, Nancy. I may have to challenge you to a shoot off."

"You're on," Nancy responded. "We might have time for that tomorrow."

Richard continued to relate his story in great detail while everyone sat quietly and listened. "I've named this project *Operation Jonah*." When Richard finished recounting his part of the plans, he stood, added a log to the fire, and turned the floor over to JoAnn.

"Since Global will own this ship for a while, I took the liberty of naming her *Stella Maris*." JoAnn began outlining the scenario she had scripted, including the cast of characters and her objective of collecting the maximum number of adversaries on *Stella Maris* and the U-Boat docked in the bay within her.

"When the U-Boat, euphemistically named *Jonah*, with its guests aboard is secure in the 'belly of the whale,' I'll initiate the action."

JoAnn then described how she planned to get each group in place and how she planned to destroy both ships and some very unpleasant people. George was on the edge of his seat. The room remained absolutely silent.

Then Richard spoke up, "JoAnn and I would welcome any suggestions, comments, or questions about the plan she just outlined."

George spoke up, "Do you plan to use the same explosives that you used on *The Lorelei?*"

"No, there are two new and better products available now," JoAnn explained. "One product I'll be using is called HMX. It works quite efficiently and effectively underwater. I'll also be using another new product. It is a relative of C4 called OMC-C8. The only unlimited opportunity I will have to plant the explosives on the ship is during its construction. I've been working closely with Israel Shipyards and *Mossad*. James used his connections to get me the materials I need. By the time *Stella Maris* arrives at the Global dockyards in Buenos Aires, all the primary and backup explosive charges and the RF receivers will be in place.

"When I appear at the 'scene of the crime,' it will be as the copilot of the Global PBY Catalina. I will bring the control panels necessary to bring our plans to a very spectacular conclusion."

Bert said, "I can't think of anything you've missed."

Alice had a question. "Do you feel confident that von Ritter and the others will want to sail on the U-Boat?"

"Richard spoke up, "Hell, yes! They're Nazis. To sail on the last known Nazi U-Boat is every *sieg-heil*-goose-stepping-flag-waving-Kraut's dream—especially during peacetime when they wouldn't come under attack. They may be a little apprehensive, but they will follow orders. After all, as we all are aware, 'orders are orders.' And we all know how well these people follow orders!"

"There is one thing that continues to bother me," Steve said. "Are we absolutely dead certain that Gunter Ehrlich is their top dog? Is he really pulling the strings?"

JoAnn immediately responded, "No, I am not. That has been really bothering me, as well."

George piped up and said, "JoAnn, let me say once again that in my book, you're still the gold medal winner in the Olympic 'Toxic Waste Disposal' category. I wish I were going with you to witness this one. *The Lorelei* was a show, but this one will really be something to see. Take some pictures for us, will you?"

Richard stood, walked over to George, slapped him on the back, and said, "George, you're a damn genius! That's a great idea! I'll bet my pilot, Zac, can rig up a camera similar to the gun cameras he used during the War in his Army Air Corps Photo Reconnaissance unit. He flew recon missions in the Pacific in PBYs. I'll get working on that right now."

Richard left the room to use the phone in the kitchen while the others talked among themselves. When he returned there was a grin on his face a mile wide.

"I'm here to announce that Zac had already anticipated our request and has already acquired two WWII gun cameras and 2,000 feet of film. He has all the high-speed aerial photo equipment in the hangar and is mounting the cameras as we speak. By the way, JoAnn, he also said that if you care to fly down to Buenos Aires, he will teach you to fly the Catalina."

Alice put her arm around George and patted his shoulder. "Great idea, George. I'm proud of you. You are good for something besides collecting and cleaning old relics."

"Poor George," JoAnn laughed, "We all love to pick on him."

Chapter 43
Happy New Year 1980

The conversation turned to the lighter side. They turned their attention to Bert. "How's your lady friend?" Alice inquired. As usual, Bert was loquacious, but somewhat evasive. Then the group made an about face and started on Nancy and Steve. They were laughingly evasive as well. James and JoAnn were also the subjects of some very pointed relationship questions. They all soon tired of badgering each other and decided to take advantage of the rather salubrious weather. They all agreed that a horseback ride around the ranch would be perfect. Each of them saddled a horse, mounted up, and took off for a two-hour ride around the ranch. Deer season was almost over, but they saw a few trophy bucks and came upon many large coveys of blue quail. There had been a bumper crop this year.

Nancy said, "According to Joe, we've had two successful hatches this year because the rains came just at the right time. There are quail everywhere. I'll call the game warden in the morning to alert him that there will be some serious shooting on the ranch tomorrow."

It was dark by the time the group returned to the barn, and groomed, fed, and watered the horses. They had leftovers for dinner and turned in early.

After breakfast the next morning, Joe loaded the trap house on the range behind the house, and everyone took a turn shooting a round of clay pigeons to sharpen their shooting eyes for the afternoon hunt. George and Nancy had an impromptu contest, but were both content with a tie.

Everyone except JoAnn had a hunting license, so she volunteered to drive the Jeep, while Joe drove the pickup. As predicted, the hunting was superb, and each shot the limit. They returned to the house late in the afternoon. Joe dressed the birds, and Maria prepared a wild game dinner including the quail and some venison from a doe Joe had harvested earlier in the season. They all insisted that Maria and Joe join them for the delicious meal, topped off by homemade pecan pies that Alice had brought. The evening was enjoyable for all. They were exhilarated by their day out of doors and the successful hunt. Retiring rather early, everyone agreed to sleep late.

Indeed, they did. They began wandering into the kitchen about 9 a.m. The weather outside was cold and rainy. It was a good thing they had already gotten in their outdoor activities. Someone put on a pot of coffee, and they all worked together to make a hearty ranch breakfast. By the time they had finished and cleaned up the kitchen, Steve had a great fire going in the living room, and one by one they settled in for a long comfy day of watching football games on television. There was no further talk of *Operation Jonah*, but everyone was thinking about it. About 5 p.m., everyone drifted off to shower and change for the New Year's Eve festivities. Joe was going to grill some grass-fed homegrown steaks. Maria brought over a large wooden bowl of salad and some twice-baked potatoes to heat in the oven—simple but delicious.

When midnight arrived, they all raised their glasses in a toast to a Happy New Year and a successful operation. They were glad to spend the beginning of 1980 with each other, and were so hopeful that their plans to eliminate some very real dangers to a largely unsuspecting world would succeed. The party quietly broke up, and everyone headed for their rooms. They were looking forward to another day of loafing and football games. Perhaps the sun would be out, allowing for another horseback ride or a hike.

After breakfast on January 2, the entire party stopped by Joe and

Maria's to thank them and again wish them a Happy New Year.

On the drive back to Austin, Nancy said, "Steve, you really had a great idea about the house party. I think everyone had a wonderful time and really appreciated being brought up-to-date about *Operation Jonah*. It will be quite a feat to micromanage all of those people into the scenario JoAnn presented."

"I agree. But if anyone can do it, JoAnn can. Changing the subject, I was thinking about that enormous trunk in 'my' bedroom—the one that you said belongs to your mother."

"Yes. What about it?"

"I was thinking that maybe someday you'll ask her for permission to open it. I would love to see if there's anything interesting inside."

"You're a nosy fellow, aren't you?"

"No, just curious."

As Richard drove toward Kerrville, he began to quiz Bert about his thoughts on the overall plan as it had been presented.

"I've been thinking about that very subject. Trying to maneuver all the players into the proper position won't be easy, for sure. It could be a very workable plan, though. I'd suggest that you start the ball rolling by meeting with Heinz as soon as possible. Describe JoAnn's scenario to him, but not in too much detail. Ask him to give it some thought and to make some suggestions. That will help plant the idea in his head. I know these people. The more he thinks about it, the greater the chance that he will begin to adopt the plan. Eventually, he'll tell you that it was his idea all along. Your chances of success will rise dramatically if that happens."

"Thanks, Bert. I may have to run more stuff by you from time to time, okay?"

"I'm here to serve."

As soon as Richard returned to Houston, he called Heinz and wished him a Happy New Year. Then he took a more serious tone of voice and said, "Heinz, things are progressing nicely. I believe we have some unfinished business to conduct. When can you come to Houston?"

There was a pause. Then Heinz said, "I agree. Is January 4 good?"

"Excellent! Call me with your flight number, and I'll have a company car meet you."

Chapter 44
The Confrontation

Heinz arrived at Richard's office at precisely 11:30 a.m. on January 4. After exchanging the usual pleasantries, Richard offered him a cup of coffee and a comfortable chair. Then looking directly into the Nazi's cold, pale blue eyes, he said, "Heinz, it is time to clear the air and tell all."

Heinz responded with an almost imperceptible flinch, he blanched ever so slightly, but said nothing.

"Let's get down to brass tacks. I feel that in order for me to continue this project, I must have answers to a number of questions. Failure to fully disclose the information I request will cause me to withdraw completely from this enterprise, and I shall return from whence I came—back to total obscurity.

Now Heinz was pale, and a few beads of perspiration began to show on his forehead. With an audible sigh, Heinz nodded his head. Their eyes were locked.

"First, who or what is Gunter Ehrlich, and what is his connection to our project? And, for that matter, why does Colonel Becker stick to him as if they are Siamese twins? Another thing disturbs me. When they stand side-by-side, they seem to have similar facial characteristics. Are they in some way related?"

For a few moments, there was no response—just silence. Their eyes were still locked.

Richard continued, "From the very start of this project, I have had the feeling that you report to someone higher up on your chain of command.

Who is it?"

Heinz adjusted himself a little in his chair and wiped away the small beads of sweat on his forehead while continuing to look Richard in the eye. He said, "I knew this moment would come. I told them that you were no fool and that you couldn't be picked up and played like an accordion in a Bavarian beer garden."

"So?"

With a sigh, Heinz began, "All right. Gunter Ehrlich calls the tune. He is my superior. Colonel Becker, as I think you have already guessed, is his son."

"Very good. Now we're getting somewhere. So which is it? Are they Beckers or Ehrlichs, and how do they fit into this puzzle?"

"They both use the name Becker when in the United States, and they both attained the rank of Colonel in the Army of the United States. They are both native born Americans of German descent. 'Gunter Ehrlich' was the name of the elder Becker's maternal grandfather. He chose it as his alias when carrying out our work outside of the United States. A few years ago, they had been heavily involved in the *Volsung Project,* a plan to initiate a modified version of the Third Reich's *Lebensborn* experiment in the United States. During the War, Ehrlich had been running his operation from the U.S. Immediately after the end of the War, he resigned his commission and went to work for Hercules/DuPont as a chemist. This gave him the opportunity to travel internationally. Something went terribly wrong, and the *Volsung Project* was terminated. I won't bother you with those details. So the answer is simply that Charles Becker, Sr., known to you as Gunter Ehrlich, is the man to whom I report. He is my superior officer."

Heinz took a long breath, sat back in his chair, and appeared much relieved at having gotten that off his chest.

"So, I must assume that *Herr* Ehrlich will be tagging along wherever we go, watching and listening to whatever we do or say. Yes?"

"Yes!"

"Very well. That is not a problem. However, I would suggest that you not tell him what you have just revealed to me. Don't you agree, Heinz? I think it would be best if he continues to think that I know nothing."

"Excellent idea," said Heinz as the color returned to his face.

Richard just sat there for a moment. He gazed out the window and thought, "He's lying. The son of a bitch is lying. There was just enough truth in his story to make it appear plausible. His body language and hand movements indicate otherwise. He's clever. He told me some truth, but then he fabricated the rest. Now he thinks he's gotten away with it, but he hasn't. I'm pretty sure he's the one in charge."

Richard looked back at Heinz for a moment and then said, "Schnapps?"

"Yes, please!"

Richard had decided not to give Heinz too much information and to offer him a little disinformation at the same time. "It is my understanding that the container ship is about 11 months away from completion and launching. I should be able to take possession by about this time next year. You can start making your plans accordingly."

Heinz's eyes lit up. He sat back in his chair and said, "Excellent!"

Richard thought, "That ought to throw his dogs off the track for a little longer. Hopefully, they won't be looking for a ship about to be completed in three or four months. As far as I can tell, I'm still squeaky clean, and the money in the numbered accounts is untraceable."

He spoke aloud to Heinz, "I'll require an additional $20 million to complete the project. Will you have any trouble with your bankers?"

"Not at all, especially when I tell them we'll have the ship sooner than we thought. I'll have it deposited to your Swiss account upon my return to Buenos Aires."

"Good. Now down to business. I've sketched out a master plan that I'd like to run past you. Give it some thought and make suggestions and alterations as you see fit. Then pass it on to *Herr* Ehrlich or Colonel Becker, whichever name he chooses to go by. When the ship is completed, it will be delivered to me at an undisclosed location, under a yet to be determined flag. When my crew and I take possession, we will sail her to Buenos Aires and dock her at the Global dockyards."

"Good! Good!"

"As far as the world maritime community is concerned, Global has purchased a new container ship, *nicht wahr?*" By the way, the name of the ship is *Stella Maris.*"

"Good name! Yes, very good. I like it!"

Richard smiled and replied, "Thank you." But he was thinking, "I really don't give a shit whether you like it or not."

"And when will we check out the docking facilities? You know, the trial run of docking the U-Boat?"

"Don't rush me, Heinz. I was just coming to that. I imagine that everyone involved in the project would want to be present to witness the historic first docking of the U-Boat—the birth of the *Fourth Reich?* At the very least, you will want as many of the officers, ratings, and support personnel as possible, yes?

"Now, I have already selected my Captain and crew for launching *Stella Maris,* sailing her to Buenos Aires, and docking the U-Boat. We will have to get your maintenance and docking crews aboard while she is docked in Buenos Aires. Keep in mind that I always work under the assumption that I'm under surveillance by some petty Argentine officials who are always looking for a handout—hush money. When she leaves our dockyard, her decks will be laden with containers heading for Cape Town, South Africa. The Captain and I have chosen the least frequented commercial sea-lane in the South Atlantic to avoid observation and detection. Another *schnapps?*"

Heinz, who was enthralled, nodded his assent, and Richard filled his glass again.

"I have been informed that you often host two representatives from the Middle East, who I assume are, or are representing, the bankers in this project? Surely you want them in attendance?" Not waiting for an answer, Richard continued, "When we all visited the U-Boat pen, *Kapitän* Kuntzelmann told me he was only taking a crew of 22 officers and ratings. He asked me if he might be allowed to take along some of his most accomplished senior cadet officers from the *Hitler-Jugand* to witness this historic event. He thought it would be inspirational to the future leaders of the *Fourth Reich*. What do you think, Heinz?"

"Excellent idea, Richard. I was just thinking the same thing. Yes, I agree."

"I'll be damned," Richard thought, "Bert was right. That Nazi is already beginning to view this whole scenario as his own creation."

He said to Heinz, "Do you want to run this past Ehrlich before we make the final decision?"

"No, no! I don't think that will be necessary. I'm certain he will approve."

"Bullshit," Richard thought, "Now I have the complete picture. You don't have to consult Ehrlich because he's not your superior officer, you not-so-clever bastard. I'm even more convinced you're the man in charge, Heinz. Confirming it will be something else, though."

Heinz sat back in his chair and abruptly asked, "Richard, how did you know about the two Arab bankers?"

Richard's response was immediate and terse. In a most authoritarian voice he said, "How I know is of no concern to you!" Immediately he changed his demeanor, and in a much softer voice said, "I've worked out a tentative logistical plan to get everyone aboard *Stella Maris* to watch the birth of our glorious *Fourth Reich*. Would you like to hear it?"

"Yes, of course!"

Now Heinz really was confused. For a moment, a faint worried look crossed his face. He thought, "Exactly who is this man? For certain, he's much more than a simple deep-cover agent."

Richard explained, "You and I, Becker, Ehrlich, and the two Arabs will fly to the colony in comfort in von Ritter's private DC-3. Strasse, Erdman, and the von Ritters will fly in one of the other DC-3s. I don't want the von Ritters anywhere near the Arabs. The four of them will join Kunztelmann on the submarine with his crew and a number of the *Hitler-Jugend*. The U-Boat's docking crew will fly to Buenos Aires in the DC-3s along with the ancillary crewmen. They will board Stella Maris under cover of darkness while she is in port and docked at Global. I doubt that your Arab guests would enthusiastically welcome or relish an underwater voyage in a U-Boat—certainly not like a true Aryan would. They would probably not be happy to be confined in such tight quarters or to soil their white robes with the grease and oil they might encounter. So, I've made arrangements for you and me, along with Becker, Ehrlich, and the two Arab bankers to fly to our rendezvous point in my PBY. The rest of the details can be worked out later. What do you think?"

"Very interesting plan. It seems to be fool proof. I like it! We will do it!"

"There will be an observation lounge on the ship's tower, one level below the Captain's bridge. From there, on large video screens, everyone will be able to witness all of the preparations for the historic docking of the U-Boat. Best of all, Heinz, at the proper moment, you will order the men on the U-Boat and the guests in the lounge to fill their glasses with champagne and to raise them in a toast to the *Fourth Reich*. Then we will all enjoy a fine party in the lounge to celebrate. Afterwards, those guests who wish to return to Buenos Aires can fly back on the PBY, which can accommodate eight passengers. Selection, of course, will be made according to rank and position. The rest will continue on to Cape Town. All the amenities for a comfortable passage aboard the ship will be provided. When the ship returns to Buenos Aires, we will help you hire and train your crew. At that time, your plans for the future can become a reality."

Heinz appeared stunned. The years of plotting and planning for Nazi supremacy now seemed to have another chance. He couldn't seem to gather his thoughts.

To break the silence, Richard inquired, "Heinz, what are your plans for the U-Boat pen and the colony in the *Golfo?*"

"Ah, indeed. They must continue to be maintained and operated just as before. Unlike *Herr* Wagner's *Der fliegende Holländer, Stella Maris* will have to come into a friendly port for maintenance and supplies. That port will be Buenos Aires. While she is there, the U-Boat will find her safe haven in her pen near our colony."

Richard shook his head slowly and said, "Heinz, you seem to have thought of everything."

Suddenly, hoping to catch Richard off guard, Heinz said, "Richard, where's your man Kreutzer? Or should I say von Kreutzer?"

"Actually, he's occupied at the university. He's preparing for the new semester. I'll fill him in on our conversation. He sends his regards."

"Yes, yes. Of course."

In a slightly more authoritarian voice, Richard said, "Finally, Heinz, understand this. The plan only works if everyone follows orders! The successful birth of the *Fourth Reich* depends on everyone—and I mean everyone—following orders to the letter. Do you think we will have trouble with anyone in our party following orders?"

Suddenly Heinz sat up erectly, assumed a new air of authority, and said, "Otto and Siegfried would be afraid to show any reluctance about sailing on the U-Boat. They will not refuse a direct order. They will sail. Strasse and Erdmann will also do as they are ordered! I agree with you, Richard. The two Arabs, Becker, Ehrlich, you and I will fly in the PBY."

"Remember Heinz, these are only my suggestions, but they will be executed as your orders, subject to *Herr* Ehrlich's approval, of course."

"Yes. Exactly! They will be my orders!"

"Very well, I believe we are finished. As the work on the ship progresses, I will inform you of the final timetable. If any problems arise call me immediately. And don't forget to transfer the additional $20 million."

Without giving Heinz a chance to say another word, Richard ushered him out the door.

Chapter 45
1980, Haifa–Some Adjustments

JoAnn flew back to Tel Aviv on January 5. She had called ahead to ask Eric to arrange for a meeting with Jake and the Israeli demolition team as soon as she arrived in Haifa. After a quick shower in her apartment, she dressed and went directly to Eric's office. The ship had been under construction for several months, but there had been some significant alterations to the initial plans. She wanted to go over them in meticulous detail with the team.

When she entered the office, Eric and Jake greeted her. The two Sergeants from the Israeli demolition squad who had helped her test the explosives in December grinned broadly when they saw her. It addition to David and Goliath, there was a new face in the office. A Captain, attired in the same battle dress as the Sergeants, stood as she came through the door.

Eric said, "Major Scarlett, this is Captain Bergmann, our metallurgical engineer."

Standing at attention, he delivered a crisp salute and promptly announced that he had some good news for her. "Major, my people, with the assistance of Eric's engineers, have redesigned and fabricated the new pump housings you requested. Each unit will contain both the primary and back-up pumps and leave you sufficient room to accommodate more than three times the explosive charge you had planned for the original units. Using your test figures, we have calculated that the new charge will tear a hole in the outer hull over nine meters across. That's a 30-foot gash in the outside wall of each compartment.

"I also made a change in the ballast chamber's entry ports for servicing the pumps. I've added a hinged circular hatch on the roof of each chamber. Explosives detonated at the latch and the hinges will blow the door off and create an ample port for air and water to exit from each chamber."

JoAnn responded, "That sounds great. I'll detonate the charges on the hatch covers simultaneously with the charges in the pump housings, insuring that *Stella Maris* will sink rather than float just below the surface. Do you have any other suggestions?"

"May I also suggest that you double the number charges on each of the eight arms of the cradle? We can call it a little insurance."

"I agree. That ought to do the job."

"I'd like to show you the plans and a model of the redesigned housing prototypes.

"And I'd like to review them with you."

"I'm at your service, Major."

The Captain unrolled the plans of the new pump housings and began a detailed description. JoAnn scanned the plans quickly as he spoke. When he finished, she said, "Captain, these plans appear to be exactly what I was hoping for."

"Great, would you like to see the prototype model?"

"By all means. How long do you estimate it will take to get the housings caste and the pumps installed?"

Eric answered, "About a month should be enough." He then unrolled another set of plans and pointed out some changes he had suggested that might save an additional week of construction without sacrificing the ship's integrity."

JoAnn studied the changes with great interest. "This all looks fine to me. Good work, gentlemen. If you'll excuse me now, I think I'd like to get some rest and do some additional thinking to be sure we've covered everything. I'm really bushed. Can we meet here tomorrow at 0830? I'll give you a rundown on my plans for blowing up this ship that you are taking such pains to build. I will be anxious to hear what you think about it."

With all the men in agreement, the conference adjourned, and they all stood up as she left the room.

Chapter 46
A Few More Details

After a good night's sleep, two cups of coffee, and a toasted onion bagel with cream cheese, JoAnn felt refreshed. She went directly to Eric's office. The men were all sitting around the conference table enjoying coffee and pastries.

"Good morning, gentlemen."

The entire company stood and returned the greeting. "We're all quite interested in your plans for *Stella Maris* and her distasteful passengers," Captain Bergmann said, "What are you thinking?"

"I believe I owe you all at least a brief sketch of my plans. Without going into too much detail, here is the first phase. If all goes as planned, the 'guests' in the observation lounge will be watching the video screens as the U-Boat successfully completes the docking procedure and is resting on her cradle. From the lounge, Heinz will initiate a toast to the birth of the *Fourth Reich*, requesting that the men on the conning tower of the U-Boat join in the celebration with champagne they brought with them. They will all lift their glasses heralding the birth of their glorious *Fourth Reich* and drink a toast. A prerecorded audiotape will then begin to play simultaneously in the observation lounge and in the U-Boat bay. As the tape plays, and the men in the lounge are watching the video screens, I will initiate the detonation. The men in the lounge will be witness to the demise of the Kapitän and the four industrialists standing on the conning tower, as well as the destruction of the U-Boat, the entire U-Boat bay, the support area and its personnel, and all of the U-Boat's passengers and crew. The explosion will take out the cameras and the video screens will go dark, but the audiotape will continue to play in the lounge."

Jake interrupted, "How do you plan to keep from detonating all the charges at once?"

"My RF transmitters and receivers are programmed to respond to different frequencies."

"Sorry. I guess I should have figured that one out myself."

"Now, here is Phase 2. The interval between the destruction of the U-Boat and the initiation of the detonations that will sink the mother ship will be around five to six minutes. I have planned a well-deserved surprise for Heinz, the two Arab bankers, and the two American-born traitors who have just had the privilege of witnessing the end of U-Boat 'S.' My surprise, however, requires four canisters of Zyklon-B pellets."

Jake exclaimed, "What?"

"I believe you heard me correctly—Zyklon-B. You remember, the canisters you captured in Syria. Surely you can spare four of them."

"My God," Captain Bergmann almost shouted. You are really planning to——."

JoAnn cut him off in mid-sentence. "Yes, that's exactly what I plan to do! You're not getting squeamish, are you? Now, do I get the canisters or not?"

"Yes, of course," Jake said. "But how are you planning to deliver it."

"I'm sure Eric remembers the plans for four nonfunctional air conditioning vents we placed in the observation lounge. They all contain ducts that are two feet deep and end blindly. Each duct will be equipped with a heater and a blower. I will place one of the Zyklon-B canisters in each duct and place a small explosive charge on each canister. When I'm ready, I'll detonate the explosive charges that will rupture the canisters. Then I will remotely start the heaters and blowers. The pellets will rapidly begin to vaporize and the gas will diffuse. When all the men in the lounge have succumbed, Phase 3 will begin. From my control panel in the PBY, I'll initiate the final destruction of *Stella Maris* with a series of tandem, sequential detonations initiated from bow to stern. Remind me to plant a heavy charge of HMX along the keel, running the full length of the bay. I want that area of the hull to split open like a ripe melon."

The room was silent.

Captain Bergmann said urgently, "What if someone sends a 'Mayday' call?"

"When we complete this exercise, Captain, there will be no one left alive on the U-Boat, in the submarine bay, or on the mother ship to send one. Now, if we have no further pressing business, I must bid you all goodbye. I have to get back to Tel Aviv to catch a flight to Houston. I need to clean up a few loose ends there before I go to Buenos Aires to begin flight training. I need to learn to fly the PBY that will be vital in bringing this nest of Nazi vipers together on *Stella Maris*. It has been a pleasure meeting and working with you, Captain Bergmann. Thank you all for your efforts. I'll be back as soon as Eric calls and gives us the green light to begin planting the explosives."

"It's been a real pleasure getting to know you, Major,"

Jake said, "A word of caution. Major, are you all absolutely confident that you have a handle on your adversaries' entire chain of command and that there are no surprises out there waiting to ambush you? You must be as certain as possible. When the submarine and ship go down, you must be sure that you've got all the rats on board. If *Mossad* can be of any assistance, please call me."

Chapter 47
The Flight to Houston

The return flight from Tel Aviv to Houston should have been uneventful. JoAnn had called ahead to ask Richard to meet her at the airport. There were a few loose ends that needed her attention, but she couldn't do much about any of them at an altitude of thirty thousand feet. She tried to doze off, but Jake's comment about being sure of having the entire Nazi chain of command on board before scuttling the ships had her worried. She asked herself the same question over and over. Each time she got the same answer: "No! I'm not 100% sure." She remained fretful, couldn't sleep, and her pulse was racing. "Who is really in charge in Buenos Aires? Was it Heinz, Ehrlich, Strasse, or Erdmann? Maybe it was none of the above. Could it possibly be that fop, the jester, von Ritter?"

Suddenly she remembered something she had learned during the *Volsung Project*. She recalled a high-level secret meeting of Nazi leaders and Nazi industrialists in Strasbourg in August 1944. American Intelligence received a report they labeled, EW-Pa 128. This document contained the agenda for the meeting. Present in Strasbourg were important Nazis who had managed to fly under the radar during the War. Their purpose was to plan the post-war funding for a *Fourth Reich*, as well as the infiltration of Nazis into world banking and industry. They were planning the establishment of a *Fourth Reich* even before the *Third Reich* had fallen. JoAnn wondered how these men thought they could pull that off. How could they get away with it? Something in that scenario bothered her for most of the flight. Then it hit her like a ton of bricks.

"Oh, my God! Those men who escaped capture and prosecution for war crimes could assume completely new identities. Identities would be created, papers forged, and false documents fabricated and issued. They could undergo plastic surgery—minor and major—to create alterations to their appearance if necessary. They could get away with it, too. Who will be there to say otherwise?"

Her mind continued to race. Suddenly she said to herself, "*Mossad*—that's who. I need pictures of everyone who attended that meeting in 1944. I'll call Jake tomorrow.

When the plane touched down at Houston International, Richard was there to meet her. "Thanks for picking me up. I'm bushed. Can I bunk at your place tonight? I'll give you a full rundown on my Haifa meetings in the morning. There are some important things that need attention."

"By all means. I'll even cook you some breakfast."

Chapter 48
Something Isn't Quite Right

JoAnn awoke to the smell of frying bacon. Still rubbing the sleep from her eyes, she entered the kitchen. Richard had gotten up early. He was anxious to hear what was on her mind as he deftly gathered his pots and pans.

"What'll you have?" Richard asked.

"How about two eggs over easy, bacon, toast, grapefruit, and black coffee?"

"Coming right up!"

After breakfast and a quick cleanup of the kitchen, both took cups of coffee into the den and got comfortable.

"All right. What's on your mind?" Richard asked.

"Before we start, Richard, I have a question. Do your pilots have their multi-engine ratings? Can they fly twin-engine propeller aircraft?"

"Matter of fact, they both do. Luther Dawson also has an instructor's ticket. Why do you ask?"

"Well, I'd like to get a little instruction and to familiarize myself with the ins and outs of twin-engine planes before I contact Zac and begin to tackle that PBY. I've logged some time in a single-engine trainer, but I've never soloed."

"That won't be a problem. Let me set up a session with Luther right now for this afternoon." He picked up the phone and set everything in motion for her flying lessons. "Now, I can't stand the suspense any longer. Out with it! What's on your mind?"

"I have a hunch—just a hunch. Before I left Haifa, Jake asked if we were sure about the Nazi chain of command. He pointed out the advantage of having all the rats on the ships before we sink them."

"I agree, but I'm almost certain that Heinz is the man pulling the strings."

"Okay, but I'd like to eliminate the 'almost' if we can."

"How do you propose doing that?"

"With the EW-Pa 128 agenda."

"Good thinking. That was the high-level secret meeting of Nazi industrialists and bankers in Strasbourg in 1944."

"Exactly. Paragraph 6 of that document details post-war plans to insinuate some important Nazis—who managed to remain under the radar during the War—into banking, worldwide commerce and industry in preparation for a *Fourth Reich*. Richard, I believe we need a complete list of those who attended that meeting, as well as their pictures. We might need to track down all of these men to see if any of them are involved in this project. While I think of it, I'd like *Mossad* to update the bios on our four South American industrialists. I believe we know all there is to know about Gunter Ehrlich, but an update there wouldn't hurt, either. It's the other South Americans that really bother me. Jake offered the assistance of *Mossad* if we need it."

"I agree. Why don't you call Jake now to get the ball rolling?"

JoAnn was on the phone in a heartbeat. "Jake, I need your assistance! Can you get me the names and photographs of every person who attended the secret meeting at Maison Rouge in Strasbourg in 1944?"

"Yes, I think so."

"Can you get us bios on all the men who attended the meeting? Then please update the bios of the four South American industrialists that we know personally—Walter Erdmann, Paul Strasse, Otto von Ritter and Wilhelm Heinz."

"I'll get on it right now."

"Thanks. I'll be staying at Richard's Houston office for now. Just fax everything here."

As they were about to hang up, Jake said, "JoAnn, a word of caution. The Nazis are masters of disguise and at changing the identities of those important people they might want to protect. To change identities, they have even used plastic surgery in some cases. But there is one thing they can't alter. At least, they haven't managed to do it yet."

"Really? And that is?"

"Our experience in *Mossad* suggests that you must look at the eyes for identification."

"We'll keep that in mind."

"You should be getting a complete list and your first pictures and biographies soon. Keep us posted."

"Thanks, Jake."

Chapter 49
The Eyes Have It

"Shakespeare said, 'The eyes are the window to the soul.' If I remember correctly, it's from *A Midsummer's Night Dream*," Richard said.

"How prophetic," JoAnn retorted. But I believe Cicero said it first around 43 B.C. Nevertheless, it's true. The eyes don't lie."

"I stand corrected. Thanks for that interesting piece of trivia."

With a big smile JoAnn said, "You're quite welcome, sir."

At that moment, Richard's secure line rang. He picked up the phone. "Richard speaking. How may I help you?" As he listened, Richard made a few notes. "Thanks for the information." Hanging up the phone, he turned to JoAnn. "Things are really falling into place now. The location for the transfer of ownership of *Stella Maris* has been determined."

"Interesting, where will it be?"

"Cagliari. A good choice, I think."

"Where is Cagliari? I'm not familiar with it."

"It's located on the southeast coast of Sardinia, and is a major port for container ships—the perfect spot for Diaz, de Silva and me to board the ship. Then we will proceed to Buenos Aires."

"What about your crew. Will they arrive when you do?"

"We haven't made that determination yet."

"May I make a suggestion?"

"Sure."

"I'm assuming the Israelis will sail *Stella Maris* from Haifa to Cagliari in order to check everything out. They will be much more familiar with the operation of the ship than any crew that we might provide. Maybe the Israelis should sail with us for the duration of the operation. We can tell the Nazis that after the trial docking of the submarine, the ship will sail on to Cape Town to deliver the containers. When we return to Buenos Aires, they can take over."

"Good thinking, JoAnn. I've already told Heinz we will help train his crew. You're as sharp as a tack. I'll discuss it with the Israelis, but I'm sure they'll agree. It will give us complete control."

At that moment, the fax machine came alive, and information began to flow. The list of names of all those attending the secret meeting in Strasbourg was first to arrive. This list would provide valuable information in the quest to identify exactly who was in charge of this new horrific Nazi project. A random mix of 8" X 10" black and white photographs followed. On the reverse of each one were the names of those in the pictures. Soon *Mossad* began sending the biographies of the men on the list, including the latest information on each one. They were true to their word, including updated biographies on the four South American industrialists. The quality of the pictures was surprisingly good, and there were dozens of them. They included photos of most of the people for whom JoAnn had requested biographies.

Richard had Rose bring in a large bulletin board. After examining the pictures for a long while, they began to choose some to pin up on the board. JoAnn pointed to one. There were two SS men, an officer and a Sergeant, standing in front of a German Tiger tank. She looked on the back. In German script on the back of the photo were the names—*Waffen-SS Hauptmann Manfred von Reimer, 1st Panzer Regiment, Group 1 and Vizafeldwebel Wilhelm Heinz, October 1944.*

"Richard, here's a picture of Wilhelm Heinz. I guess *Mossad's* database spit it out because we asked for his bio. Doesn't *Vizafeldwebel* mean 'First Sergeant'?"

"Yes, it does."

"Well, how would you translate *Waffen?*"

"It means 'armed.'"

"So *Waffen-SS* means 'armed *SS?*'"

"Exactly."

"Yeah, I thought so." JoAnn shivered as a cold chill ran up her spine.

The fax machine continued to spit out more pages. Richard said, "Well, here are the bios you requested." He handed JoAnn the four new bios of the South American industrialists she had just received from *Mossad*. Richard pulled the old biographies of the same men from his file on the *Volsung Project*. First they compared the old texts relating to Walter Erdman, Paul Strasse and Otto von Ritter to the newly-received biographies. They were virtually the same—no changes to speak of. The biography of Wilhelm Heinz from Richard's file stated that Heinz was born in Stendal, Germany, and immigrated to South America in 1946 or 1947. It made no mention of service in the *Wehrmacht*. However, the most recent *Mossad* bio told a different story. Suddenly Heinz is a First Sergeant in a *Panzer* unit. But they have no record of him after the War. "Richard, look at this again." JoAnn pointed to the picture of Heinz with his tank commander.

Richard's eyes went wide as he turned the picture over again and read the inscription on the back. "Good god, JoAnn, this is all wrong. The Sergeant Wilhelm Heinz standing next to Captain von Reimer in this photograph is not the man I know from South America. The date on this picture is 1943. The Heinz I know in Buenos Aires behaves like a Prussian aristocrat. He's officer material! He's no common soldier and most certainly not a Sergeant in a *Panzer* unit. Let me get the picture from the hunting trip last fall. Nancy made sure that all the Nazis were in it."

In a few minutes, Richard returned with the group picture and handed it to JoAnn. "The Heinz in this picture reeks of cold, hard arrogance."

JoAnn asked, "Could there be two Wilhelm Heinz's, both from Stendal?"

"Doubtful. That would be too much of a coincidence. Let's have another look at those pictures, JoAnn. Put them on the desk."

"JoAnn placed the pictures side-by-side. "Here's Heinz and von Reimer standing by their tank. Now let's compare that with the picture from the hunt."

Richard gazed at the photos and actually shouted, "Look, JoAnn. Not only is Sergeant Heinz not 'our' Wilhelm Heinz, but I think there is a real possibility that Captain von Reimer is. Something is not right. We need to get to the bottom of this!"

The fax machine started up again, and another picture emerged. JoAnn picked it up. "Richard, take a look at this one." She placed it on the desk next to the two they had been examining.

The photo showed five men standing in front of a German Tiger Tank that was flying a regimental leader's pennant from the radio antenna. Two men were dressed in *SS* uniforms. The other three were civilians. *Mossad* had written their names and the date on the reverse side: *Herr Doktor Haberkorn, Reinmetall-AG; Waffen-SS Oberst Joachim Peiper; Herr Doktor Johann von Kreutzer, I.G. Farbin; Waffen-SS Hauptmann Manfred von Reimer; Herr Doktor Rolf Kaspar, Krupp. 11 August 1944.*

JoAnn pointed out that the three industrialists' names were on the list of participants at the secret meeting in Strasbourg. "That's probably why this picture was selected. Can you read the inscription on the front?"

"I think so. It says 'Our bravest and our best: *Standartnführer Waffen-SS Oberst Joachim Peiper, Commander, 1st Pz. Rgt. and Waffen-SS Hauptmann Manfred von Reimer, Group Leader, 1st Pz. Rgt.*' It's obvious from the picture that the industrialists took great pride in being photographed with military heroes of the *Third Reich.*"

"If von Reimer turns out to be *Heinz,* who is Peiper, and what is so special about them? They look like a nasty pair."

"The name 'von Reimer' is not familiar to me, but Colonel Joachim

Peiper is one of the most infamous Nazis of the War. If I remember my history correctly, Peiper's *Panzer* unit captured about 80 unarmed American soldiers who had surrendered during the Battle of the Bulge in December 1944. They were all summarily executed on the spot. For this barbarous act Peiper became known as the 'Butcher of Malmedy.' Somehow, word of the atrocity got out, and, after the War, Peiper was immediately sought out and arrested by the Allies. He was put on trail for war crimes. As I said, I don't know anything about von Reimer. However, I wouldn't be surprised if he had a part in that travesty as well."

JoAnn nodded. "Richard, look closely at these three pictures. Here are von Reimer and his Sergeant Heinz in front of their tank in 1943. Next, are von Reimer and Peiper with the industrialists in 1944. Now compare von Reimer in those two pictures with last year's photo of the 'Heinz' we know. Look at the eyes, Richard. Look at the eyes!"

"I'll be damned. Wilhelm Heinz from Buenos Aires and von Reimer in those photographs are the same man! I believe we'd better find out just who this guy is. JoAnn, call Jake and ask him if they have anything on von Reimer. If they do, tell him to send it quickly! This guy makes me more than a little nervous."

JoAnn made the call. "Jake, do you have any information on a Manfred von Reimer? His picture showed up in conjunction with Heinz and the industrialists on the list from the Strasbourg meeting. We know he's connected to Joachim Peiper."

"Oh, 'The Butcher of Malmedy.' That guy was ruthless. I'll check von Reimer out and get back to you as soon as I can."

"Great! If possible, can you send an age-progression photograph of von Reimer? We may have just solved a big mystery."

"I'm on it!"

As she hung up the phone, JoAnn said, "Richard, I think they really are the same person. We may have just serendipitously hit a home run with the bases loaded! Jesus, look at those eyes!"

They stood transfixed, looking at the photographs. Richard said, "It's uncanny. We seem to be looking into the face of *Waffen-SS Hauptmann* Manfred von Reimer in the first and second pictures, and his identical twin brother, South American industrialist Wilhelm Heinz in the third picture. There seems to be no doubt. But will we be able to prove it?"

Still staring at the second picture, JoAnn answered, "We'll have to be patient until we hear more from Jake. But, why does the name Johann von Kreutzer sound familiar. Is he important to us?"

"Hell, yes! You bet he is. He was a hardcore Nazi chemist working for I.G. Farbin during the War. He also happens to be Steve's uncle."

"Well, here he is. He's the civilian in the center."

"So that's the connection. Heinz knew von Kreutzer during the War. I wondered why Heinz took such an interest in Steve after becoming aware his last name was Kreutzer. That explains why he insisted Steve join us for the hunt in Argentina. The invitation came completely out of the blue.

"Before we jump to any conclusions, let's see what *Mossad* digs up on von Reimer." JoAnn looked at her watch. "I've to go. I don't want to be late for my flying lesson."

Chapter 50
Surprise Package

After dinner, they were quite relieved when they returned to Richard's office to find *Mossad's* report on von Reimer waiting for them in the fax machine. They sat on the couch and read it together:

"When the War was over in 1945 and *SS* officers and noncommissioned officers feared the very real possibility of imminent capture and arrest, it was common practice for them to exchange uniforms with those of regular army privates. In the post-surrender chaos, they melted into the landscape. Many important and notorious Nazis used this practice successfully. After the German surrender, the Allies had their hands full sorting and tracking thousands of military prisoners. Colonel Joachim Peiper was caught and arrested by the Allies and put on trial for his culpability for the massacre at Malmedy. It now appears, however, that von Reimer slipped through the cracks and returned to Stendal. We have also determined that his Sergeant, Wilhelm Heinz, returned to Stendal, his hometown as well. Now the story becomes a bit convoluted.

"Stendal police records state that on 16 July 45, Wilhelm Heinz left his home located about four miles from Stendal. He told his family he was going into town to have a few drinks with an old army buddy, and he left on foot. According to the missing person's report filed with the police a few days later, he was never seen or heard from again.

"Coincidentally, on that same day there was a terrible automobile accident involving a single car a few miles west of Stendal. The car was totally demolished, and the occupant was thrown from the vehicle. Both the car and the occupant were burned beyond recognition. A short distance from the body, papers and some personal letters were found. From the papers, the body was identified as that of Manfred von Reimer, formerly a Captain in the 1st *SS Panzer* Regiment."

JoAnn said, "My God, that's a bit too much for a simple coincidence."

Richard answered, "Apparently that's what *Mossad* thinks as well. They seem to be surmising that von Reimer enticed his old Sergeant to meet him in Stendal. Instead, he picked him up on the road to town. Somehow he engineered Heinz's death and then set the scene as if it were an accident. That enabled von Reimer to switch identities with Heinz. The body the police found was really Wilhelm Heinz, but they identified it as von Reimer's."

"Well that explains a lot of things. The eyes don't lie."

"There's more."

They read on together. "Further investigation reveals that von Reimer had attained an advanced degree in Metallurgical Engineering from *Technische Universitat Berlin*."

JoAnn exclaimed, "So he was one of those 'valuable' men who remained below the radar during the War and who escaped to Argentina, most likely with a little assistance from *Odessa*, the Nazi escape organization. *Odessa* probably helped him pull of the accident and identity switch as well. Now the picture is becoming crystal clear."

"I believe we have the bastard now. I have an idea that may stir the pot. It's risky, but I believe it's worth the gamble. Try this on for size, JoAnn."

As Richard slowly began to reveal his plan, JoAnn sat and listened. What began as a hint of a smile on her face grew into a broad grin. Then she said, "I like it, Richard. Let's make that phone call and put your little plan into action."

"I agree. What time is it now in Buenos Aires?"

"They're actually three hours ahead of us, but that's of no importance."

Richard picked up the phone and dialed a number that he knew by heart. JoAnn just sat back with a grin that could have put a Cheshire cat to shame.

"Wilhelm, I'm calling to give you an update on our little project. I've been informed that the construction is progressing well and is on schedule, but I still have not been given a delivery date. How are things at your end? Any problems? Oh, by the way, a couple of very interesting photographs have come to my attention."

"Really?" What kind of photographs would they be?"

"One appears to be a photograph of three civilians, all high level German industrialists, and two *SS* officers. It's dated August 1944. The other photograph, dated 1943, shows First Sergeant Wilhelm Heinz standing in front of a Tiger tank next to his tank commander, *Waffen-SS Hauptmann* Manfred von Reimer. It's quite a nice photo of you—Manfred. Or should I address you as *Waffen-SS Hauptmann* Manfred von Reimer, second in command of the 1st *SS Panzer* Regiment?"

There was a distinct pause in the conversation, followed by a guttural whisper. *"Gott im Himmel!* How did you get that information? All those records were destroyed!" Another pause in the conversation followed. Then came the question, "Who ARE you?"

Richard could tell immediately that Heinz's impenetrable armor had been mortally pierced. "Never mind, that's of no importance to you. I'll be in touch again—soon. Oh, one more thing. As the time gets closer, we can afford no slip-ups. Every man must follow his orders to the letter! *Nicht wahr?"* Richard hung up the phone without waiting for a response.

"He'll need a change of underwear after that little exchange, Richard."

"Probably, but now he'll be guessing how I found out, or if I knew all along. Where I stand in his chain of command will be unclear to him. I want him to be confused. That should give us a little breathing room. To beat those bastards one must think like they think. Don't you agree?"

"Indeed. No one will dare fail to follow orders now."

The fax machine came to life and one more photo landed in the tray. It was the age progression photo of Manfred von Reimer. It was Wilhelm Heinz as plain as day.

"There is no more 'almost.' Now we are sure who's in charge!"

Chapter 51
The Stolen Arms Investigation

Sitting in his office at the HQ building at Fort Hood pondering his next move, James was now in full uniform wearing the insignia of an Infantry Colonel. He had been on the job for only two weeks, but he had come to the conclusion that it was time for him to insert an undercover agent from CIC, the Army's Criminal Investigation Command. He picked up the phone and dialed the number on a card he had taken from his wallet.

"Headquarters, CIC, Quantico."

"This is Colonel James Hill at Ft. Hood. Put me through to Colonel Alford, please."

"CIC, Colonel Alford speaking."

"Jack, it's James Hill. How are you these days?"

"Couldn't be better, James. My promotion to full Colonel has just been approved."

"Great! I'll buy you a drink at the 'O Club' when we get together."

"I'll take you up on that. What's on your mind today?"

"Are we on a secure line?"

"Yes. Shoot."

"I need your help. Are you free to follow up on anonymous phone tips and leads and keep it under wraps?"

"With my new promotion, there'll be no problem. Now I can cut the red tape, and I have the authority to follow leads and travel at will."

"Okay. Consider this an anonymous tip. Here's the situation. I'm in-volved in a delicate operation that is totally off the books. As a by-product of this operation, I believe we may have uncovered the first of many major sources of stolen government weapons that are being sold worldwide to revolutionary and *jihadist* groups on the black market. I'd like your help in infiltrating the conspirators, starting here at Fort Hood. The base commander knows I'm on to something, but if our operation here on the base is uncovered, he will have to disavow any knowledge of it. I'm putting my job, my retirement and my ass on the line. If you get involved in this, and it goes south, your tenure as a chicken Colonel may be short-lived as well."

"Say no more. It sounds to me like the CIC needs to take a hand in this project. Count me in. Is it just the two of us?"

"For now."

"Okay. When do you want me there?"

"ASAP."

"I'll be there next week. What do I need to bring?"

"Just your conjured-up orders, new identity, and military records stating that you are 'a chronic foul-up, untrustworthy, and a persistent embarrassment to the Army. You're suspected of being involved in a number of shady deals but have never been caught. You've been busted from E7 to E5 for marginal performance of duty. Unfortunately, you're in possession of information that might be considered detrimental to the careers of some of the brass, so the Army frequently moves you from base to base."

"I've got it. I can fill in the blanks. I'll fly to Dallas a week from today and take a Greyhound to Belton. If *Katie's Koffee and Kolache Korner* across from the bus stop is still there, we can meet at 0900."

James chuckled, "It's still open. Some things never change. See you there and thanks."

Jack Alford was a native Texan. His dad was in the military, and he had spent quite a few years at Fort Hood. He knew the place like the back of his hand. James was drinking coffee and munching on a sausage kolache when he saw Jack step off the Greyhound, cross the street, enter *Katie's*, and come directly to his booth. They were each dressed in jeans, cowboy shirts, denim jackets, and fancy boots. They looked like the rest of the locals, and greeted each other like brothers. Jack ordered one sausage and one strawberry kolache with black coffee.

"I sure miss these. You can't get anything like them back east. They're big on bagels with a schmear!"

James laughed. "Say, where's your duffel?"

"Don't have one. Somehow it all got 'lost in transit.' That way there's nothing to trace. I'll draw a new issue when I arrive on post. I don't even have a comb or a toothbrush with me. All I've got are my orders and my records. Take a look." He handed them across the table.

As James scanned the papers, he whistled. "You really are a scoundrel—a real foul-up. We have information that there is a lot of funny business going on here in the QM Supply Depot. As you know, Fort Hood is an active post where field exercises are constantly in operation. A sprawling base like this offers ample opportunity for upper echelon enlisted and officer personnel to traffic in illicit weapons, munitions, and military gear of all types. Hopefully, you'll be able to obliquely insinuate yourself into their organization, however long it takes. Remember, I only want you to gather information for the time being. Until the primary mission has been successfully completed, I can't give you the green light to act. It's imperative that you sit on the information you gather. This is only the first of many military bases where these illicit operations are occurring."

"Can I assume that I may be transferred to other trouble spots later?"

"Yes, but by that time you and your CIC agents will be in total control of the operation. I'll be long gone. If you need to contact me, here's my number. Be sure you call from a pay phone. I'll contact you through the office of the Sergeant Major. Well, good luck. How are you planning to get to the base?"

"I'll take the military bus."

"Right. Then I'll be seeing you, old buddy. Thanks for your help and congratulations again on your promotion."

Chapter 52
The Green Light

Construction of *Stella Maris* was progressing well, and the pumps had all been installed in their reconfigured housings.

Eric called JoAnn. She was still in Houston practicing her flying skills in the twin engine Cessna. "It's time to place the explosives and receivers. We need you back in Haifa. Also, you asked me to remind you about placing HMX along the keel in the U-Boat bay.

"Thanks, I'll be on the first flight out of Houston tomorrow. By the way, I have decided to plant charges of ONC-C8 in the Captain's bridge and the radio room—just in case. Will my demolition team be available when I arrive?"

"They will. Captain Bergmann wants to meet you at the airport. He appears to have something on his mind."

On the flight, JoAnn reviewed her plans for placing the explosives. She realized she was solely responsible for the plan but was looking forward to consulting with her Israeli team. Captain Bergmann was waiting for her in a black diplomatic limousine when she arrived.

"Nice to see you again, Captain. What's on your mind?"

"Major, I'm concerned about the reliability of RF reception through the steel hull of *Stella Maris*. While you were away, I consulted our top electronics experts. I explained my concern that the charges may fail to detonate due to the thickness of the steel hull. I asked if they thought the signal would be strong enough to penetrate."

"I'm listening. Please continue."

"In the 1960s, the British had problems with RF signals not penetrating the hulls of their Oberon Class submarines. They decided to change the steel in their new subs from OT28 to UXW. They also developed an improved, more sensitive RF receiver. Fortunately, we have constructed *Stella Maris* using only UXW steel. My consultants suggested that just to be doubly sure our charges will detonate, we add one of the more sensitive British receivers to each one of the charges. They can be detonated at the same time from the same control box that you're going to use. The original receivers might work, but it's better to be safe than sorry."

"Captain Bergmann, I like the idea. I agree. Let's incorporate the additional receivers in each charge."

The limo arrived at the shipyards, and JoAnn and Bergmann went directly to Eric's office. They exchanged greetings with Eric, Jake, Little David and Goliath.

"Before we get to your 'demolition derby,' I'd like to go over some other details," Eric said. "We have just installed and tested the two pneumatic doors—one on each end of the observation lounge. Once inside, there should be no reason for any of the guests to leave the lounge while the U-Boat bay is being prepared or when the U-Boat begins its docking procedures. When Richard leaves the lounge to take a call in the radio room, he will lock the doors. I've also added two additional video screens. That will make a total of four and will give everyone an excellent view of the events as they occur."

"Good. That arrangement should please the financial backers in the long white robes, as well as the other guests. I want a sumptuous buffet in there and plenty of champagne on ice for the toast."

"All of that is planned as you specified. The lounge will be furnished just like a cruise ship. There will be ample food and libations available to please all palates and dietary preferences. The guests should be sufficiently entertained watching the crew prepare to flood the ballast tanks and the docking bay for receiving Submarine 'S.' After the U-Boat has docked, they will watch as the ballast tanks are emptied and the stern plate rises, leaving the U-Boat on its cradle arms out of the water. Then, the crew and the guests on *Jonah* will spill onto the deck and ready themselves for a toast to the *Fourth Reich*.

"Who will take care of the champagne on *Jonah?*"

"I'm sure Heinz will attend to that logistical exercise. I have another important question. Do you still plan to place the Zyklon-B pellets in the observation lounge?"

"Yes, in the four closed ducts. Each will contain a canister of pellets, a pan of water, a heater, and a fan. A light explosive charge will be placed on each canister. The detonators will be rigged to respond to a signal from the control box causing the canisters to rupture. The pellets will fall into the water, the heater and fan will be activated, and the gas will begin to diffuse into the room."

Bergmann was almost at a loss for words. All he could say was, "They deserve it."

"Good, now what have we missed? Oh my God—the obvious. The crew and personnel that will be servicing *Jonah* will arrive in Buenos Aires in von Ritter's squadron of DC-3s. They will be instructed not to interact with the other crewmembers. But what if they do? I'm pretty sure they only speak German. I doubt they can even speak Spanish. They've all lived in that isolated community of Nazi ex-patriots. They don't live in our world, and they have a single purpose, which is to service and sail that damn U-Boat into the *Fourth Reich*. If we all do our jobs, maybe we can help them sail into oblivion."

"We're good. We'll have some German-speaking crew on board, and all of the signage on those decks will be in German, Spanish, and Arabic."

"Not in Hebrew?"

"Very funny, Major, very funny. Here's some other information for you. As you know, the ship now has two unsinkable, covered, ocean-going lifeboats as well as two launches. One of each is located on the starboard side. The others are on the port side. The winds in the South Atlantic can be tricky. Depending on the wind direction, the PBY will have a choice of approaches and will land according to the most favorable wind direction. Captain Diaz will choose the launch on the appropriate side to facilitate a smooth transfer of the passengers from the plane to the ship. He won't want to make our guests nervous. We have designed hand-held controls to lower the launches and lifeboats. We have also installed two rubberized gas tanks—one on each side of the ship. Each will contain 600 gallons of high-octane aviation gasoline to refuel the PBY. Flexible extension refueling hoses will be attached."

"I like it! We will have ample options for our plan to work. We are definitely on the same page. Now, Eric, tell me how you plan to effect the transfer of the ship to Richard."

"Sure, it will be a simple, straight forward operation. An Israeli Captain and I will sail with her after her quiet launch here in Haifa. She will leave here under a Panamanian flag, with Panamanian papers, and the name *Aztec Queen* painted on her stern. A couple of days out into the Mediterranean, we'll rename her *Stella Maris*. We'll paint her new name on the stern and destroy the original papers, exchanging them for those of Liberian registry. We'll hoist the Liberian flag and sail on to Cagliari, Sardinia. I took your recommendation—that our crew remain with the ship for the entire operation—to the Israeli government, and they consented. The crew will all be military, with training equivalent to your American Seals. Richard, Captain Diaz, and 1st Officer de Silva will fly to Naples. We have eyes and ears there. If all is clear, they can take a day ferry to Cagliari, board *Stella Maris*, and take 'ownership' of her. Once they are aboard, they will sail for Gibraltar. An Israeli patrol boat will rendezvous with *Stella Maris* southeast of Gibraltar. The Israeli Captain and I will leave the ship and head back to Haifa. Captain Diaz will take command and continue to Buenos Aires."

"It's that simple?"

"Yes, I'm afraid it is."

"Kind of a let down, don't you think?"

"Dammit, Major. Not everything on this project can go boom, bang, and light up the night sky!"

"JoAnn smiled. I don't see why not—but first things first. How soon can we obtain the new receivers? When do you think we can begin to place the explosives?"

Bergmann said, "Everything we need is already in the basement. We can start in the morning."

"See you at 0700," JoAnn replied. All of the men stood as she left to go to her apartment.

Chapter 53
Placing the Charges

The next morning, the group reconvened on the after deck of *Stella Maris*, which was now looking like a ship. JoAnn began, "Now that we have the green light to complete the installation and arming of the explosives, allow me to review my plan of action with you. Then you can evaluate and critique it. We will run the checklists together, just like a pre-flight check on a plane. Agreed?"

"Agreed!"

"I had originally planned to arm each explosive charge with two RF receivers. Captain Bergmann has convinced me that it might be prudent to add one of the newer, updated receivers to each charge. I have also decided to double the number of receivers in the engine room. I think the vibrations in that area could dislodge some receivers there, so I want to cover that possibility. A large charge of HMX that I plan to place along the keel in the U-Boat bay will be included in the initial sequence of detonations. I'd like at least six original receivers spaced evenly between each charge and an additional six of the new ones placed in the same way. Is that feasible, Captain?"

"Yes, Major. We have an ample supply of the new receivers. It might be overkill, but this will act as insurance since we only have one chance to get the job done."

"I've numbered and indicated the location and size of each charge and its receivers. I'll call out the number circled in red on the plans, and you will check off the type and pre-weighed amount of explosive. The hinges and latches on all 48 hatch covers are located on top of the ballast compartments and are above the waterline. We can use ONC-C8 there and in the Captain's bridge and radio room.

"Below the waterline, I have decided to pack all of the pump housings with a mega charge of HMX. The eight cradle arms will be packed with ONC-C8.

"So far, so good," the Captain said.

"Well then, here's the sequence of detonation. First the U-Boat in the cradle and the keel will be detonated. Those explosions will totally demolish the U-Boat, completely obliterate the bay, and probably kill everyone there. It might also cause a secondary detonation of some of the torpedoes. Then I will activate the Zyklon-B pellets. Another series of detonations will destroy the Captain's bridge and the radio room.

"Next, I'll activate the receivers in the pump housings. That should initiate 24-paired explosions. They will tear 30-foot gashes in each compartment. Simultaneously, I will blow off every hatch cover located on the top of each ballast compartment. As the ship sinks, water will rush in and force the air out. The pressure of the seawater rushing in and the air and water being expelled through the rupture on top of each compartment will cause the ship to begin to come apart as it sinks.

"Once the ship is launched, we're committed. We can't make adjustments. One master control box will remain with me at all times. The second will be attached to the bulkhead behind the co-pilot's seat in the PBY. If we incur any problems with the plane or complications of any sort, there will be a third master control unit in Captain Diaz's safe with instructions for its use. Diaz will bring it with him when he leaves the ship."

Bergmann said, "Our electronics people have assured me that all three master control units are identical and will be rigged to send the proper signals in the required strength to initiate detonation of all the charges—either in sequence as planned—or, in case of emergency, all at once."

"In that case, the whole shebang will go up simultaneously," JoAnn, said. "It's a bit messy, I'll admit, but quite effective. Are we all still on the same page, gentlemen?" Comments? Questions? Suggestions?"

They all nodded in agreement.

Eric said, "As they say in the States, 'This ain't our first rodeo.'"

JoAnn replied, "Glad to hear that! Oh, but first, Eric, I want to give you and Jake the fail-safe code that will activate the three electronic control units. Your electronics people need to program the number into each of them."

Eric handed a piece of paper and an envelope to JoAnn. She took out a pen and began to write:

106-612-151-492-177-619-411-944

JoAnn passed the sheet of paper to Eric. He looked at it before he passed it on to Jake. They exchanged looks of total confusion. Jake said, "These numbers are really random."

"Not so. Break them down by fours. The first four digits are 1066, the Battle of Hastings. Then 1215, the Magna Carta."

Eric said, "I've got it now. 1492, Columbus. 1776, the Declaration of Independence, and 1941, Pearl Harbor. 1944 is D-Day."

"Precisely. Well done!"

JoAnn folded the paper, inserted it into the envelope, and said in her best southern drawl, "Now Eric, lock this up real good in the Captain's safe. You hear?"

"'Deed I will, Miss Scarlett! 'Deed I will."

Suddenly, all of the frivolity in JoAnn's voice disappeared. With an intensity that surprised none of them she said, "Now, let's get to work!"

Chapter 54
Plans to Consider

JoAnn had just returned to Houston. She was walking into Richard's office when his secure line rang. She had spent three grueling weeks in Haifa with her demolition team on *Stella Maris*, placing explosive charges and RF receivers—then checking and rechecking them. The task had been long and tedious, requiring many 14-hour days. Richard motioned for her to take a seat as he answered the phone. He looked at JoAnn and said, "It's James. I'll put him on speakerphone.

"What's on your mind, James?"

"While I've been up here at Fort Hood seeking out felons and illicit arms merchants, I've been doing some serious thinking. I have an idea that I'd love to discuss with you, Steve, and JoAnn if she's available."

"She just arrived from Tel Aviv. As a matter of fact, she's sitting here now listening to you."

"Great! I can't wait to see you, JoAnn. Richard, could you ask Rose to set up a meeting for the four of us ASAP?"

"Of course, I'll get her on it."

"Thanks, see you all soon."

"Wow," JoAnn laughed. "I didn't even get a chance to say hello. I guess we're all totally focused on the task at hand. Speaking of which, have you been alerted that *Stella Maris* is about six or eight weeks away from completion and launching?"

"Yes, I spoke to Eric a couple of days ago, and he told me. He also outlined his plan for transferring the ownership of *Stella Maris* to my company.

As soon as the ship is launched, Diaz, de Silva and I will fly BOAC to Naples, take the day ferry to Cagliari, and take possession of *Stella Maris* when she docks there. An Israeli Captain and crew will staff the ship. Eric will also be on board. From Cagliari, we will all sail to Gibraltar, where we will be met offshore by an Israeli patrol boat that will take Eric and the Israeli Captain off the ship. At that point, Diaz will take over command and bring her home to Buenos Aires. The Israeli Government has given us the nod to retain the Israeli crew, and they have orders to remain with us for the entire operation."

"I like that plan."

"JoAnn, you look bushed. Why don't you bunk in upstairs and get some rest before the meeting James requested? I'd like you fresh and rested by the time James gets here to tell us what he has on his mind."

"That sounds like a great idea!"

Twenty-four hours later, Rose had everyone assembled and seated in Richard's conference room. He said, "Now James, tell us about your operation at Fort Hood. How's it going?"

"Right on target. I have a high level CIC agent inside Ft. Hood collecting data. We've agreed that no action will be taken until *Operation Jonah* has been completed. Then, I'll notify him, and he will take over and expand the operation to other bases. The CIC will be taking over rounding up the bad apples on our end.

"Two things have been bothering me. Have any arrangements been made for the disposition of the contents of von Ritter's warehouses? You can bet your ass the U.S. government doesn't want that stuff returned. It would be too embarrassing. On the other hand, we sure as hell don't want the Argentine government to get hold of the contents. In my view, they're no more than Spanish-speaking Nazis."

Steve said, "You've got that right."

"I suppose we could just dump it all into the ocean, but I may have a better solution."

JoAnn asked, "Would you care to share it with us?"

"Yes, I would. Thinking hypothetically, just suppose that immediately after *Operation Jonah* has been successfully completed, a company of 15 or 16 Arab-speaking Israeli commandos wearing *keffiyehs* arrive in the *Golfo san Matias* on one of Richard's coastal freighters. The Israeli officer in charge would have to be a native German speaker who also speaks fluent Arabic. Steve, it is essential that you accompany the party. You are known at the compound and can converse with them in German. You will show the Nazis 'orders' to remove von Ritter's planes, munitions, and arms to the freighter. You will give the Israeli Captain directions in German. He will then relay orders to his men in Arabic."

Richard responded a little hesitantly, "Now, that's a very interesting scenario. Just where will you obtain such a force, James? Or need I even ask?"

"That's where I hope Steve and JoAnn could use their *Mossad* connections and convince them to lend us a team."

JoAnn said, "It's a very interesting plan. However, invading a sovereign nation at peace with the world might just precipitate World War III. That being said, I'd be glad to run it by Jake. He seems to have some clout with *Mossad*. What do you think, Steve? Could we pull it off?"

"I like the idea! Let's call Jake right now. Your plan is just crazy enough to tweak their interest but risky enough to offer *Mossad* a challenge."

James jumped in and said, "Wait a minute. Before we all go off half-cocked, we have a second problem to address."

Richard said, "And that is?"

"That is—what's the plan for dealing with the remaining citizens of the colony? They're all faithful Nazis."

Richard thought for a minute and softly said, "They must be terminated."

An awkward silence followed.

JoAnn said, "I guess there's no other choice, is there?"

Steve said, "They'd do it to you in the blink of an eye if our positions were reversed—and they have."

JoAnn answered, "Who will draw the short straw on this action? Will it be our people or the Israelis that pull the trigger?"

Once again, the silence was deafening.

JoAnn continued, "Okay. When we talk to *Mossad*, we had better inform them about that decision as well. They may be the ones who will have to do the dirty work in the end."

"Right," Richard responded. "Anything else? If not, JoAnn, it's time for you to hook up with Zac for those flying lessons. We'll head down to Buenos Aires tomorrow."

"That'll be fine."

"Well, if there's no further business to discuss, the meeting is adjourned. Lunch is on me."

Chapter 55
The First Lesson

Comfortably seated in first class, JoAnn said, "Richard, after *Stella Maris* is launched and as soon as Diaz can confirm her actual cruising speed, we'll contact Zac and Kuntzelmann. They already know their cruising speeds, and we can begin to develop a timetable for the departures of the U-Boat, the PBY, and *Stella Maris*. We all need to rendezvous at the same place at the same time. I don't want the PBY bobbing around all alone in the South Atlantic waiting for the others to arrive."

"Good idea. I'll let them know as soon as we know."

When their plane landed in Buenos Aires, JoAnn and Richard went directly to the offices of Global Import/Export, where Zac sat reading a magazine while waiting for them.

"Why don't you and Zac head down to the docks to begin your flying lessons?"

Zac grinned as he got up and opened the door for JoAnn. "Do much flying, Major?"

"A little. I've had a few hours in a flight simulator. I've flown the Army T-34 Mentor, and recently I've become familiar with Richard's twin prop Cessna 411."

"That's great! As we make our external preflight check and before we climb aboard this venerable veteran of WWII, I'd like to prep you with a bit of information. I'm sure you've already noticed that the PBY is not an ordinary plane."

"Yes, that's obvious."

"In other words, it's actually a flying boat with the bottom of the fuselage shaped and configured like a boat's hull. While the PBY is on the water, it's a boat. However, once it's in the air, it becomes a plane. The proper term naval aviators use to describe the short transition period from the boat phase on the water to the plane aloft is 'getting on step.'"

"Very interesting. Thanks, I'll remember that."

"If you're ready, we'll enter through the waist blister and climb into the cockpit." Zac took the pilot's seat while JoAnn settled into the co-pilot's seat. They both strapped themselves in, and Zac explained each dial, gauge, and lever as they went through the internal preflight check together.

"This plane is powered by a pair of 1200 horse power Pratt and Whitney radial engines. They have quite a bit more juice then the Cessna 411 engines can muster."

He pressed the starter for the starboard engine. It coughed twice and turned over. As Zac adjusted the fuel mixture—the air-to-gasoline ratio—he explained, "Most planes carry their batteries on the starboard side, so we start the starboard engine first."

"Hold on a minute, Zac. Since when is the right side of a plane called the starboard side?"

"When you're on a Navy plane," Zac laughed. "I forgot you're Army. You're right. In the Army, it's just right or left. May I continue?"

"Sure, please do."

"As I was saying, I'll start the starboard engine first. Then I'll switch on the generator to build up a good charge in order to start the port engine. Once the starboard engine is running smoothly, I'll start the port engine."

The noise level in the cockpit was horrific. Zac pointed to the engines, put on his headphones, handed JoAnn a pair with an audio cable and jack attached, and pointed to the input on the control panel.

"That's better. Now we can talk over the engine noise. Once the engines are in sync, we can take off."

He released the brakes and began to taxi the PBY down the concrete ramp into the water, heading for the channel marked by red and green lights on buoys. Once clear of the concrete ramp, he retracted the wheels. Suddenly, there was a new sensation. The resistance, or drag was gone, and the plane seemed to glide across the water like a speedboat. He checked the windsock and pointed the plane into the wind as he began to slowly advance the throttles. Moving swiftly and smoothly across the surface of the water into the well-marked sea-lane, he lowered the flaps and further advanced the throttles. The plane gathered speed, 'got on step,' and was soon in the air. The plane circled once to gain altitude and then headed out to sea.

"I'm going up to 5,500 feet. Then your lesson will begin." Zac pointed to the compass and called out a heading of 095°. Then he pointed to the altimeter and said, "Take the controls, bank to starboard and change course to 110°. Remain at an altitude of 5,500 feet. Keep your air speed at 105 knots." They were now headed out over the ocean.

"You're now in control, Major. I'll have my hands on the controls as well. Just maintain your altitude. Don't overcorrect. There's a short lag time for the plane to respond to any change of course, and remember, there's lots of space up here. You won't hit anything. By way of review, when you're not flying by instruments, and visibility is good, you are on what we call 'visual.' While on visual, when taking a compass heading, from 0° to 179°, use an odd thousand plus 500 feet for your altitude. When on visual from 180° to 359°, use an even thousand and add 500 to the number. If you forget, just remember, 'It's odd to fly east.'"

Five minutes passed, but to JoAnn, it seemed an eternity. He continued to coach and instruct her. "You're doing fine. You have a nice touch for a novice. Now, bank to starboard and come to 210°, level off, drop down to 4,500 feet and hold course. Look at your instruments occasionally, but don't stare at them continuously. Just glance at them now and then."

After another fifteen minutes and a few course changes, Zac took over the controls and said, "Time to head back. You're getting the hang of it. These high-winged planes are usually more forgiving and easier to handle. Remember, don't be afraid to use your rudder pedals. Learn to rely on your instruments. Learn your instrument panel and its dials and gauges so well that you can tell at a glance if there's something amiss. Learn to scan the panel."

JoAnn watched his every movement and took mental notes as he made his approach between the red and green lit buoys and touched down as smoothly as a duck on a pond with just a slight flare at touch down. As he approached the ramp, he dropped his wheels and cut back his engines. The plane slowed, taxied out of the water, and came to rest on the concrete apron. Zac cut the mixture levers to idle cutoff, removed his headphones, and said, "Well done, well done. Tomorrow at 0900 good for you?"

"Yes, that'll be fine, thanks."

Chapter 56
Lesson Two

JoAnn arrived at the dock precisely at 0900. She was anxiously anticipating her next flying lesson. Zac was waiting for her on the concrete ramp, relaxing in a canvas deck chair. They went through the external preflight check together, climbed into the cockpit, completed the cabin preflight check, and then buckled up.

"Today, Major, I want you to learn to synchronize the engines. We use the term 'sync the props.' Then we'll water taxi out into the channel and take off. I'll have my hands on the controls as well."

They both donned and plugged in their headphones. After starting the starboard engine, she turned on the generator and adjusted the fuel mixture until it was correct and the engine was running smoothly. Then she started the port engine. Once again JoAnn adjusted the fuel mixture, slowly advancing the throttle until she could feel both engines running in sync.

"Now, release the brakes and taxi down the ramp," Zac said through the headphones. "After retracting the wheels, bring the plane into the channel marked by the red and green lights on the buoys and check the wind direction."

She brought the nose of the plane into the wind, lowered the flaps, and advanced both throttles. The PBY gained speed, and JoAnn said, "She's about to break free from the surface."

"Major, the correct terminology for that is 'getting on step.'"

"Oh yes! I mean she's 'getting on step.'"

"That's better. That term indicates you're making the smooth transition from a watercraft to an aircraft. Once you're 'on step,' it's like the hull of a speedboat getting 'on plane.' Advance the throttles, and you're off. You're doing just fine."

When she had attained air speed of 110 knots, Zac said, "Make a slow turn to starboard and come to a compass heading of 075°. Keep your air speed at 110 knots. Take her up to 5,500 feet. Now let's just hold this heading for about ten minutes."

After she had implemented Zac's instructions, JoAnn adjusted the controls slightly, keeping the plane on course as she listened to Zac recount the history of this venerable old war bird. She continued to follow instructions to the letter. After a few course and altitude changes, Zac called out a compass heading and instructed her to point the ship toward home. "It's time to make your first landing."

Zac kept his hands very lightly on the controls and continued to give her instructions. JoAnn made her approach, dropped her flaps, reduced her speed, and, just as the PBY made its first contact with the water, she pulled back on the control column, ever so slightly. When the plane made full contact with the water, she cut back the power and pushed the control column forward. The plane settled and slowed. Dropping the wheels, she water taxied onto the ramp and out of the water. She brought both throttles back as far as they would go. The fuel mix went lean, and, as the engines used up the remainder of the fuel, they stopped and the props stopped turning. With a sigh of relief, JoAnn said, "Well, that's that!"

"Well done, Major, well done! If anything happens to me, just look for the big red X on the charts and head for home!"

As they exited the plane, one of the ground crew who was placing chocks behind each wheel called out to Zac, "Richard just called. He wants you both in his office as soon as possible."

Chapter 57
A New Rendezvous Point

It was only a three-minute walk to Richard's office. Zac said, "I wonder what's up?"

Richard and Captain Diaz were chatting when Zac and JoAnn opened the office door. Richard welcomed them. "Come in, close the door, and grab a chair. We have a few logistical problems to work out, and I believe now's the time to address them. Our first plan of action was to have *Stella Maris, Jonah,* and the PBY rendezvous at a point above a five-mile deep trench in the middle of the South Atlantic. That's where we had planned to destroy the two vessels. But Captain Diaz and I have had second thoughts about that. What do you say, JoAnn?"

"I do understand that we would have to travel farther to get to that point and also that the weather in the South Atlantic is frequently unpredictable. A flight of that length could be risky. In my opinion, the longer our guests remain on the PBY or the U-Boat, for that matter, the greater chance of a major mishap, malfunction, or a SNAFU. I would certainly consider another rendezvous point."

"Good. Then we are all in agreement. Captain Diaz has suggested an alternative. I spoke with Kuntzelmann earlier today, and he has also agreed—although, in truth, we didn't give him a choice. The new rendezvous point is 250 nautical miles southeast of the coastal town of Viedma, Argentina. It's in an area that Captain Diaz calls an 'empty zone.' There are no commercial maritime traffic lanes in that area. We will be able to conduct our business unobserved."

Juan Diaz spread out a nautical map on the table and said, "The co-ordinates that I have chosen are 58° 5' W longitude and 42° 7' S latitude. They intersect right here." He pointed to the spot that he had marked with a red pencil on the map. "At a cruising speed of 106 knots, the PBY can easily fly from Buenos Aires to *Golfo san Matias* in less than six hours."

"JoAnn said, I've also been considering another slight variation to the plan. I think Richard, Becker, Ehrlich, Heinz, and the two Arabs should fly the first leg of the trip from Buenos Aires to the colony in the comfort of von Ritter's private DC-3. I can get in a few more hours of practice at the controls while Zac and I ferry the PBY to the colony the day before *Operation Jonah* commences. Then we can pick up our passengers and fly them to *Stella Maris*. How long will it take the PBY to get to the new rendezvous point?"

"At 106 knots, it's only a two-hour flight," Zac responded, "Good idea. I like it, too!"

Chapter 58
One More Time

As they left the meeting, JoAnn said to Zac, "Now, I really believe this is going to happen, but I'd feel much more confident if we could have one more session. When it comes to getting my ass safely back on terra firma, I'll spare no effort. Are you up for it?"

"You bet! I'll see you at 0900."

The next morning they met at the plane. Once again they began the external preflight inspection. They climbed aboard, and JoAnn recited every item on the preflight checklist. Then she initiated ignition and the starboard engine came to life. She turned on the generator. Then she initiated ignition of the port engine and adjusted the fuel mixtures until she had both engines running smoothly and in sync. JoAnn thought, "Constant repetition is necessary if one expects to get home again—alive." She released the brakes and the plane taxied down the ramp into the channel. She retracted the landing gear, checked the windsock, and lined the PBY up between the markers. After adjusting the flaps she pointed the plane into the wind and advanced the throttles. The plane picked up speed, got on step, and they were off. Zac just sat quietly, watched, and said nothing. Soon they had the desired air speed and altitude. They were headed out to sea on a compass heading of 075°, climbing to an altitude of 5,500 feet, with an air speed of 110 knots.

JoAnn said, "I think I'm getting the hang of it now. Zac, after we land, I must give you a copy of the fail-safe code in case you need to detonate the explosive charges. There will be a master control box mounted on the bulkhead behind my seat. If for some reason it malfunctions, there will be a backup unit located in my flight kit that will be stored under my seat. If I'm incapacitated, all you will have to do is punch in the code and hit the big red button. It will detonate everything at once. Just be sure to get this old bird out of the way first. Get as much altitude and distance from *Stella Maris* as possible. I have no idea how high or how far the debris will travel if all of the charges detonate at the same time. You will do this only in case of emergency. In a nonemergent situation, when I'm controlling the box, I'll be able to sequence the detonations individually as planned."

"Understood! Hey, you're doing a great job up here, even while you're talking my ear off. Now take her up to 9,500 feet and hold your course for ten minutes. Put on your oxygen mask just in case. The mask probably isn't necessary at 9,500 feet, but it's mandatory at 10,000 feet and above." After ten minutes Zac said, "Now bank to port, descend to 4,500 feet, acquire a compass heading of 225° and take her home."

The PBY came in smoothly, landed with an ever-so-slight flare, and settled in the water. As JoAnn approached the ramp, the wheels came down, and she taxied up the ramp.

As they left the cockpit and the ground crew began turning the PBY around for her next takeoff, Zac said, "A very pretty bit of flying, Major Scarlett. Congratulations. I'll fly with you anytime!"

"Many thanks for the lessons, Zac. You're a great instructor. By the way, here's the fail-safe code to activate the black box—just in case."

Zac took out his little pocket notebook. He was never without it. If one were to guess, it probably held the phone numbers of every eligible female in Buenos Aires. He knew that the number he was about to add was hotter than any of the Argentine *señoritas*. "Okay, shoot!"

JoAnn methodically began to repeat the sequence that she had committed to memory:

"106-612-151-492-177-619-411-944"

"Got it." He repeated the code just to be sure he had correctly recorded it. "But, JoAnn, it's totally random. How will anyone be able to remember it?"

"It's easy. They're all famous dates in world or American history. Break the numbers into groups of four."

"Well, I'll be damned! You are one clever lady, Major."

"They don't call me Major for nothing! Many thanks for the flying lessons, Zac. See you when I get back!"

Chapter 59
April, 1980—Wheels in Motion

Although far from an accomplished pilot, JoAnn now had the required fundamentals and touch to keep the PBY in the air and on course if the need arose. In case any inquisitive eyes were wondering who his good-looking pupil was, Zac's cover story was simply that he was just trying to impress the lady and that his intentions were, as usual, dishonorable. To the locals around the docks who knew his reputation, the story was quite plausible.

Richard and JoAnn returned to Houston. Back in his Houston office she continued to go over each and every detail of her plan, looking for flaws in timing, logistics, and movement of personnel. Attention to detail was critical to the success of the entire enterprise.

In Haifa, the finishing touches were being applied to *Stella Maris's* tower and electronics. Finally, Richard received a call from Haifa. "Hello Eric, JoAnn's here with me. Let me put you on speakerphone."

"I'm glad you're together. I have great news. The package will be ready for shipping in about 10 days. We're going to get this show on the road—or the water."

"I want to be present for the launching," JoAnn said. "I'm sailing to Buenos Aires on the ship."

"I thought you might," Richard said. "There's a first class ticket on *El Al* with an open date waiting for you on my desk. Good luck—to us all."

"Hold on a minute, Jake has news as well," Eric said.

"Hello, Richard. I wanted to let you know that my superiors at *Mossad* have considered the sensitive issue James had JoAnn and Steve bring to me. It's a go—a green light all the way at this end. It's considered a high-risk operation, but apparently they believe that it's worth the gamble."

"Thanks. I'm delighted Steve will be working with them."

Richard buzzed Rose on the intercom, gave her some dates, and said, "Please book two first class tickets from Buenos Aires to Houston for de Silva and Diaz. Then we'll need four first class tickets on BOAC to Naples the following day.

As soon as Richard received the confirmations and flight numbers, he called Juan Diaz. "Diaz, you and de Silva have tickets on an 8 p.m. flight out of Buenos Aires to Houston in two weeks. They will be waiting for you at the check-in desk at the airport. It's a nonstop flight and will take about 11 hours. Travel light and get some sleep."

The following days were filled with anticipation and anxiety. When the two men arrived at Houston International each carrying a hand-held travel bag, they were met by a black Suburban and taken directly to Richard's office.

Richard greeted them and said, "Gentleman, I suggest you go upstairs, shower, change and get some rest. Be ready to leave for the airport at 0530 tomorrow. We're going to Naples. It's time to go yachting on the Mediterranean with the rich and famous. I'll give you both a complete set of updated specs for *Stella Maris* so you will be up to speed by the time we board her. I've booked four first class seats. We don't need anyone looking over our shoulders."

The flight to Naples took almost 12 hours and would prove to be very productive for the Captain and his First Officer. After the flight was underway, Diaz said to Richard, "I believe we have a logistical problem that we haven't addressed. A fully-automated container ship of this size usually requires a minimum crew of 15 to 19 able-bodied seamen. How are we going to manage after we take control of the ship?"

Richard responded in a low voice, "The entire crew who will bring the ship from Haifa will remain with us until the mission has been completed. We will, of course, get them off the ship before the fireworks begin."

"How?"

"Captain Diaz, that problem has already been anticipated and solved by JoAnn. The ship is now equipped with two twenty-man, unsinkable, motorized lifeboats—compliments of our very generous Arab benefactors. As soon as all the guests are in the observation lounge, you will give the order for a routine lifeboat drill. It will apply to your crew only and will be explained as a test of the lifeboats; therefore the guests won't be involved. Right after that announcement, de Silva will call me on the observation lounge phone to tell me that I have a call in the radio room from my office in Houston. By then everyone should be totally absorbed watching the proceedings in the U-Boat bay. As soon as I get the call from the radio room, I'll leave the observation lounge and trigger the electronic locks on the lounge doors. By that time the Israeli crew will be off the ship in both lifeboats, sailing Northwest on a compass heading of 320° where they will rendezvous with one of my smaller ocean-going freighters which will be shadowing *Stella Maris*, just over the horizon. By the way, I intend to salvage those lifeboats for Global Import/Export."

"That settles the logistical problem," Diaz said. He cracked a rare smile, while de Silva grinned from ear to ear."

Once they arrived in Naples, they were picked up by *Mossad* agents and taken to the docks where they boarded a ferry to Cagliari. Private accommodations for them had already been made. They were under continual surveillance by *Mossad* until they boarded *Stella Maris*. Arriving two or three days early was prudent and smart. Richard had plenty of time to update Diaz and de Silva on the timeline and plans for *Operation Jonah*.

Chapter 60
The Delivery

Just as planned, *Stella Maris*, flying a Liberian flag, arrived at the port of Cagliari at sunrise on April 23. Maintaining a speed of 20 knots, she had sailed 1,330 nautical miles without incident. There was nothing special or unusual about her. She appeared to be just another container ship waiting for her turn to enter the port. A tug nudged her gently toward the quay, and she was secured to the bollards by three huge hawsers at her bow, stern, and amidships.

Out of the shadows, three men appeared. Each of them carried a canvas seaman's bag. They slowly ambled down the quay in the general direction of the ship that had just been secured. They ascended the gangway and boarded. They entered the elevator at deck level and pushed the button marked Captain's Bridge. When the door opened, they stepped out into the modern, high-tech, fully automated control room of *Stella Maris*. The wings of the Captain's Bridge extended beyond the ship's beam, allowing the Captain a clear view of the ship: fore, aft, port and starboard. Eric, JoAnn, and the Israeli Captain were waiting to greet them.

The Israeli Captain stepped forward and introduced himself. "Welcome aboard. I'm Captain David Kuhn."

Diaz stepped forward, extended a hand, and said, "I'm Captain Juan Diaz, and this is First Officer de Silva."

Then Richard stepped forward, extended his hand, and said, "Captain Kuhn, I'm Richard Eherenfeld. Thanks for getting our ship here."

"It's an honor to meet you. We are happy to give you all the support we can. We believe in your mission. Please follow me to the wardroom. We've assembled the crew there."

When the door opened to the wardroom, all 15 of the Israeli crew rose to their feet. They were all English-speaking and dressed as ordinary seamen. Diaz gave the crewmen a quick assessment and thought, "These men don't have the look of ordinary seamen to me. They look more like an Israeli Special Forces Unit. Oh well, what the hell!"

"It's a pleasure to meet you all. You obviously know more about this ship than I do, but I'm sure I'll be up to speed in no time. We all appreciate your being here."

Kuhn dismissed the crew and said, "They are all military trained. As you know, they will remain with the vessel and serve as your crew until you reach your final destination."

Eric spoke up, "Richard, I believe it is time for us to complete our paperwork transferring ownership of *Stella Maris* from our Greek friend, Nicholas Alexander Poulos, to Global Import/Export."

"Yes, we'd better take care of that now. How did your little art project go?"

"I assume that you're making reference to the former *Aztec Queen* suddenly deciding to change her name in the middle of the Mediterranean. Two days out of Haifa, by the light of the moon, we lowered the Panamanian flag, painted *Stella Maris* on her stern, and raised the Liberian flag. It went well, no one is the wiser."

"Well done! Let's destroy *Aztec Queen's* papers and put the new ones in the safe."

Captain Kuhn asked, "Richard, have you been informed that we will be acquiring the assets you requested?"

Richard nodded his head, indicating that he had. Kuhn continued, "We plan to rendezvous with one of our patrol boats off the coast of Gibraltar. She will approach us flying a British Naval Ensign. You may recognize it as a German WWII 'E' Boat. Our people captured her intact near one of the Greek islands in 1944. Eric and I will be leaving *Stella Maris* at the rendezvous point at the same time your commandos will be boarding."

Captain Kuhn turned to Diaz and said, "The ship is being refueled as we speak. The Harbor Master has given us the green light to clear the harbor at 0700 tomorrow, if you wish to do so."

"Excellent. By the way, who did the cooking for you on the trip so far?"

Eric said, "Funny you should ask. We have no cook aboard. JoAnn volunteered to try her hand in the galley. That was really an 'experience.' I hope she is better at demolition then she is at cooking for a bunch of hungry sailors. We have provisions aboard to feed an army, but so far the fare has been barely edible."

"That bad?"

"Eric laughed, "Richard, can you cook?"

"Not for a crowd, but I've been told that de Silva is a fair hand in the galley."

"Great! Let's draft him quickly, or it will be a long, hungry voyage!"

Chapter 61
Better Fare

The alarm clock went off in de Silva's cabin at 0430, and he bounded out of the rack and hurriedly dressed. He made his way to the galley and in no time had whipped up a couple of huge stacks of flapjacks, scrambled three dozen eggs, and had made toast and coffee. He was ready to feed the first watch of the day going on duty, and the night watch as they were coming off. Needless to say, breakfast was a dramatic improvement, and JoAnn was all too happy to relinquish her responsibilities as the ship's cook.

By first light JoAnn, Richard, Diaz, Kuhn, de Silva and Eric were on the bridge listening to the Harbor Master's instructions over the loud speakers. The three hawsers were lifted from the bollards and cast off. With the aid of the ship's lateral thrusters, the harbor tug nudged *Stella Maris* into the shipping channel and guided her out of the harbor that she cleared at precisely 0750.

As they were sailing toward Gibraltar, Diaz and de Silva, under the watchful eye of Captain Kuhn, spent their time becoming familiar with the ship's controls and the equipment in the radio room.

Eric watched the activity and beamed with pride as the new Captain took control of the ship he had built. "It's a damn shame to destroy this ship, he thought. It's a work of art! At least they plan to salvage the new life boats."

At dusk, 30 miles southeast of Gibraltar, de Silva received a call from the waiting Israeli patrol boat. "The 16 additional assets you requested are aboard and approved for service. We are ready to deliver them and take Captain Kuhn and Eric Benjamin aboard. Good luck."

Less than 15 minutes elapsed before Captain Kuhn, binoculars up to his eyes, said, "Here she comes." He had spotted a patrol boat flying a British Naval Ensign approaching.

As the patrol boat approached *Stella Maris's* starboard bow, the British Ensign was suddenly lowered and replaced by the Israeli Naval War Ensign. When the patrol boat came abeam, *Stella Maris* lowered her gangway. The 16 new arrivals boarded the ship. They were dressed as ordinary seamen. Each carried a black waterproof sea bag. They were escorted directly to their quarters without a word being spoken, and began to set up housekeeping in the area marked U-Boat Officer's Quarters. They had specific orders to take their meals in their quarters, not to socialize with the officers or any members of the crew, and to take their exercise each day on the forward deck.

Eric turned to Richard and said, "Sure wish I could stay with you to see the fireworks, but I have some other important business to attend to. Duty calls."

Captain Kuhn added, "I'd like to see the action as well, but orders are orders. I must leave with Eric."

Eric turned to Captain Diaz and said, "Remember, you must watch the weather diligently during the crossing. Avoid any serious storms in the South Atlantic if at all possible. I don't know how much stress *Stella Maris* will withstand in a violent storm at sea. She wasn't engineered for the long term."

Richard said, "Eric, it was a pleasure working with you. Please give my best regards to Jake."

Eric said, "JoAnn, take some pictures for me."

She walked over to him and whispered in his ear, "You can bet your ass we will. It's the least we can do. Thanks again!"

There were handshakes all around. After delivering a crisp salute, Captain Kuhn said, "Captain Diaz, take the helm. She's your ship now. Best of luck." As soon as Eric and Kuhn were on board the patrol boat, her three diesel engines immediately roared to life, and she sped away into the dusk at a dazzling 43 knots, leaving only a wake of diaphanous plankton behind.

Diaz set a southwesterly course for the Cape Verde Islands. From there, he would sail to the Coast of Brazil and then home to Buenos Aires. Suddenly, de Silva realized he had just acquired 16 more hungry men to feed. He mumbled, *"Hijo de puta!"*

Chapter 62
Transatlantic Crossing

Time passes slowly on a ship if there's nothing to do. Richard, JoAnn, and Captain Diaz kept the crewmen busy checking and rechecking the equipment and instrumentation. Any mechanical problems, no matter how minor, were to be reported immediately to Richard, Diaz or JoAnn and dealt with on the spot.

Richard and JoAnn spent their days between Gibraltar and the Cape Verde Islands reviewing every detail of the plan. JoAnn asked, "Captain Diaz, how many knots can *Stella Maris* comfortably make on the open sea?"

"Right now, she's making 20 knots with ease. The real test will be the transit from the Cape Verde Islands across the South Atlantic to the Brazilian coast. Those waters can be rougher than the Mediterranean.

"Okay, I'll use that information along with the figures that Kuntzelmann gave me for *Jonah*, and Zac gave me for the PBY to calculate the tentative departure times for *Stella Maris* from Buenos Aires and the U-Boat and PBY from the *Golfo san Matias* so we can precisely coordinate our rendezvous time. We need to be as accurate as possible."

JoAnn worked for several hours. She met with Richard and Diaz. "Kunzelmann assured me the U-Boat can make 16 knots on the surface. When submerged, it only makes seven knots. If the U-Boat leaves her base at dusk she should be able to reach the rendezvous point in 12-1/2 hours. She will have to run on the surface all night, submerge at first light and continue under water until she's on station. *Stella Maris* will require just under 48 hours to reach the designated spot. Zac and I will fly the PBY from Buenos Aires to the *Golfo* the day before *Jonah* leaves. According to its specs, a PBY Catalina 5A can fly at a maximum speed of 164 knots and cruise at 109 at an altitude of 7,000 feet. Depending on the wind, the first leg of the trip should take only five or six hours. The next morning, we can fly our six dignitaries to the rendezvous point in less than two hours. Check my math. If everyone is in agreement, we have our plan." They studied her calculations and readily concurred.

When they were one day out from the Cape Verde Islands, JoAnn requested another drill. The Captain announced it to the crew. "I've been informed that you are now familiar with the docking apparatus. It's time for us to test it. You're going to flood the ballast compartments and take on enough water to drop 35 feet. We'll lower the stern plate as well. Then we'll pump all the compartments dry and sail on. If we have any problems, we need to correct them now. Everything must work perfectly for the successful completion of our mission. There will be no second chances."

The pumps filled the ballast chambers evenly. When the two enormous hydraulic pistons were activated, the stern plate went down smoothly. When the pumps were reversed, the ship rose evenly, and the pistons returned the stern plate to its original position. Everyone on board let out a loud cheer and breathed a sigh of relief.

While refueling at the Cape Verde Islands, the crew conducted another very important exercise. They wanted to check the davits—the cranes that raise and lower the lifeboats and launches from the boat deck into the sea below. Their proper operation would be essential to the crew's exodus from *Stella Maris* before the fireworks began. The davits worked perfectly and were lubricated as soon as the boats had been recovered. JoAnn checked another box off her list.

Mindful of Eric's warning about the weather in the South Atlantic, Captain Diaz studied all the meteorological data pertaining to their route. He decided to alter his course to the coast of Brazil. After refueling, he gave the order to sail with the morning tide. The crew continued to monitor every detail, and JoAnn and Richard were more than pleased with the ship. She was performing admirably. It was de Silva who alerted the ship's company that they were approaching the Equator. They decided to forego the traditional "Crossing the Line" ceremony for first-timers, but Richard had anticipated the event and had stocked the ship with enough champagne for everyone to partake in a toast. On Diaz's command, they all raised their glasses. "To *Operation Jonah*." The company of men—and one woman—repeated, "*Operation Jonah*."

The voyage was largely uneventful for the next few days. The weather was good. They all kept their fingers crossed that they wouldn't encounter any sudden violent storms before they reached port. When they were three days from Buenos Aires and 75 miles off the Brazilian coast, *Stella Maris* made a rendezvous with one of Richard's small coastal freighters. A motorized launch approached from the starboard side. At the helm was a boatswain's mate, and at his side was Steve Kreutzer. As the launch came along side, the 16 silent men who had boarded at Gibraltar assembled on deck. Without a word, they went down the gangway and boarded the launch. Steve waved to his friends on *Stella Maris*, and the launch returned to the freighter. The small freighter made a slow 180° turn to starboard and steamed south. On her stern one could clearly see her name—*Estrellita*. On the bridge Captain Diaz plotted a course toward the dockyards of Global Import/Export in Buenos Aires.

One day out of Buenos Aires, a very anxious JoAnn suggested that both pneumatic doors in the observation lounge be tested, "Just one more time. Once we have them caged, I don't want any of those animals to get loose." They worked perfectly.

Diaz followed the coastline to the mouth of the *Rio de la Plata*. As he turned *Stella Maris* into the river's mouth, the anticipation on the bridge was palpable. *Operation Jonah* was soon to become a reality.

Chapter 63
A Bold Venture

The 16 men who had just boarded the *Estrellita* stowed their gear and reported to the seaman's mess where Steve was waiting to greet them. When they were all seated, he stood and addressed them. "Gentlemen, welcome aboard. I'm Dr. Steve Kreutzer. By trade, I'm a college history professor. How I became involved in this venture is a story for another day. I'll be your guide for this expedition."

One of the Israelis stepped forward, extended his hand and said, "I'm Colonel Karl Baumann."

"Pleased to meet you, Colonel. We are grateful to you and your men for volunteering for this mission. Allow me to give you some background and possibly some insight into what we are about to do.

"Since the end of World War II, there has been a community of ex-patriot Nazis located 600 miles south of Buenos Aires living in total isolation from the world. In 1944, before the War ended, the Nazis constructed a U-Boat pen there to house one of their Type VII/C U-Boats that had transported purloined gold to South America. The sole purpose of the community was to preserve, maintain, and provide crews for the U-Boat that the Nazis believed would be instrumental in establishing a *Fourth Reich* when the time was right. The people of the community were completely isolated from the rest of the world. They maintained the language, customs, and ideology of their Fatherland. Several Nazi industrialists, who had relocated to Buenos Aires after the War, kept them supplied. They built a camouflaged airstrip for their fleet of DC-3s that ferried in those supplies, and they also constructed several warehouses to store the black market weapons that were being acquired by one of the Nazis. The proceeds from this illicit trade were earmarked for their dream of a *Fourth Reich*. They even developed a unique system for extending the docking facilities from shore to allow a ship of this size to anchor and take on or discharge cargo.

"Apparently, the Nazis have decided that now is the time to put their plans for establishing the *Fourth Reich* into effect. They have joined forces with several powerful *jihadist* groups and have promised to provide them arms and transportation on their beloved U-Boat to launch clandestine raids and wreak havoc around the world. While everyone is preoccupied with the bedlam created by the *jihadists*, the Nazis will begin to establish their *Fourth Reich* without the loss of a single man.

"The ship that brought you here is actually a giant decoy. As you already know, *Stella Maris* is a floating drydock disguised as a container ship. The Nazis plan to transport the U-Boat to strategic spots around the world to deposit *jihadists* and their arms. It's a one-way trip for the *jihadists*. The U-Boat will then return to her secret floating dock to ready for the next mission. In reality, we are planning a big surprise for them.

"*Stella Maris* is going to dock in Buenos Aires. There she will take aboard all the support personnel from the U-Boat base that have been flown there in the DC-3s in preparation for the rendezvous and first docking of the U-Boat in the South Atlantic. The DC-3s will then fly a group of Nazi industrialists and two Arab bankers to the U-Boat base from Buenos Aires. Some of them will be transported to the rendezvous site by a PBY and then transferred to *Stella Maris* for a gala party to witness and celebrate the historic event. The rest of the participants, including senior members of the Hitler Youth, will travel to the rendezvous aboard the U-Boat.

"I will give you more details in a minute, but in a nutshell, our mission will begin after the U-Boat and *Stella Maris* have been destroyed. We will empty the warehouses of stolen materiel, and load the contents into this freighter to be transported to Buenos Aires. The last task that must be performed is essential, but very distasteful. We must eliminate everyone who has been left in the compound."

Although everyone in the room had been listening attentively to Steve, his final statement seemed to suck the air out of the room. Finally one of the men asked, "Who will be left?"

"Remember, these Nazis have been living in South America for over 35 years. The colony is virtually self-sustaining. The original residents were former U-Boat men, their wives, and children. They left a militant country and created a militant community. As the children grew up, some of them married and had children of their own. Most of the men and Hitler Youth will be on the U-Boat. There will probably be close to 100 left in the compound. Most of them will be women and children. There will be some older and disabled men as well."

Another Israeli spoke up in disbelief, "What? You want us to kill them all? They're damn civilians! That will make us no better than the Nazis!"

Steve spoke quietly. "Is there anyone in this room whose family wasn't affected by the atrocities committed by the Nazis in Europe during the War?" There was no response. He continued, "Believe me, these people cannot be rehabilitated. It is far too late for that. I can assure you that if the situation were reversed, they wouldn't hesitate to kill you, your men, your women, and your children. Let me remind you that they are planning to establish a *Fourth Reich* to carry out what they failed to do during the *Third Reich*. If we don't put a stop to it now, they might succeed in starting World War III. In fact, one of their primary missions is to wipe the State of Israel off the face of the earth."

Colonel Baumann stood up and said, "It's a dirty business, but remember—they are all hardcore Nazis living in the past. The War was over a long time ago, yet they are still steeped in hatred and an over-riding sense of Aryan superiority."

Heads nodded among the men, and the company mumbled their assent.

"Good. I'll be leading the team on this part of mission, and I'll ask for volunteers when the time comes."

Chapter 64
More Details

Steve once again took charge of the meeting. "I know you all volunteered for this mission not knowing anything about it. Now you do. Your government has disavowed any involvement in this action and will declare that it has no knowledge of the plans. That gives them plausible deniability on the world stage. This is purely a renegade operation orchestrated by *Mossad*. For the time being, we are all orphans—men without a country. What we are about to undertake is dangerous, illegal as hell, and, if we are caught, our presence could precipitate a major international incident. I understand that you are all fluent in Arabic and that you are all armed with Russian-made AK-47s and ammunition. You have been issued camouflage jungle fatigues, traditional Arab headgear, the *keffiyeh*, prayer rugs, and *Qurans*. In other words, if stopped or detected, we want it believed that you are part of a *jihadi* mission. As a matter of fact, after you leave this meeting, you are to communicate with each other only in Arabic.

"There are two reasons for this ruse. The first is obvious. Your country will not be implicated in this scheme if it doesn't go as planned. The second is to dupe the people at the colony into believing that we are acting on orders from their Nazi superiors.

"Is any one of you a native German speaker?"

"I am," Colonel Baumann spoke up. "I was born in Magdeburg, in 1945. A German family hid my parents and me until the War ended. We immigrated to Israel when I was 16, and I speak fluent German."

"Perfect. The residents of the compound know me and speak only German. I will converse with them and you only in German, Colonel Baumann. You will not wear a *keffiyeh*. I want them to think you are a German officer. You will address me as '*Oberst*,' and give your men orders in Arabic. It will be my job to convince the Nazis left in the compound that a foreign government has purchased the contents of the warehouses, and that I have been given the authority to transfer all the weapons and munitions to the freighter. I will have the proper paperwork to show them. If things go well, we may even get an opportunity to empty the hangar of any spare parts for the DC-3s. We also have reason to believe they have some canisters of poison gas.

"That reminds me. I understand that one of you can fly a DC-3?"

"That would be me. I'm Marcus," said a lanky young man as he stood up. "I've logged a couple of hundred hours in those crates. They're solid, dependable planes."

Colonel Baumann spoke up, "I've also logged some time in a DC-3, but it's been a while. I may be a little rusty."

Steve was elated. "Marcus, why don't you give the Colonel a short refresher course before this operation starts? Then we can ferry both of them back to Buenos Aires.

"Last item for this meeting. How many of you have any experience operating forklifts and cranes and have worked on the docks?" Six hands went up. "Great, you can help instruct your buddies so we can get the job done as efficiently as possible. Are there any questions?"

The men responded in a tongue that was unintelligible to Steve. He assumed it was Arabic. Colonel Baumann turned to him, saluted, and said, "*Alles ist in Ordnung, Herr Oberst.*"

"Colonel Baumann, you may discharge your men for the time being, but I'll need you to meet with me privately. We have a few more things to discuss."

Colonel Bauman stood, called his men to attention in Arabic, and dismissed them. Steve studied his new "recruits" as they left the mess. He was very pleased with what he saw. These were trained professionals. He was sure they would get the job done.

Steve poured drinks for himself and the Colonel. As they sat down, he said in his best German, "*Oberst Baumann, welche Art von Seitenarm werden Sie tragen?*"

"*Ein neun milimeter Luger. Man mus so authentisch wie möglich sein.* One must remain as authentic as possible."

"You're correct, we want you to look as German as possible. We will remain on the freighter and out of sight of the *Golfo* until we get the word from those on the PBY that *Stella Maris*, the U-Boat, and all of their occupants have been destroyed and are headed to the bottom of the ocean.

Karl looked Steve in the eye and said in a hushed whisper, "Who's the half-witted, lard-assed desk jockey that dreamed up this mission? I'd like to kick his ass! Do you realize that on your command, I'm going to lead an armed Arabic-speaking, military force of 15 men, and that we are invading the sovereign shores of a nation presently at peace with the world? Then we are expected to steal a couple of warehouses full of arms and ammunition, load it onto this ship, and then quietly sail off into the sunrise?"

"Let's not forget the DC-3s we plan to hijack and the bodies we'll be leaving behind, Karl."

"Yes, of course! Let's not forget the planes and the bodies."

"That's it in a nutshell. And, just for the record, Colonel Baumann, I'm one of the half-witted, lard-assed desk jockeys who came up with this plan."

"*Ach scheisse!*"

"Forget it! If our positions were reversed, I'd would probably have said a lot worse than that. But it has to done. We've got to remove the contents of the warehouses. Most of it has been stolen from U.S. military bases. Believe me when I tell you that the U.S. government doesn't want it back. It would be totally embarrassing and humiliating. We sure as hell don't want the Argentines to have it. As far as I'm concerned, most of them are nothing more than Spanish-speaking Nazis. That leaves us with the option of either dumping it all into the ocean or appropriating it for Israel, and there is no question that we've got to eliminate everyone involved. *Is das nicht so?*"

"It seems that it is. Sorry again about the 'lard-ass' comment. By the way, what the hell are you calling this little adventure?"

"I call it *Operation Cojones.* It's the best I could come up with on the spur of the moment."

"Kreutzer, you do realize we're all crazy as hell for doing this. If we're caught, the repercussions will be monumental!"

"Well, let's plan very carefully not to get caught. After all, Israel can hardly afford to make any more enemies."

"I've just had a thought. We should leave a *keffiyeh* or two as calling cards."

"Great idea. I don't believe you actually count the Argentines among your friends, but it would probably be best if they don't find out who has actually carried out this mission. Do you really give a damn about the Argentines?"

"No I don't. We've been short of friends for over 5,000 years. If we lose one or two more, I doubt we'll notice the difference."

Nodding his head, Steve said, "I promise that when this mission is complete, I will thoroughly debrief you and your men. There may even be a movie for you to see. I predict it will be spectacular.

Steve began to outline the location and details of the airfield, warehouses, docks, loading facilities, and various buildings in the compound. Then he and Karl began some serious planning.

Chapter 65
Buenos Aires

The day before *Stella Maris* arrived in Buenos Aires, Richard called Heinz. "My friend, the big day is at hand. It is time to make the final preparations. I suggest you alert Kuntzelmann to assemble the men from the compound who will be sailing on *Stella Maris*. Send DC-3s down to pick them up and get them here by tomorrow night. As soon as we dock, I would like a meeting with you in my office. We need to discuss the timetable and final logistics for our glorious event."

"Richard, I couldn't be more pleased with the way things are progressing. I don't know how you pulled this off so quickly, but I am delighted. As soon as I hang up the phone I'll get the ball rolling at my end. *Bis morgen!*"

True to his word, Heinz immediately called Kuntzelmann. "*Kapitän,* the time has finally come! Assemble those men who will be needed on the *Stella Maris.* Include the docking crew, machinists, mechanics, and any other crewmembers that won't be needed on the U-Boat. Let me know the total number as soon as possible. I need to know how many DC-3s to send to pick them up. They need a day or two on the ship to get familiar with the equipment in the docking bay. Instruct them to stay below decks and in the area of the U-Boat bay. After all, we have to keep up the appearance that we are a container ship. They will be picked up tomorrow, flown to *Herr* von Ritter's airfield, and then transported to the ship under cover of darkness."

"Very good, sir. I already know 93 men will be needed. They are ready and anxious to go."

"Good! I will send three planes. You and the rest of the crew must be on alert. Your orders to sail will be forthcoming."

As soon as the ship docked, Richard hurried to his office where Heinz was anxiously waiting. Almost as if needing to please Richard, Heinz announced, "The DC-3s are on their way and will have the crews here by 0100."

"Great. I'll have buses there to meet them. Have a seat, Heinz. We have much to discuss."

Richard pulled navigation charts and a sheaf of papers from his brief-case. He spent the next few hours going over every detail of the plans that he, Diaz, JoAnn, and Zac had formulated. These included the point of the rendezvous, the exact timeframe, and the passenger lists for each vessel. Heinz listened intently and took copious notes. He became more and more excited. By the time Richard was finished with his presentation, Heinz was pacing around the office.

He exclaimed, "We are actually ready to begin! I will make calls now and have everyone in my office tomorrow at 1900 hours. The Arab bankers are already in Buenos Aires, but they need not be at this meeting."

"Excellent, Heinz. I will see you then. Please excuse me now, I have some pressing details of my own to take care of."

The next evening, Richard was the first to arrive at Heinz's office. Erdman, Strasse, von Ritter and his son, Ehrlich, and Becker soon followed him into the office. When everyone was present and seated, Heinz, standing erect with his hands clasped behind his back and looking every bit like the *SS Hauptmann* he had once been, began to speak. Heinz had taken control of the operation—or so he thought.

"Welcome gentlemen. We are now in the final countdown to the commencement of our plan to attain worldwide domination for our cause. The time has come for our U-Boat to enter her floating dock for the very first time. If we are successful in this endeavor, we will be on our way to establishing the *Fourth Reich*. Here are your orders!

"I will fly to the compound in von Ritter's private DC-3. Eherenfeld, Ehrlich, Becker and the two Arab bankers will join me. We want our Arab 'friends' to travel in comfort, and it's the only DC-3 outfitted for the level of comfort to which they are accustomed." Otto von Ritter briefly considered raising his hand to protest not being included on his own private plane. However, he thought better of it when he received a withering stare from Heinz.

"The rest of you will fly on another DC-3. You will be honored to sail to the rendezvous on our U-Boat. The three DC-3 pilots will join you and Kapitän Kunzelmann, the crewmen who have devoted their lives to sustaining and operating her, and the senior members of the Hitler Youth who are the future of our party.

"The remainder of the party—Ehrlich, Becker, Eherenfeld, the Arabs, and I will board the PBY for the flight to the rendezvous with *Stella Maris*. Our new ship makes 20 knots and will require 46 hours to reach the rendezvous point, which is 250 nautical miles southeast of Viedma. The U-Boat will arrive in 15 hours. The PBY can fly there in about two. The U-Boat will leave at dusk and travel at 17 knots on the surface, under cover of darkness. At dawn, she will submerge and finish the trip at 7 knots. Our departures times will be staggered so that we will all reach the rendezvous point simultaneously. Captain Diaz has assured me that the targeted spot is well away from any commercial sea-lanes. Those of us on the PBY will be transported by launch to *Stella Maris* and escorted to the observation lounge. The pilot of the PBY will be in the air, filming the approach and entrance of the U-Boat. Then we will watch the delicate maneuver on closed circuit cameras and audio that have been installed in the docking bay. After the successful docking of the U-Boat, those who have been aboard her, the docking crew, and those of us watching in the lounge, will all celebrate with a champagne toast to the birth of our *Fourth Reich!* Then you, Kuntzelmann, and the U-Boat officers will join the rest of us in the lounge for a joyous celebration.

"At the conclusion of our onboard activities, you will have a choice to make. Eherenfeld and I will remain on board for the voyage to Cape Town, South Africa. There I will sign papers to formalize the official transfer of *Stella Maris* to us. You may choose to stay with me, or return with the Arabs to the compound and then on to Buenos Aires. *Stella Maris* will sail tomorrow morning. You all have your orders and timetables. This meeting is concluded."

Heinz stood transfixed for a moment. His chin was up and his chest was out as if he were reviewing his old *SS Panzer* Regiment. Then he suddenly raised and extended his right arm, clicked his heels together, and said, *"Heil Hitler!"* Everyone in the room dutifully and enthusiastically returned the all-too-familiar salute.

As the men left the room, one could identify a new sense of pride, military bearing, and purpose in each man's demeanor. Richard followed after them and went directly to his office at the Global Import/Export dockyard. Diaz, de Silva, JoAnn, and Zac were waiting.

"How did it go?" JoAnn asked.

"Just like a third grade 'repeat-after-me' exercise. How little it takes to revive a lost cause. You wouldn't believe how child-like these people can be. They are like wind-up toys. Hats off to Bert. He was right on the money. Heinz delivered the message as if all the ideas were his own, and he really believes that they were. He still hasn't figured out who I am supposed to be. On the other hand, this group of Nazis is just as dangerous as ever. Don't doubt for a minute that they have to be stopped!" The group murmured their relief that the meeting went well. They were ready to get the ball rolling.

Richard asked, "Juan, you'll be sailing in the morning. Is everything ready?"

"We are more than ready. We've even loaded 50 or 60 empty cargo containers just for show."

"Then I'll see you at the rendezvous. Smooth sailing. Zac and JoAnn are you all set?"

"Roger that," Zac responded. "We have extra batteries, full fuel tanks, RF units, and plenty of film."

"Is there any need to review our plan?"

JoAnn was totally serious when she responded, "If we don't know it by now, it's too damn late!"

Richard replied, "Well then, it's a green light all the way!"

Chapter 66
Golfo san Matias

Operation Jonah was now in motion. There was no turning back. *Stella Maris* left Buenos Aires at first light. Steaming at 20 knots, she had to cover almost 900 nautical miles to reach the rendezvous coordinates on-schedule. By Tuesday morning, she had covered half the distance. At 0900, Richard, Heinz, and the other passengers boarded the DC-3s in Buenos Aires. About five hours later, they landed on the camouflaged airstrip at the compound. As they stepped out of the planes and into Jeeps, Heinz very proudly gave them an extensive tour of all of the facilities. He was very proud of it all—especially the warehouses chock-full of weapons and ammunition. Of course, the industrialists had seen it all before, but the Arabs seemed sufficiently impressed. They were absolutely amazed at the U-Boat.

"*Herr* Heinz," one of the bankers said, "everything is as you described. We are very pleased. I am convinced our collaboration will be successful!"

"Of course it will. I wouldn't have it any other way! Gentlemen, we will now take you to our guest facilities where you may refresh yourselves before dinner. Kapitän Kuntzelmann plans to sail this evening, so we will eat earlier than usual."

Richard was the first to enter the banquet hall where the pre-departure banquet was to be served, and was as awed by it now as he had been when he and Steve had first visited the *Golfo*. The great medieval hall was decorated with Nazi flags and banners, and the huge *swastika* inlaid in the floor was brightly polished. They had pulled out all the stops for the

Arabs. Richard thought, "I'm convinced they really believe all of this stuff themselves. We need to put an end to it!"

Kuntzelmann, his officers, and selected members of the Hitler Youth marched in with Prussian precision and stood behind their chairs around the massive round table. The industrialists were the last to enter. Everyone sat and was served a delicious German dinner by the women of the compound. The Arabs were offered food that adhered to their dietary convictions. After the meal's completion and many toasts, Kuntzelmann, his crew, and the Hitler Youth left the hall to ready the U-Boat for departure.

Soon the von Ritters, Strasse, Erdman and the three DC-3 pilots were escorted to the U-Boat. Kuntzelmann eased her out of her pen at 2030. Making 17 knots, he planned to run her all night on the surface. She would then submerge and travel the remaining distance under water. A snorkel had been added to the U-Boat months before to allow her to stay submerged for longer periods of time. That might be the case on this mission.

The other guests—the two Arabs, Ehrlich, Becker, Richard, and Heinz— would stay the night at the compound and fly to *Stella Maris* the next morning in the PBY. Zac and JoAnn had quietly arrived from Buenos Aires while the others were feasting in the hall.

Just as planned, the PBY was primed and ready to go at 0930 the next morning. They walked out on the dock and boarded the plane through the waist blister, donned their life vests, and strapped themselves in for the flight. None of the passengers—except Richard—noticed the co-pilot. With her hair covered by her cap and headset, JoAnn was about to embark on the most important mission of her career. Zac passed a bag full of noise-suppressing headphones to his passengers. He said, "Relax gentlemen. This is the safest plane in the world. It's noisy but safe. Put these on and save your eardrums." Zac closed the blister canopy and climbed into the pilot's seat. The PBY's engines were turning over in sync. He revved the engines slightly, nodded to JoAnn, and taxied the plane into the protected water of the *Golfo* which was as smooth as glass. He thought, "I hope the ocean looks like this when we land."

Advancing the throttles, he dropped the flaps, and as his speed increased, the PBY got on step and transitioned smoothly from boat to plane. When they were airborne, Zac looked back in the passenger cabin and saw that the two Arabs were almost as white as the robes they were wearing. He and JoAnn could converse with each other through their headsets. "Steal a look at those guys, JoAnn. Those Arabs are terrified."

JoAnn did just that and grinned from ear to ear. "Not as terrified as they will be in a few hours," she replied. The plane attained an altitude of 7,500 feet and cruised at 110 knots for about two hours. Suddenly their headsets crackled. Only Zac and JoAnn could hear the transmission. It was de Silva. "Wind is off the port beam at six to eight knots. The U-Boat has arrived and is submerged 1,000 yards astern. She is awaiting instructions. You may initiate landing."

"Roger that," Zac replied. "Let's get this show on the road." Without warning, the plane banked to starboard and the Arabs let out audible gasps. Below, through a thin wispy layer of clouds, the passengers could see *Stella Maris* on station, awaiting the arrival of the other characters in the drama that was about to unfold.

Chapter 67
Go

The PBY circled, descended slowly, touched down on a friendly sea, and settled like a duck on a pond. Zac eased back on the throttles and cut the engines. The plane came to rest about 400 yards from *Stella Maris* and rocked gently in the swells of a very calm South Atlantic. Heinz was his usual officious self as he addressed the Arabs, "See what you have financed. This ship is the key to our success. She is worth every penny." The robed men returned tight smiles. They were not men of the sea, or small planes.

As the plane was landing, de Silva had lowered the Captain's launch and motored out to the PBY to meet and receive her passengers. When it drew close, de Silva cleated a towline to the PBY. The other end of that line was attached to the nozzle of the refueling hose. As the men released their seatbelts, Zac went aft and raised the blister's canopy. His passengers climbed out of the plane and boarded the launch for the short ride to *Stella Maris*. Zac exited the hatch above the pilot's seat and shackled his lifeline to the safety ring on the wing. He unlocked the gas tank's intake cap while JoAnn leaned out of the waist blister, gathered in the towline, and threw it up to him. "Be careful," she yelled, "those damn props are still wind-milling."

"Right, I've got my life jacket on and my life line is hooked up." As soon as he finished pulling in the towline, he grabbed the nozzle and began the refueling process.

When de Silva returned to *Stella Maris* and guided the launch alongside, he reconnected the davit lines, pressed the remote control, and the boat rose and was deposited in its cradle on the boat deck.

As soon the last man exited the launch, de Silva said, "Gentlemen, please follow me to the observation lounge." He ushered them into the lounge that was darkened by the sunscreens that had been lowered so that the guests would direct their attention to the video screens. All of the external cameras were focused on the refueling of the PBY, and everyone seemed fascinated by the procedure. "Make yourselves comfortable, please. I am happy to announce that the U-Boat has arrived and is on station. The Captain has asked me to inform you that he has called for a lifeboat drill for his crew only. The external cameras will also pick up this activity for you to observe. I think you will find it very interesting. When the docking procedure is about to begin, we will switch to the internal cameras so you will be able experience it in comfort. Please take advantage of the food and drink we have provided for you. There is also a lavatory for your convenience. Remove your life vests. Relax and enjoy the show."

They hardly noticed when de Silva left the lounge. He went directly to the radio room and made the prearranged call to Richard, who had accompanied the other 'guests' to the lounge. They were so absorbed in the action on the screens that they didn't notice the phone when it rang. Richard answered it and said, "Yes? Thank you. I'll be right there." He replaced the receiver, quietly opened the door, and made his exit. As the pneumatic door closed behind him, he reached for the tiny RF control in his pocket. Six almost inaudible clicks followed. No one would ever enter or exit the lounge again.

Heinz, Ehrlich, Becker, and the Arabs were watching the screens intently as the crew entered the lifeboats. They murmured their approval at the speed at which this maneuver was carried out. Very Teutonic! They had no idea that the men or the lifeboats would never return to *Stella Maris*. Their destination was another one of Richard's freighters, *Lola Montez*, waiting just over the horizon.

In the radio room, de Silva focused his attention on a panel with three switches. All the lights were red. The first one represented the signal to deactivate the external cameras. The second one would activate the audio and video systems in the docking bay that were linked to the observation lounge. Number three would alert the U-Boat bay to prepare for the recovery and docking. With a single motion, de Silva flipped all three switches, and the entire panel went green. He left the radio room and locked the door behind him.

In the docking bay, Klaus Kreuger, the crew chief, shouted over the loud speaker. "We have a green light! I repeat! We have a green light. Start the pumps and lower the stern plate." His message and the activity in the docking bay that was now visible on the video screens mesmerized everyone in the observation lounge. Kreuger immediately radioed the news to Kuntzelmann who gave his own set of orders. "Prepare to surface!"

With the external cameras deactivated, no one saw Richard, de Silva, and Diaz—with JoAnn's third master control box under his arm—climb aboard the launch. Once again, it was lowered into the ocean and motored out to the PBY. As the last man out of the launch, de Silva opened the seacocks, and the boat rapidly began to fill with water and sink. "Damn shame to sink such a fine craft," he thought.

JoAnn said, "Welcome aboard, guys! Put on your headsets, and we'll be able to hear everything going on down there. Now, Zac, let's get this old girl in the air for a ringside seat. If everything goes as planned, the entire docking procedure should take between 25 and 30 minutes. From then on it will be action central down there. The fat's in the fire now!"

Chapter 68
So Far So Good

When Zac had the PBY aloft, he started to fly lazy eights over *Stella Maris*. The radio was now tuned to the frequency the U-Boat and *Stella Maris* were both using. It was an open line, and every word between the U-Boat bay, the U-Boat, and the lounge was now being monitored through their headsets. Less than 15 minutes had passed since de Silva had given the U-Boat bay the green light. Kreuger radioed Kunzelmann, "The ballast tanks are full and our ship is down 10.7 meters. The stern plate has been lowered. Surface and advance slowly."

When that order was heard in the lounge, the men were overjoyed. They were transfixed by the activity they were witnessing on the video screens.

Zac said, "Keep a weather-eye open for the U-Boat."

"By the way," JoAnn said, in a rather offhand way, "I've left an audio gift for the gentlemen on the U-Boat, in the docking bay, and in the lounge."

Richard asked, "Now what has your twisted mind conjured up? Did you leave them a recording of Wagner's *Flying Dutchman?*"

Just then, the PBY's radio picked up a signal from *Lola Montez*. "Your crew and lifeboats are safely aboard. We are proceeding to Buenos Aires."

"Good news," Richard replied. "So far, so good."

Suddenly, JoAnn pointed excitedly, "Look about 800 yards behind *Stella Maris!* Can you see that disturbance on the surface? It's *Jonah* blowing her ballast tanks! She's coming up! Start the cameras, Zac! She's about to breach! Here she comes!"

All aboard the plane cheered as the ocean began to roil and the surface became more chaotic. They could see the radio antenna, periscope housing, snorkel, and the crown of the conning tower break the surface. As she emerged, they noted the new 88mm gun on the foredeck, complements of Otto von Ritter.

Chapter 69
The Toast

At an altitude of 1,200 feet, Richard could see the ship below quite clearly. With the stern plate down, the gaping maw of the docking bay could be seen from the air. All this action was caught on the screens in the lounge. Everyone heard Crew Chief Kreuger give Kuntzelmann the order to advance. The U-Boat was aligned with the docking bay and slowly approached. On the conning tower, along with Kapitän Kuntzelmann, stood the von Ritters, Erdman, and Strasse. The U-Boat entered *Stella Maris* and, in short order, was totally engulfed within the cavity of the docking bay. It was akin to watching a python devour its quarry whole.

No longer visible to the PBY, Zac stopped filming. They had to rely solely on audio communication to follow the activities below. The eight cradle arms were advanced to capture and stabilize the hull of the U-Boat. Then, the pumps were reversed, and the ship began to rise evenly and the hydraulic pistons elevated the stern plate. *Stella Maris* had returned to her original configuration. She now appeared to be merely an ordinary container ship.

The mood in the docking bay was euphoric. The U-Boat crew and Hitler Youth poured onto the deck and joined the docking bay crew in a celebratory chorus of cheers. The roar was deafening. Through their headsets on the PBY, they could hear Heinz give the order that the champagne be opened. The men in the docking bay were watching Heinz intently on the huge video screen in the bay. "Gentlemen, fill your glasses. Join me in a toast to the birth of our glorious *Fourth Reich*."

"To the Fourth Reich."

There was a pause, and the airborne eavesdroppers imagined the champagne being drained from the upturned flutes.

"Now, refill your glasses and join me in a second toast—to our allies from the Middle East. May they be successful at last in waging worldwide *jihad* and wiping the State of Israel off the face of the earth."

In the PBY, JoAnn retrieved the black box from under her seat and flipped the small switch on its right side. Richard said, "JoAnn, do you need the black box we brought from the ship?"

"It's a back-up, Richard. Just stand by in case we have a problem with this one. Zac, call out the code, and I'll arm it."

He complied, "106-612-151-492-177-619-411-944."

She repeated the code and entered it on the keypad. "We're armed and ready for business. Take her up another 300 feet. When I initiate detonation, I have no idea how high the debris will fly."

The successful docking and the champagne that continued to flow, created a festive mood and everyone was a little giddy. The *Fourth Reich* had been born. Wilhelm Heinz thought, "I always thought it was just a dream. Who would have ever thought it would become a reality?"

Chapter 70
The Message From Hell

As soon as the code was entered into the black box, a single blue light appeared above each of the four toggles, indicating that the circuits were programmed in and ready to fire. The quarter-sized failsafe button in the center of the box glowed an ominous red.

JoAnn replayed the firing sequence in her mind. Zac announced, "We've reached 1500 feet, JoAnn. Whenever you're ready. It's your show now."

"Restart the cameras, Zac," she replied as she flipped the first toggle on her master control. Her pre-recorded message began to play. Her most sultry and seductive voice was heard clearly in the lounge and in the entire U-Boat bay.

"Good day, gentlemen. Congratulations. You, *Herr* Heinz, or if you prefer, *Hauptmann* von Reimer and your friends have just created and witnessed the successful birth of the *Fourth Reich*, thanks in part to the generosity of your Arab bankers. Congratulations are also in order to Kapitän Kunzelmann and his fine crew for their excellent seamanship and for successfully docking the U-Boat. Indeed, you have all made history.

"Unfortunately for all of you on the U-Boat, in the docking bay, and in the lounge, your odyssey is about to come to an end befitting a Wagnerian opera. You men in the lounge will hear four soft pops. Don't be alarmed. It's only the gas being released. Momentarily, you will begin to detect the odor of bitter almonds. Yes! You are right. It's Zyklon-B, courtesy of your Syrian brothers. It's exactly the same gas used in your camps to carry out the 'final solution.' Both pneumatic doors have been electronically locked and are airtight. There is no escape, gentleman. Welcome to hell!"

Panicky voices in high-pitched Arabic and guttural German created a sudden cacophony emanating from the lounge. Everyone in the docking bay was stunned. They all stood transfixed in abject horror by what they had just heard. The festive mood had suddenly become a nightmare. On the screen in the docking bay, the horrified men witnessed the activity in the lounge. All five trapped men began tugging, beating, and pulling at the doors. They were yelling and screaming as the gas diffused and permeated the airtight room. The last words of JoAnn's message were, "*Auf Wiedersehen.*" As the caterwauling in the lounge increased in intensity, JoAnn's fingers were poised momentarily over the toggle switches.

In a barely audible whisper, JoAnn said, "God bless America."

Then she very deliberately flipped the second toggle. In milliseconds, the charges in each of the eight cradle arms supporting the U-Boat detonated in rapid succession, obliterating everything and everyone there. The explosions turned the U-Boat and docking bay into a giant funeral pyre. Simultaneously, the charge of HMX that JoAnn had laid along the keel of *Stella Maris* detonated and split her hull like a ripe watermelon. The ship rocked violently, and her stern rose nearly 50 feet in the air before slamming back down to the ocean's surface. The screaming in the lounge continued for a few seconds longer. Those inside were literally 'out of breath,' but not before they witnessed the explosion. The audio went silent.

Richard thought, "*Auf Wiedershehen,* my ass. For those bastards down there it's '*Götterdämmerung*'—'The Twilight of the Gods.' It's the end of their dreams of a *Fourth Reich.* Thank God!"

Zac exclaimed, "JoAnn, you sounded just like 'Axis Sally.'"

At that moment she flipped the third toggle, and multiple explosions occurred on the ship's tower that destroyed the Captain's Bridge, radio room, and the lounge. At 1,500 feet, the PBY was buffeted by the shock waves caused by the explosions. The aft compartments of *Stella Maris* were totally destroyed. Scattered throughout the remnants of the docking bay, dozens of crewmen's bodies and body parts were being incinerated.

"When she finally goes under, the sharks are going to have a field day down there. I hope they like their dinner well done," JoAnn said matter-of-factly.

For a moment, there was a stunned silence in the plane as they watched the inferno below. The only audible sound in their headsets was the muffled roar of the PBY's engines. The camera was still running as the plane banked to port. Zac paused for a moment and then exclaimed, "By God, Major Scarlett, you really hone the essence of vendetta to a fine edge, don't you?"

Diaz and de Silva crossed themselves and whispered, *"Madre de Dios."*

Richard just smiled.

Chapter 71
"D" is for Destiny and Destruction

The afterdeck of *Stella Maris* was now a complete wreck, with fires burning furiously in the docking bay. The U-Boat was history. JoAnn finally spoke. "That's the end of that nest of aquatic vipers. However, gentlemen, the job is only half finished. Now we must send her to the bottom. If we leave her as she is, partially submerged, she might eventually drift into the commercial sea-lanes and become a menace to shipping and maritime navigation. We also don't want to leave any evidence that she ever existed. She has too much air trapped inside her compartments to go down, but I intend to remedy that."

JoAnn flipped the last toggle on the master control box, initiating at two-second intervals, a sequence of 24 paired detonations in the pump housings in the ballast compartments located just below the true waterline. Each pair of detonations—port and starboard—began at the bow and traversed the length of the ship. Simultaneously, the charges on each corresponding hatch cover detonated as well. With each paired detonation, *Stella Maris* rose and fell, undulating like a giant sea serpent. All 48 hatch covers on the ballast tanks were blown off. The force of the explosions caused some of them to rocket through the deck plates and sail like steel Frisbees more than 500 feet in the air. Some of them penetrated the cargo containers, while others ricocheted in all directions. Cargo containers and large, jagged hunks of steel flew everywhere. Zac asked, "My god, JoAnn, what the hell did you use? Depth charges?"

"Not quite, but close. Just call it insurance."

Following each detonation, a geyser of trapped air and water shot skyward, resembling a pod of whales surfacing to clear their blowholes. As the trapped air was released from each ruptured bilge compartment, the ship continued to take on more water and slowly settle. Viewed from the PBY, the fountains of water emitted by the stricken ship seemed to subside and soon ceased. There was no doubt that all of the ship's compartments had been breached. The ship began listing to port, and as the angle increased, everyone in the plane could see the ship's waterline and the results of JoAnn's expertise with explosives. Just below the starboard waterline, 24 jagged, gapping lacerations in the hull were visible. Each one was easily 30 feet across.

Richard said, "That's some serious damage, JoAnn. I'm impressed. I expect the port side will look the same."

"She may go down before we get to see it. She's about to capsize. Those new explosives really work wonders. A little seems to go a long way. Remind me to send a thank you note to Hercules Powder Company when we get home."

The ship continued to release small pockets of air. Her tower finally went under, and she capsized. Diaz mumbled, "Never saw anything like this before."

JoAnn exclaimed, "Look at that split in her keel. It's over 150 feet long. That's much better than I expected! As the ship went over and began to sink, JoAnn breathed a sigh of relief. "It's done."

Zac said, "Damn, I think the gun cameras ran out of film just before she went under. Richard, did you get any of that on the hand-held camera?"

"Never fear, Zac. I'm still rolling."

"Quick thinking, Richard. Thanks. We'll circle until the last of the debris has been sucked under."

JoAnn sat back in her seat. She finally dared to relax a bit. "We can all thank Commander Eriksson and Eric, and his staff of engineers for all their good work. They came up with the perfect ship and made my task a lot easier. She only had to last for one Atlantic crossing. We were lucky we didn't run into any severe storms. Mother Nature could have destroyed her before we accomplished our mission. But as Mr. Shakespeare put it, 'All's well that ends well.'"

The American and Israeli marine engineers had taken months to design and build *Stella Maris*. JoAnn had destroyed her in just a few minutes, with a U-Boat thrown in to boot.

Richard asked Zac to get *Estrellita* on the radio.

"Roger that."

In a few moments, Steve's voice was heard on the headsets. "How'd it go? I've been anxiously awaiting your call, Richard."

"*Operation Jonah* was an unqualified success. Believe me when I say it was quite a show. JoAnn did a bang up job."

"Richard, you do have a sense of humor after all."

"Never mind that. You now have a green light, Steve. I repeat. You have a green light."

"Read you loud and clear, Richard. We're on our way. Hope you got some good pictures. Congratulations to you all. Over and out."

JoAnn let out a loud sigh of relief. "So much for the maritime branch of the *Fourth Reich*. Now it's up to Steve and the commandos to finish it."

Zac smiled broadly as he said, "JoAnn, would you like to fly her back to Buenos Aires?"

"Yes, I'd like that," was her response as she took the controls.

Chapter 72
The Beginning of the End

Emile Schiller stood on the dock at the compound. He had been unable to sleep and had gotten up before first light to stand near the empty pen where his beloved U-Boat had remained hidden for almost 40 years. Just being close to it comforted him. He had devoted his entire life to the *Kriegsmarine*. In 1944, he was the First Officer on a U-Boat in the Mediterranean Sea serving under Kapitän Kuntzelmann. When a British destroyer sank it, he lost his left leg to a shark while being pulled onto a life raft. At the end of the War, Schiller was rewarded for his bravery and loyalty by being chosen to be part of the compound where a hidden U-Boat was to be conserved in preparation for a then-unknown role. Now the U-Boat was to be a key weapon in the founding of the *Fourth Reich*. Although his prosthesis made it difficult for him to navigate the tight passages of the U-Boat, he was able to serve as an instructor and mentor to the younger men as they began to take over the jobs performed by those who had originally sailed it to South America.

Emile had known he would not be participating in the historic docking of the U-Boat in the belly of *Stella Maris*. Yet, even as he stood alone on the dock, he was proud that Kuntzelmann had left him solely in charge of the inhabitants and facilities in the *Golfo san Matias*.

Almost 38 hours had passed since the U-Boat had departed for the glorious venture. The PBY with Heinz, Eherenfeld, Ehrlich, Becker, and the Arabs had been gone for 26 hours. The radio room was locked. In true Nazi tradition, he had every confidence in his superiors, but Schiller was beginning to worry.

As dawn began to break, he was startled by the presence of the *Estrellita* a short distance off shore. He thought, "It must have entered the *Golfo* by mistake." Soon he observed one man in a lifeboat motoring toward the dock. As the small craft drew closer, Schiller recognized Steve at the helm, threw him a line, and said, "What's the occasion for this unscheduled visit, *Herr* Kreutzer?"

As Steve stepped ashore, he responded with a question of his own. "Unscheduled? Did *Herr* Heinz not leave any orders with you? Were you not told to expect us?"

"*Nein! Nein!* He gave me no orders!"

"Schiller, do I need to contact *Herr* Heinz on the ship?"

Schiller responded emphatically, "*Gott im Himmel! Nein!* That isn't necessary." For a moment there was a look of panic on his face. Then he regained his composure and responded, "I am in charge here!"

Steve waved a sheaf of papers in front of Schiller, and said in his most authoritarian voice, "*Herr* von Ritter has made an arrangement with a client in the Middle East. All munitions and weapons are to be removed from the warehouses and transferred to the *Estrellita*. He wishes us to accomplish this as quickly as possible. Extend the pier, Schiller, so we may start to load. We must begin immediately!"

The old man saluted Steve and responded, "Yes sir." Then he limped toward a small, squat, well-camouflaged building at the shore-end of the dock.

Steve followed closely behind. "I want you to show me how to extend the pier."

Schiller said, "It's very simple. To extend the pier, just pull this lever down. This will turn on the power. Then you must push the black button." As he pulled the lever down and pushed the black button, the pier began extending out to the ship. He continued, "To retract it, push the red button.

When the pier is completely retracted, simply push the lever back up to cut off the power."

Estrellita was positioned so that the pier made contact with her gangway on the starboard side. Assembled on her deck were 15 Arab-speaking Israeli commandos, each wearing boots and camouflage fatigues. Each man sported facial hair and a *keffiyeh*. They stood at attention awaiting orders from Colonel Baumann. The commandos were unarmed. Karl and Steve had agreed that they would initially present themselves that way. "We don't want this looking like an invasion," Steve had said. Their Russian-made AK-47s remained stacked in their quarters aboard ship.

As soon as the ship's gangway had been secured to the pier, Colonel Baumann led his company of commandos off the ship and onto the dock. "Emile Schiller, allow me to present *Oberst* Karl Baumann." Attired in the full dress uniform of a World War II *SS* Colonel, Baumann clicked his heals and gave the old man a short, curt nod."

Pointing to the commandos, Steve announced, "Those men speak only Arabic. I give orders to Colonel Baumann in German, and he relays them to his men in Arabic. *Verstehen Sie?* By the way, Schiller, how do you communicate with Buenos Aires?"

"The only radio transmitter in the colony is in Kapitän Kuntzelmann's office. The room was locked when he left. Entrance there *ist verboten*."

Of course, Steve was already aware that was the case. He just wanted confirmation. He continued to wave the papers in Schiller's face. Then in a more conciliatory voice, Steve casually asked, "Emile, how many people are left in the compound?"

"About 100 women of various ages, six or seven Hitler Youth cadets, a dozen old men, eight children, and me. That's all."

Rather brusquely, Steve announced, "I will be overseeing the transfer and loading of the munitions and weapons." He then turned to the Colonel, pointed to the forklifts and the warehouses, and barked a few orders in German. In turn, Baumann addressed the men in Arabic. Work parties began in earnest. The men worked 14-hour days. They took all their meals aboard ship and observed the call to prayer five times daily.

The residents of the colony went about their usual routines, taking little notice of what was going on at the pier. Schiller never challenged Steve's authority or asked to examine the papers he was carrying. He had no inkling that the entire operation was a sham.

At the end of the second day, Steve took Baumann's arm and said, "Walk with me, Karl. Just who is that fellow you call Marcus? He's no Israeli. That's obvious to me."

"You're very perceptive, Steve. His real name is Will Franke."

"Franke? That sounds like a German name."

"Yes. He is of German descent, but he's actually a member of an American Delta Force Black Ops unit. He's kind of 'an exchange student,' you might say. He's on loan to us for a year. I believe the American's call it TDY—'Temporary Duty, Yonder.' He's been assigned to our special ops unit to learn how we do things. I believe he hails from some place in the middle of Texas—Waco or Dallas or someplace like that. We decided to call him Marcus, like the store Neiman-Marcus. There's less confusion that way."

"Well, I'll be damned. By the way, Karl, are you sure you're up to flying one of the DC-3s?"

"You bet. Marcus gave me a crash course on the ship, remember?"

"A crash course? That's comforting. Would you like to rephrase that?"

"Oops, poor choice of words on my part. Sorry, but fear not my friend. I'll fly her to Buenos Aires. I also plan to take my men out with us. There's more than enough room for all of us."

"Good idea! Now that we have a few minutes alone, let me run some ideas by you. When the ship is fully loaded, which should be around noon tomorrow, come looking for me. I'll be hanging out with Schiller. Appear to be in an agitated state. Tell me that *Estrellita's* radio room has just intercepted a message sent from the PBY. The message should read, 'Explosion on U-Boat in docking bay. U-Boat and *Stella Maris* sunk. All hands lost.' I'll show the message to Schiller, and order him to summon everyone in the compound to the banquet hall so that he can make the announcement. He's to tell them that I'm giving them a brief moment to absorb the bad news and that I will be coming to the hall to inform them of the plan that Heinz had prepared in case of an emergency. As soon as Schiller goes inside, it's your show.

"Right, I'll station three men at each of the two side exits and the one in the back."

"I agree. Three men at each door should do it. Just to be clear, Karl, the 'kill all' order still stands. No one is to be left alive. Have you picked your team?"

"Yes. I'll lead my five-man team through the front door. You stay with me. We'll synchronize our watches and start the countdown after the last colonist has entered the hall. We'll give them exactly ten minutes to absorb and react to the shock of the news. I'll give the signal to go. Marcus will be at the airfield, and the rest of us will hit the doors simultaneously."

Chapter 73
No Loose Ends

By noon the next day, just as Steve had predicted, the commandos were loading the last crates from the warehouses onto *Estrellita*. He and Schiller were standing by the dock when Baumann came running down the pier, waving a piece of paper. He looked grief-stricken as he handed the ersatz communiqué to Steve. Steve glanced at it and appeared to be absolutely crestfallen. In fact, his reaction was worthy of an Academy Award.

"Schiller, there has been a catastrophe. The *Estrellita* has intercepted a message from the PBY. Just as the U-Boat completed docking, something went terribly wrong. The U-Boat exploded inside *Stella Maris*. Both vessels burst into flames and went down. There are no survivors." With shaking hands, he offered the message to Schiller. "Here, you read it."

Tears streamed down Schiller's face as he read. He looked at Steve and said softly, *"Mein Gott!"* Almost imperceptibly, his demeanor changed. In a stronger voice he said, "I must tell my people."

"Yes!" Steve said. "Assemble everyone in the banquet hall. Do it now, Schiller! Before this operation started, *Herr* Heinz made some contingency plans in case of an emergency such as this. They are in a sealed envelope on the ship. I'll retrieve them and meet you in the hall."

Schiller stared quizzically at him for a few moments. Then he turned and limped toward the bronze bell in front of the hall as fast as his artificial leg would allow and began ringing it furiously. Everyone in the compound had been programmed to immediately gather in the great hall at the sound of the ringing bell. In a surprisingly short period of time, they had all gathered inside. Schiller was the last one to enter. As the door closed behind him, Baumann signaled his men to begin their ten-minute countdown. They ran to the ship to retrieve their weapons. Along with his gun, Marcus picked up a satchel and made a quick detour to the U-Boat pen. Then he dashed to the airfield and the rest of the men took their positions at the exits as ordered.

Not a sound issued forth from the hall. There was no crying, no moaning, no weeping, nor wailing. There was only silence. Steve took a step closer to Karl, who was now carrying an AK-47. "It's awfully quiet in there. Too quiet for my liking."

A whispered voice behind Karl Baumann said, "Colonel, this just doesn't feel right."

"It has to be done. We'll wait the full ten minutes. Then we'll go in as planned."

The commandos were all in position and keeping a close eye on the time. After six and a half minutes elapsed, a single muffled sound from inside the hall broke the silence. "What the hell was that, Steve? Was that gunshot?"

"Could be, I'm not sure."

The last three and a half minutes seemed like an eternity. An eerie, unnatural silence returned to the hall. A cataclysmic event had just occurred in these peoples' lives, yet there was no audible sign of any emotional response.

Each of the men locked his magazine into place and chambered a round. Baumann was ready to lead his men to carry out a mission that would probably haunt all of them for the rest of their lives. "This is a dirty job, but I know I can count on my men to carry it out."

Colonel Baumann kept his eye on his watch. As the last second ticked off, he gave the hand signal to go. Like clockwork, the commandos burst through the doors. The silence was deafening. They all froze at the sight before them. Everyone lowered their weapons and stared in disbelief.

The great ceremonial hall was still festooned with Nazi flags and banners, just as it had been a few days ago for the pre-departure celebration. *Swastikas* covered nearly every inch of the walls. Bodies were draped over the huge ring-like table and completely covered the huge inlaid *swastika* on the floor in the center of the room.

"Good God," Steve mumbled. "This is insanity!"

Everyone stood transfixed by the grizzly scene. Before them, every single one of the women, children, and old men who had been left in the compound lay dead. Their faces were contorted. Many of them had white froth oozing from the corners of their mouths. Emile Schiller sat propped against the front wall, a Luger in his right hand. Blood trickled down the side of his face from a hole in his temple. His cold, dead eyes stared vacantly into space.

"They've all committed suicide," Baumann said. "Look at the foam at the corners of their mouths. It's cyanide. They all took cyanide—women, men, and children. All of them committed suicide."

"Karl, no wonder Schiller gave me such a cold stare at the dock. Obviously, in true Teutonic tradition, they already had a contingency plan in place. At that exact moment, Schiller knew what had to be done. They needed no help from us."

"Yes, their behavior leaves no doubt in my mind that they were all true believers. They were fanatical Nazis to the end. Thank God they saved us the unpleasant task of eliminating them. For that, all of my men will be eternally grateful."

Baumann backed out of the front door and said, "Two or three of you men drop your *keffiyehs* on the front steps. If someone eventually discovers this mess, they will point the finger at some renegade *jihadist* group."

Turning toward the DC-3s, Baumann yelled to Marcus, "Check the fuel gauges. Top off the tanks, and let's get ready to roll."

He responded, "Colonel, the tanks are full. Let's get the men aboard. I've already had their gear transferred from the ship."

Baumann called out to his men, "Drop a few more *keffiyehs* in the warehouses as you pass by, and let's get the hell out of here." He headed toward his plane as his men formed up into two seven-man squads and jogged to the planes. Before boarding, they unloaded their weapons and cleared the chambers. The Captain of the *Estrellita* gave two blasts on her whistle indicating that the ship had a full head of steam and was ready to sail.

Karl extended his hand and said, "Well, Steve, it's time for Marcus and me to crank up these old crates and head for Buenos Aires."

"See you there, Karl. Nice working with you all. By the way, that guy Marcus is a real piece of work. You ought to keep him around."

Karl just smiled.

Steve jogged back to the dock and retracted the pier. He wanted the compound to remain as hidden as it had been when de Silva first discovered it those many months ago. Then he climbed aboard the lifeboat, started the engine, and motored out to the ship. As he boarded, he gave the Captain a smart salute and went directly to the radio room to send a message to Richard. It was short and sweet. "*Operation Cojones* successful. Coming home."

When he left the radio room, he heard the roar of the planes' engines. As they flew over the ship, they waggled their wings. As soon as the crew secured the lifeboat and hoisted her anchor, *Estrellita* sailed out toward the mouth of the *Golfo san Matias*. Her next port of call would be Buenos Aires. Steve turned for a final look at the compound. At that precise moment, a series of explosions emanated from the U-Boat pen. Even though it was broad daylight, the sky lit up like the 4th of July. Steve smiled and thought, "Who knew Marcus was also a wizard with explosives?" He went directly to the officers' wardroom, where he poured himself three fingers of 15 year-old Macallan. He found a soft chair, put his feet up on the table, took a sip of his scotch, and said, to no one in particular, "Damned if we didn't pull it off!"

Epilogue

Both of the DC-3s made it safely back to Buenos Aires, as did Steve with the *Estrellita* and her cargo of weapons and munitions. There was a happy reunion with Richard, JoAnn, and Zac. All of the Nazi contraband purloined from the *Golfo*, as well as the remainder of von Ritter's fleet of DC-3s, was transferred to Global Import/Export's transoceanic freighter, *Evita Peron,* to be delivered to *Mossad* in Haifa. The evening before she sailed, Richard hosted a dinner for all the mission's participants in Buenos Aires, including the Israelis, Juan Diaz, and the newly-promoted Captain Fernando de Silva, who would be sailing *Evita Peron* to Haifa.

The highlight of the evening was the premier of Zac's film depicting the dramatic demise of *Stella Maris* and the U-Boat. "I still have some editing to do, but I think you can get the general idea," Zac said as he turned the lights back on. The quality of the photography was excellent, and they all seemed enthralled. "As soon as I finish the editing, I'll send copies to you."

"Many thanks for a job well done, Zac," Richard said. "I owe you big time."

"And I as well," JoAnn added. I can't wait for Eric and Jake to see this. Had it not been for them, there wouldn't have been a mission at all."

On the plane back to Houston, JoAnn said, "Richard, I have an idea."

"JoAnn, knowing you, that can only spell trouble."

"Seriously, I think the film could be even more interesting for our group at home if we narrate it as they watch."

"I agree. As soon as we get back to the office, I'll have Rose gather everyone for a wrap-up meeting and, of course, a steak dinner at *Arthur's*. We've finally solved the 36-year-old mystery.

With so many schedules to accommodate, it took a week before the much-anticipated gathering could be arranged in Houston. Classical music was playing softly in the background as Alice and George entered the room. George cocked his head and said, "*Götterdämmerung*, an excellent choice for the occasion, Richard. Do I detect a touch of allegory?" Richard just smiled.

A few minutes later, Bert, Steve, and Nancy arrived with an unexpected guest. Much to the surprise of her parents, it was Becky Ames. Last to enter was James, with JoAnn on his arm. He was sporting a cat-that-ate-the-canary grin. When everyone was seated. Richard called on James to begin.

"As you know, we all suspected that the main source for von Ritter's weapons and munitions business was the United States military—illegally, of course. I initiated an investigation at Fort Hood to prove this and track down those involved in the theft. I seemed to have hit the 'motherlode.' The operation has now extended to several other military facilities. I've turned it over to Colonel Jack Alford and his undercover CIC agents. Even though von Ritter is out of the picture, I'm sure there will always be those willing to sell and buy contraband. We're on them now. Let's move on to Zac's film. I hear it got great reviews in Buenos Aires."

Richard turned down the music and started the projector. Once again *Operation Jonah* came to life on the silver screen. This time, however, JoAnn and Richard expertly narrated the black and white "news reel." For the next 46 minutes, the audience sat spellbound. Once the U-Boat had been engulfed in the belly of *Stella Maris*, the action below decks couldn't be filmed. However, those in the PBY heard everything through their headsets. Richard and JoAnn were able to convey what had taken place in exquisite detail. JoAnn even included a repeat rendition of her sultry

"Axis Sally" address to the men in the lounge. The film action picked up again as the explosions completely demolished *Stella Maris*. When the last pieces of debris were sucked under and disappeared from view, everyone in Richard's office stood and offered a spontaneous round of applause and boisterous bravos.

Next, Steve stood and addressed the group. He seemed a bit reserved as he detailed *Mossad's* clandestine operation that had wiped out the Nazi colony in the *Golfo*. "The scene when we entered the ceremonial hall was one that none of us will every forget. Sure, it signaled the end of their plans for a *Fourth Reich*, but more than that, it proved just how single-minded and fanatical they were."

"Did you take any photographs?" Bert asked.

"Not a one. We didn't want any evidence that we had even been there. I guess we figured that those of us who saw it would never be able to forget it, no matter how hard we tried."

When Steve had finished, Richard stood up and acknowledged Colonel Garnett Hill who had slipped into the room just after the film had started. "Great to see you, Colonel. It's fitting that you should be here, since you were the one who always admonished us to leave 'no loose ends.'"

"Hello, Dad. I'm really glad you're here," James added.

"I'm so honored to be in the company of such a clever and resourceful group of people. Each one of you has contributed to the success of this mission. But this evening, I have the honor and privilege of making a presentation."

Colonel Hill approached JoAnn and said, "Your exploits and achievements have not gone unnoticed." He handed her a small gray box. "Please accept this as a token of appreciation from the United States Army and from the grateful nation you proudly serve." The Colonel took two steps back, came to attention, and gave her a crisp salute. JoAnn was taken totally by surprise. She opened the box. Inside were two silver oak leaves.

"This must be a mistake. These can't be mine. These are silver, and I'm a Major."

"There is no mistake. They most certainly are yours, Colonel Scarlett. You've been promoted. Congratulations!" JoAnn was too dumbfounded to respond. Once again, everyone stood, gave her a crisp military salute, and a well-deserved round of applause.

James stood and turned to JoAnn. He proffered a second small gray box that was almost identical to the one she had received. Accepting the box, she opened it. Tears suddenly welled in her eyes. In a hoarse whisper, she said, "Yes!" She held the ring up for all to see and handed it to James, who slipped it onto her left ring finger. A third round of applause followed as she kissed him. Then the room went silent.

Nancy spoke up and said, in her best West Texas drawl, "Appears to me ya'll had more fun than a West Texas rattle snake hunt. You found them in their den. You smoked them out. You killed them. Good work. The problem is, there's always more of them hiding under the rocks waiting to strike."

"Yes," JoAnn said, "that's true. But the next phalanx of vipers we'll meet won't be goose-stepping in black boots, wearing red armbands with black swastikas, chanting '*Sieg Heil*,' and singing '*Deutchland Über Alles*.' Instead, they'll all be wearing *keffiyehs*, carrying copies of the *Quran*, and yelling '*Allahu Ackbar*.'"

"You just hit the nail on the head, JoAnn!" Bert interjected.

"James, Richard said, "I have one more job for you. Destroy this film. *Mossad* has orders to do the same with their copy."

"I most certainly will. None of us will ever forget what we have seen here tonight."

Richard stood and said, "Well, that's about it for loose ends. The opera is over and the fat lady has sung her final encore. I suggest we adjourn to *Arthur's* for dinner."

As chance would have it, George was seated directly across the dinner table from Nancy. Throughout dinner, she noticed he couldn't take his eyes off the gold coin pendant she wore around her neck.

Richard ordered several bottles of fine champagne. When they arrived at the table, he stood and offered a toast, "To a job well done by all." They repeated the toast and drank. "To JoAnn and James on their engagement." They repeated the toast and drank. "To Colonel JoAnn Scarlett and no loose ends." They repeated the last toast, and, in celebration, they drank several more bottles. They had a lot to celebrate.

At one point Nancy said, in a voice loud enough for all to hear, "Steve, tell me again. What was your little caper called?"

"*Operation Cojones*, dammit. You just wanted to hear me say it so you could have a good laugh," he said with a smile.

"You're right, and it was well named and worth it."

After dinner, Alice and Colonel Hill reminisced about "the good old days. He asked, "Did I hear you say something about government service, Becky?"

"Yes, as soon as I get my Ph.D."

"When you're ready, please give me a call."

Alice listened and just smiled while watching history repeat itself.

Nancy took George aside and said, "George, you've been staring at the pendant around my neck all evening. What's up?"

"That gold coin. It's a bit unusual. May I have a closer look at it?"

Nancy removed the necklace and handed it to George. He removed a small magnifying glass from his pocket and said, "See here, on the face of the coin? It reads 'California Gold.' Nancy, this is an 1849, $5, United States Territorial gold coin. On Miss Liberty's coronet it says 'Moffat & Co' instead of 'Liberty.' Where did you get it?"

"When I was a student at the University of New Mexico, a friend of mine gave it to me. She was a Pueblo woman whose name was Anita Two

Crows. Look on the pendant's rim. Her trademark is two crows standing back-to-back."

"Interesting. Very interesting."